D0200730

A Crafter Quilts a Crime

Also available by Holly Quinn

Handcrafted Mysteries

A Crafter Hooks a Killer
A Crafter Knits a Clue

A Crafter Quilts a Crime

A HANDCRAFTED MYSTERY

Holly Quinn

NEW YORK

This is a work of fiction. All of the names, characters, organizations, places and events portrayed in this novel are either products of the author's imagination or are used fictitiously. Any resemblance to real or actual events, locales, or persons, living or dead, is entirely coincidental.

PUBLISHER'S NOTE: The recipes contained in this book are to be followed exactly as written. The publisher is not responsible for your specific health or allergy needs that may require medical supervision. The publisher is not responsible for any adverse reaction to the recipes contained in this book.

Published in the United States by Crooked Lane Books, an imprint of The Quick Brown Fox & Company LLC.

Crooked Lane Books and its logo are trademarks of The Quick Brown Fox & Company LLC.

Library of Congress Catalog-in-Publication data available upon request.

ISBN (hardcover): 978-1-64385-290-4
ISBN (ebook): 978-1-64385-311-6

Cover illustration by Ben Perini
Book design by Jennifer Canzone

Printed in the United States.

www.crookedlanebooks.com

Crooked Lane Books
34 West 27th St., 10th Floor
New York, NY 10001

First Edition: February 2020

10 9 8 7 6 5 4 3 2 1

Mark, your unwavering support and love amaze me. This one's for you.

Chapter One

Sammy Kane clutched the navy scarf closer to her neck, hoping to rebuff the frigid air threatening to penetrate any air pocket in her winter coat. Her auburn hair had grown a few inches in the last few months and now hung in soft waves from underneath a matching hand-knit winter cap, collecting ice crystals. She didn't allow the chill to dampen her spirits, though, as she briskly walked the snow-plowed sidewalk toward Community Craft, a retail store and gathering place she owned and managed on Main Street in Heartsford, Wisconsin. As a matter of fact, the frosty air and the snow falling and swirling in glittering patterns above her head delighted and only added to her already uplifted spirit. Mother Nature had decided to bless the town with a postcard evening, despite the bone-chilling cold. It was that kind of night—sparkling and magical.

"Hey, there! Can you believe our luck?" Annabelle Larson, Sammy's business neighbor a few doors down, popped her curly red head outside her storefront and acknowledged the falling snow with an outstretched hand. "A perfect evening for the best shopping night of the year. Wouldn't you say?"

Sammy nodded her head in agreement toward the Yarn Barn. "I know, right? This looks like something out of a Hallmark movie." Her eyes lifted to the indigo sky. The Fire and Ice event was the only time snow *encouraged* the crowds to show up in droves past Christmas, Sammy thought silently. Otherwise, folks bundled up and hibernated from January second until the last possible hint of frost, which often wasn't until late May (if they were lucky). Years ago, specifically the year 1990, they'd had a paralyzing blizzard in May. Sammy hoped this year that would *not* be the case.

"The weather will definitely work in our favor tonight," Annabelle agreed, snapping her chewing gum hard. "I'll be over in a few minutes with the knit socks. I was up until the wee hours last night knitting. My hands are raw from the wool slipping through these poor old fingers, I tell ya! This last week I picked up the needles any spare moment I had. Please tell me you'll have time to price them and have them out on the shop floor tonight?" she asked with a hint of concern.

"How many do you have?"

"I only made a dozen pair. I thought maybe you could hang one as a sample display and then stock the rest. If you sell them all, we can just take orders after that. What do you think?"

"I think you're going to catch a cold if you don't hurry back inside." Sammy smiled. "Sure, we'll work it out. Bring over whatever you have."

"Thanks. You're a doll!" Annabelle retreated into the Yarn Barn as Sammy waved a glove-covered hand and hurried toward her own shop door.

A Crafter Quilts a Crime

The fading light of day only brought more excitement to the craft shop owner. The sight of the lampposts suddenly sparkling with twinkling white lights brought a smile to Sammy's frozen lips. The commencement of the Fire and Ice event was only an hour away, and the town was coming alive with festive decor. It was the only night every storefront lit a direct path to its doors with intricately cut snowflake-designed luminary paper bags weighted down with sand. In addition, battery-operated flaming candles glowed in each storefront window, and glittering white lights surrounded every doorway. The Main Street stores and businesses remained open only one late night a year—until midnight—when the town's official bonfire would light up the park square. The town's recycled holiday trees would be burned and the townspeople would gather around with cocoa or spiked coffee (though some refused to admit it) in their mitten-covered hands, chatting happily with their neighbors.

Most of the townspeople participated in the celebration, held on the second Saturday in January, as it kicked off the first official event after the new year and had quickly become an annual town tradition. The last few years, the event seemed to have grown, along with the anticipation. And the pressure to add more festivities and make the night even more memorable weighed heavily on Sammy's petite shoulders. She wanted her store to host something special. Something unforgettable that would outdo the rest. If she was being honest, her competitive nature might be part of the problem.

After all, Marilyn, the owner of Sweet Tooth Bakery, had convinced a local choral group to serenade patrons outside her shop, where she was prepared to sell her hot cocoa, cookies, and other fine treats to passersby. Horse-drawn carriage rides through the town would be available again this year, along with free roses for all the ladies, compliments of the Blooming Petal flower shop. Douglas, the owner of Liquid Joy, the coffee shop across the street from Community Craft, was selling coffee with a "hint" of whiskey, sugar, and thick cream.

Sammy thought she'd come up with the perfect idea to encourage customers to want to peruse her shop. It was the only night of the entire year that the town stayed awake with such enthusiasm and gathered together despite the frigid air. The craft store owner knew it would take something big and bold. This year Sammy had, in her mind, hit the mother lode of ideas. Her face lit in a smile.

While pondering what to display in the front windows of her store for the event, her heart had fluttered with excitement. She'd asked the vendors from Community Craft to participate in a live-mannequin contest inside the storefront display window that faced Main Street. Her vendors would have the opportunity to display their own creations in real time. The winner of the contest would be chosen at eleven PM, immediately before the bonfire, and would receive a substantial gift card to use on anything in the store, perfectly timed for the one-night-only shopping event. She had hoped this would entice participants to stand inside the window of Community Craft. Well, the buzz had taken off on Facebook, and the excitement had grown to a level that had surpassed even Sammy's wildest imagination.

The coveted window spot that normally displayed the best handcrafted items for sale within her shop would now be filled with live performers on this very special night. Each participant would perform inside the display window for a twenty-minute time slot, and this would continue throughout the entire Fire and Ice event. Sammy had spent wasted energy worrying that her idea would flop and she wouldn't be able to fill the window space, but her doubts had been unfounded. She had ended up with a wait list, in case someone should "chicken out" at the last moment and decide they couldn't stand to be in the display due to cold feet—and not because of the below-zero temperatures. What Sammy Kane didn't know was that filling the window on that snowy winter night would be the least of her problems.

Chapter Two

Sammy swung open the front door of Community Craft, transporting a swirl of snow inside the shop with her. The cloud of glistening ice powder landed on the floor as she stomped her feet on the welcome mat to remove the excess from her practical winter boots. The last thing she wanted to do was drag snow through the stocked store, prepared meticulously for the night's event.

The scent of cinnamon and orange spice greeted her, and the welcoming smell filled her senses and lifted her lips in a smile. Besides the holiday season, this was her favorite time of year to be a Main Street shop owner. Although enormously busy, she loved the spirit of the townspeople coming together and felt it a privilege to be surrounded by their beautiful handcrafted items.

Sammy mentally tried to find the perfect spot to hang a pair of Annabelle's hand-knit socks for display. Her eyes scanned the impeccably decorated shop that she had spent hours the previous night preparing. She had splurged this year and purchased hand-blown glimmering icicles to hang from the ceiling, where they gave off an impressive sparkle. Her eye bounced from the hand-sewn quilts, perfectly folded and stacked beneath the red-and-muslin nine-patch-variation quilt displayed on the wall, to the Wisconsin-map-embroidered pillows that flanked the sides of Miles's newly crafted wooden bench. Miles, the well-known woodworker in town, had begun selling his hand-carved items over the Internet. His creations had caught the eye of someone in the art world, catapulting his pieces to sell for exorbitant amounts of money. Because of his love for the town and Community Craft, he continued to offer Sammy a few pieces for prices the locals could afford.

Her inspection of the storefront led to the hand-knit and crocheted scarves in bold hues of green and gold, signifying the Green Bay Packers, scattered throughout the shop and draped on various endcaps holding handmade soaps, candles, and mason jars packed with dilly beans, tomatoes, and pickles. Patchwork-quilted squares and stuffed, plumped pillows, hand-sewn by the quilting group in geometric patterns, lined the wall. Intricately painted wooden slabs adorned with winter scenes, deer, and pinecones hung on the wall above the polished wooden cash-register counter. A small round table displayed rustic wooden disks hand-burnt with a soldering tool to show various designs of trees, chickadees, and snowflakes.

Sammy looked to the ceiling, noting that the ice ornaments made rainbows when the lights hit them. She was glad she had made the decision to decorate with them. Along the wall, a sturdy shelf exhibited her part-time employee's wineglasses, hand-painted with whimsical cheery snowmen, left over from Christmas. Deborah had also left behind a few formal designs, of winter birch trees, which were popular and sure to sell. Sammy chuckled aloud when she eyed the painted wooden word signs—a newer edition to the shop—with various phrases such as *If you're waiting for a sign . . . this is it*, or *If our dog doesn't like you, we probably won't either.*

This reminded her that she hadn't seen her prized golden retriever when she noted the empty dog bed that lay waiting for him by the cash-register counter. She secretly wondered if she should bring Bara home before the event; the growing crowd might be too much for him. Even though he loved her customers, many with kind hearts often brought treats for him, and she was afraid her dog would leave the event with a stomachache.

The winter display of quilted table runners was presented in front of the glass-enclosed craft room. The quilting group loved to hand-quilt, as it allowed them to sit inside the lovely space, gather around the table, and visit while they sewed. Sammy had even taken part in the group occasionally when time allowed.

After she finished surveying the shop, she finally settled on the perfect location for Annabelle's knit socks. She would hang them along the gleaming polished wood countertop that housed the cash register. That task managed, she maneuvered past the rack stuffed full of hand-knit scarves and mittens lined with soft fleece and finally reached her older sister, Ellie, who was standing with a customer at the register. Instead of stopping to talk, Sammy rushed past her sister, sharing an acknowledging nod of the head, before stepping into the small private office behind the counter. She removed her gloves, plucked the knit hat from her head, and tossed the wet mass onto a nearby metal chair. After removing her scarf, she shook the snow from it and hung it on a nearby hook behind the door along with her wet coat.

Unexpectedly, she heard the sound of singing moving closer. "*Dashing through the snow, is a baker on her way, delivering treats to all, on this joyous happy day . . . ba da da daaa!*"

Marilyn, the friendly baker from next door, whose yummy treats expanded Sammy's waistline, popped her head inside the office. She abruptly stopped singing and said, "I brought the cookies you ordered, darlin'." The baker filled the office door with her ample frame. Her hairnet was covered in patches of snow, and the shoulders of her pink bakery frock were wet and glistening.

"Still can't get the Christmas songs out of your head, huh?" Sammy chuckled as she regarded her neighbor. "Thanks so much. I was going to come over and grab them in a bit; I've gotten a bit sidetracked, and the afternoon seems to have gotten away from me."

"No worries." Marilyn popped the lid of the large pink box to show off her perfectly baked cookies sprinkled with edible glitter.

Sammy breathed them in and then closed the lid. "Please don't tempt me."

The baker smiled. Her chin lifted in satisfaction.

Sammy removed her boots and slid her feet into a pair of dress flats hidden beneath her desk, which she could wear for the entire evening to avoid a backache. "I'm saving the cookies for my customers. My plan is to keep refilling a plate at the register. A little sweetness while the patrons wait in line might help them be a little more patient this year." Sammy silently recalled the previous year when the line had wrapped around the corner and two shoppers had gotten into an altercation. Sammy had almost needed to seek police assistance due to their lack of maturity, as one of them nearly ended up with a bloody nose. She hoped the treats would help quell any potential restlessness this year.

"Well, I can't stay a minute longer. Lois usually helps me for Fire and Ice, but she's gone and caught the flu." Marilyn frowned, and she laid a chubby hand that suffocated a silver ring aside her rosy cheek.

"Oh, don't tell me the flu's going around already."

Marilyn's shoulders rose, and she threw up her hands. "I sure hope she's not claiming flu to get out of work tonight, but sometimes I don't know with that one." She shook her head in disgust. "As soon as we're expecting busy crowds, she seems to vamoose and disappear," she added with an animated face and a swift clap of her hands.

Sammy was unsure how to reply. She had heard Marilyn's grumblings about the older woman in the past and wasn't sure if it was due to a feud or if there was a hint of truth to the allegations, or both.

"Well. You have fun tonight, darlin'. I hope your customers enjoy the treats." Marilyn disappeared from the office, leaving a melted path in her wake as if Frosty had just liquefied. The wet path Sammy herself had been trying to avoid. But she guessed she'd have to give up the idea of keeping a dry store. It probably just wasn't possible with the current weather conditions.

No sooner had the baker left than Ellie popped her head in the office door. "I'm so glad you're back. I'm really surprised at how busy it's been the last hour. I thought for sure everyone would wait until later in the evening to show up, but apparently people are anxious to get tonight's party started. Heidi's in the bathroom primping. Just wait until you see her!" Ellie grinned.

"Primping?" Sammy knew her cousin didn't need much primping. She was one of the most attractive women in Heartsford, at least by Sammy's standards. And out of the three of them, the most physically fit. The annoying part was, Heidi hardly had to work at it; she was naturally beautiful, the only unnatural exception being that she dyed her hair blonde. Heidi's blemish-free complexion and milky skin were stunningly flawless. Sammy self-consciously tapped her finger to her chin where a red mark was beginning to form. A blemish undoubtedly caused by the double-dipped chocolate cupcakes from Sweet Tooth Bakery and a week of stress preparing for the event was now evidently bubbling to the surface.

Ellie stepped inside the office and whispered, "Seriously. Let's just say she's taken your window mannequin competition thing to a whole new level." Ellie brushed her shoulder-length auburn hair—which closely resembled her sister's, though it was highlighted a deeper russet—off her face to expose dazzling hazel eyes.

Suddenly the door opened wider and their cousin appeared out of nowhere, presenting jazz hands. "Ta-da!"

Sammy's hand flung to cover her gaping mouth for fear she would speak out of turn. Her cousin stood before them in a tightly fitted blue velvet dress. Blue-and-white-striped leggings elongated her long, lean legs, and the dress lifted a few inches from her knee, leaving little to the imagination. Her shapely round bosom was front and center, with a tight silver belt sucking in her already narrow waist. The costume, a far cry from Heidi's normal oversized scrubs that she wore working as an ER nurse at the local hospital, took Sammy completely off guard.

"You don't like it." Heidi dropped her jazz hands, placed them on her slender hips, and forced a laugh.

Ellie cracked up immediately, and fat tears began to roll down her cheeks. Sammy wanted to join in, but Heidi looked suddenly crestfallen. Sammy inhaled a deep breath, placed a hand to her heart, and said, "Wow."

"Wow bad or wow good?" Heidi's ruby-lipsticked bottom lip came out in a pout. "This isn't exactly the reaction I was hoping for."

"I'm not sure." Sammy answered honestly. "There are going to be children here tonight." Her pencil-thin eyebrows knit together, and she held back a smile.

Heidi shook her head in disgust, and Ellie hiccupped in laughter before saying, "Yeah, she'll surely get the votes from the thirteen-year-old boys."

"Well, at least I'm making an honest effort to win the contest; isn't everyone? Since I'm the first one in the window, I thought dressing like an Ice Princess would give me a leg up!" Heidi threw her arms into the air in defeat. "Do you know how hard it's been for me to grow my nails working at the ER with gloves on over washed hands all day?" Heidi flung her silver-glittered manicured nails in front of her cousins. "I've worked really hard on this costume!"

"Where's the hat?" Ellie giggled. "You have to show Sammy that part of the costume too!"

"Hat?" Sammy's attention turned from her sister back to her cousin.

"Yes. It has jingle bells on it. I'm not wearing it yet; it makes too much noise. The bells attract too much attention." Heidi waved a hand airily.

"I think you're a little past that." Ellie bent over at the waist in laughter. Sammy couldn't help but join her sister in laughing aloud as a snort leaked out of Ellie's nose. Her amusement was catchy.

"You guys suck." Heidi turned on her heel and stomped away from the office in a huff, while Sammy's round hazel eyes met her sister's and the two roared until they were both crying.

Ellie lowered her voice. "You know, she even brought something for Bara to wear. I'm not sure your dog will go for it."

"I meant to ask you, where is Bara?" Sammy rushed past her sister to look for her golden retriever.

"Randy and Tyler stopped in, and I had them take him for a walk. I figured, with all the excitement tonight, you wouldn't have time to take him out."

Sammy breathed a huge sigh of relief, grateful that her brother-in-law and young nephew would take the time to do that. She hugged her sister tight and then released her. Holding Ellie at arm's length, she said, "Thank you. You know how overwhelmed I get before these big events."

"Yes, I do. That's why family is here to help," Ellie responded, patting her sister lightly on the shoulder as a sign of encouragement. "But it always works out just fine. And besides, the store looks *b-e-a-utiful*. You did a great job decorating; it looks like a storybook in here. Don't forget to breathe and have fun—you earned it," Ellie added with a smile.

Heidi approached from the bathroom and eyed the large clock on the wall above the cash register. "I don't have time to come up with another costume," she said with disgust.

Sammy and Ellie rushed to her side.

"It's okay; I think it's actually starting to grow on me." Sammy reached for her cousin's arm and encouraged Heidi to spin in front of them. "You just surprised me is all. I wasn't expecting participants to show up in costume. Honestly, the thought had never crossed my mind, but you're right, it was a great idea. And hey, we need to get you inside the window. You're the first out there to perform. Let's go and get you set up before the others show up and it gets crazy busy in here."

"But I need Bara! I brought a costume for him to wear," Heidi said over her shoulder as they maneuvered like a train of cars through the merchandise racks toward the front of the store.

"It's snowing pretty heavily. I think he'll be soaked by the time he gets back from the walk," Ellie said firmly, encouraging Heidi with a quick pat on the backside to move at a quicker pace so they could shove her into the large storefront window.

"I wasn't self-conscious until you two started picking on me. Now I'm not sure I can go through with it!" Heidi slowed her steps and backed away from the window. The strong look of second thoughts crept across her face.

"Get in," Sammy ordered with a pointed finger. She didn't have time for nonsense. The event was about to begin! The last thing she wanted was folks to pass on the sidewalk and see nothing but an empty window display.

Heidi took a timid step up the small footstool into the front window of Community Craft before looking back at the sisters hesitantly. "I don't know . . ."

"You're fine," Sammy said, dismissing her cousin's concern and waving her hands to mimic a push, prompting Heidi to step inside the makeshift winter scene ornamented with fake snow.

A slender, artificial fireplace, adorned with handcrafted finery sold within the store, was tucked in the corner, which Heidi was cautious not to bump.

Sammy and Ellie closed the makeshift black velvet curtain so the display would not be visible inside the store. Then the two hurried out the front door into the cold to see the window from the street side. Heidi remained poised in a mannequin position, her head tilted to one side and eyes wide open with childlike wonder.

"She looks adorable." Ellie shook her head and nudged her sister. "The costume actually turned out to be a great idea. I shouldn't have teased her, because in the window, her costume really works!" Fat frozen flakes began to land on the sisters' heads as they stood, eyes fixated on the window.

"I think we're just jealous of her figure." Sammy looked down to eye her flatter chest and her stomach that had rounded out a bit in the past few years. "And besides, that's what we do when we're in each other's company: revert to our youth." Her eyes returned to the window.

"Yeah, whatever." Ellie waved a hand in disgust, never one to be able to stick with a diet plan herself, and then changed the topic. "The artificial felt snow that you put on the floor looks good. It kinda sparkles in the light, doesn't it? I love it."

Sammy nodded and pointed to Heidi's silver ballet slippers that stood atop a blanket of white. "Speaking of light, I think we should adjust the light a bit; the curtain looks as if it's blocking one of the up-lights. But the display definitely has the effect I was looking for." Sammy clasped her hands together in delight. "Yay! I'm so happy!"

Crowds began to form around the window, and she could hear laughter and cheers over her shoulder: "There's a real person in there!" "Oh my, look! *Sooo* cool!" "I think she's the Ice Queen for Fire and Ice!"

Sammy looped her shivering sister by the arm and led them back inside the warmth of the shop.

"Success! It's going to be the hit of the evening. I just know it!" Ellie said as she shook the snow out of her hair and combed her fingers through it.

Sammy opened the velvet curtain for a moment and adjusted the up-light. "Heidi, we were wrong to tease you. You look ah-mazing! Now don't move a muscle," she reminded as she closed the curtain tightly.

Community Craft was slowly filling with customers, and those who were next to take a turn in the window display were gathering inside the glass craft room located in the interior of the store. The noise and chatter soon exceeded the background instrumental mood music overhead. Sammy encouraged her sister to return to her spot behind the cash register. "You only have to work the register a few minutes longer; Deborah is going to release you as soon as she gets here. I sure hope I left the roster for the window display inside the craft room. I need to make sure my mannequins rotate every twenty minutes." She said this more for her own confirmation than Ellie's. "Thanks so much for your help today. I couldn't have pulled all this off without you."

Ellie disregarded the thanks with a casual wave of her hand. After all, it was probably the third time that day Sammy had expressed her appreciation to her sister.

Sammy made her way to the craft room in the center of the store. The glass-enclosed space allowed craft classes to be seen from inside, prompting visitors to want to participate in learning a new skill. The room also held numerous fund-raiser and community events that had been started by the previous owner, Sammy's best friend from high school, Kate. When Kate had died unexpectedly, Sammy had taken over the store, and she wanted to continue her best friend's legacy by promoting community involvement. Sammy organized fund-raisers, gathered knitters to knit baby caps for the newborns at the hospital, made lap quilts for the sick and elderly, and hosted meetings for the Beautification of Heartsford Committee—the amazing group of locals who covered the town with flowers, plants, and seasonal decor. It was a ton of extra work, but in the end, it brought people together in a way that encouraged and uplifted the community and made Heartsford a very special and unique place to live. Sammy was only sorry Kate wasn't around to take part in the mannequin challenge. She would've loved it.

The craft room door was ajar, and several participants had already seated themselves around a long table in anticipation of their performances. The chatter stopped suddenly when Sammy entered the space.

"Thanks so much for coming and your willingness to take part in the contest!"

The room erupted in applause. The excitement for the evening was palpable.

Sammy cleared her throat before continuing. "Some of you might want to take a peek at Heidi performing in the window so you have an idea of what you signed yourself up for. No backing out now!"

Collective laughter filled the air.

As soon as the room quieted, Sammy continued, "The voting box will be by the front door and customers will be encouraged to vote, so let's see who can hold the best mannequin pose without moving the longest." Sammy smiled as she reached for a clipboard off a nearby countertop aside the table. "Wanda, looks like you're up next."

A slender, middle-aged woman with deep-brown hair styled fashionably in a pixie cut stood and reached for a quilted bag next to her feet. "I brought props!" Wanda Wadsworth opened the bag to reveal a beautifully crafted lap quilt that looked like a family heirloom painstakingly pieced and sewn by hand. "I want to sit in the window and pretend I'm quilting this one. Is that possible?"

"Sure! What a great idea. I'll grab a folding chair from the office and meet you by the storefront window, okay?"

"*You're* going to sit?" another participant named Cheryl piped up. "Seriously? You're a yoga instructor. I thought for sure you'd strike an uncomfortable pose. Then maybe someone would want to try out your impossible classes." There was a hint of snarkiness in her tone. "I don't know how anyone is expected to contort their body that way; it's not natural."

Sammy hoped this wasn't an indicator of how people were going to behave tonight. Couldn't everyone play nice in the sandbox? Especially for one of the best nights of the year, the night of Fire and Ice! Sammy stepped in front of where Cheryl was seated in hopes of deflecting any more irritation, but her block was ineffective because of her mere size.

Wanda shot Cheryl a dagger look and impatiently snapped back, "I'm not exactly feeling up to par tonight. In fact, I'm going to make a run for the restroom before I go." Wanda gathered her props and moved past Sammy, then turned and handed her a stainless travel mug. "I almost forgot, I can't take my peppermint tea with me. I drink it when my stomach acts up like this. Guard it with your life!" Wanda winked a lightly mascaraed eyelash and then handed the travel mug over to Sammy before making her way toward the restroom. Meanwhile, Sammy's eyes quickly darted to the clipboard and scanned the next name on the list. "Mary, it looks like you're up after Wanda. Twenty minutes, people! Twenty minutes . . . so please don't disappear!"

Sammy placed the travel mug on the counter along with the clipboard, then quickly exited the craft room and moved purposefully toward the office to retrieve a metal folding chair. There was a large line beginning to form at the cash register, and Ellie was feverishly making sales. Apparently, the mannequin idea was working and drawing customers into the shop. This brought a smile of satisfaction to Sammy's lips as she rushed through the growing crowd to bring Wanda the chair. She'd have to get that dish of Marilyn's cookies out soon, she thought as she opened the velvet curtain to relieve her cousin from the display.

"That was so much fun!" Heidi said as she stepped down out of the window. Her face flushed crimson and a big smile revealed her dimples. "The up-lights do feel hot after a bit. It's a good thing you're only keeping us in there for twenty minutes. Any longer and I might have roasted to death." Heidi waved a hand to cool her face. "Oy! I need a cooldown. Or maybe a cocktail?" she hinted.

Sammy rolled her eyes at her cousin and said, "Cocktails later. First, we have a big night to get through." She unfolded the metal chair in the display, situated the fake snow around the bottom to hide the unsightly metal legs, and then Wanda appeared. The yoga instructor gracefully stepped up on the footstool and into the window, where she took a seat and covered her lap with the quilt. "Have fun!" Sammy gave her a thumbs-up before closing the black velvet curtain.

"Oh my goodness. That was *so* fun!" Heidi said again. "People were trying so hard to make me laugh, but I wouldn't crack. You should've seen the funny faces they were making at me. One guy even put his lips on the window and blew up his mouth like a blowfish! But I stood my ground. I didn't break character. No sirree!"

"I hope you didn't blink those eyes of yours," Sammy teased. "Boy, they really pop green with that glitter eye makeup you're wearing . . . and that *costume*." Sammy chuckled. "Do you think you can stick around and hand out candy to customers? You look so jolly! My sweet little Ice Queen." Sammy threw her arm around her cousin's shoulders and gave her a light squeeze.

"Oh sure, *now* you're loving my costume!" Heidi laughed as she continued to fan her face with her hand.

"Yes, Ellie and I agreed we were wrong to tease you. Sometimes we just can't help but act like children around each other. I apologize for both of us."

"No worries." Heidi grinned and continued to fan her flushed face with her hand.

"Step outside and check out Wanda in the window. You'll get a chance to cool off and an idea of what you looked like from the outside. Now that it's getting darker outside, the display really pops. If I do say so myself, I hit the mother lode on this great idea. I have to run back to see if Mary is going to need anything for her turn."

Sammy turned from her cousin and rushed toward the craft room. Twenty minutes wasn't really a lot of time between mannequins. The rushing around was making Sammy rethink her time schedule and whether she should have made it thirty minutes instead, although after what Heidi had said about the heat of the lights, maybe not. As she was mulling this over and going over the list on the clipboard, Heidi rushed back in her direction.

"Oh, I think I'm already beat in this contest. Wanda is doing an amazing job! People are even tapping the window and she isn't budging! Not even a little! Hasn't moved a muscle!"

Sammy's eyes lifted from the clipboard, and she regarded her cousin. "Yeah, but as Ellie mentioned, all the young guys will vote for you. Am I right?" Sammy winked and poked Heidi in the side with the end of her capped pen.

Heidi batted her long natural lashes in response. "Okay. Where's that candy you want me to hand out?"

"Lollies are on my desk in the office. You mind grabbing them?"

Just as Heidi was about to leave to retrieve the candy, Sammy heard loud arguing coming from the front of the store, and she reached for her cousin in alarm. The quarrel seemed to be quickly escalating. "Do you think I need to go break that up?" She stepped out of the inner craft room and lifted onto her tiptoes for a visual.

"Who is it? Can you see?" Heidi raised her thin frame, mimicking her cousin, to see if she could catch a glimpse over the merchandise racks.

"You're taller than I am. Surely you can see better." Sammy stood barely five feet. What was her cousin thinking? Heck no, she couldn't see a thing. And darn it, she had even bought cookies to avoid any altercations! What was wrong with people? Sammy's face tightened.

"I guess you should go and encourage them to take it outside. Do you want me to call Tim?" Heidi continued to crane her neck and swayed from side to side to see who was causing such a ruckus.

Sammy didn't think they needed to call Heidi's police officer boyfriend, Tim Maxwell. At least she hoped not. She took a deep breath and then decided she had no choice but to confront the disruption within her store. As she made her way toward the couple, she noticed it was Cheryl arguing with her husband, Craig. Cheryl was obviously no longer waiting inside the craft room; instead she was flying into a rage, and her voice had risen to an uncomfortable decibel. Craig must have noticed Sammy approaching, and quickly the pair moved outside. The argument continued, though, and those who were standing outside watching Wanda in the display window turned their attention and became engrossed in watching the couple argue. The crowd slowly began to dissipate, and Sammy and Heidi stepped outside as well to encourage Cheryl to either return to the craft room *alone* or kindly take her marital argument home with her. Sammy glanced at the window, and through all the commotion, Wanda still didn't move.

"You're right, Heidi. She is good." Sammy flicked her finger toward Wanda, who sat completely still, seated in the chair, quilt covering her lap.

Heidi moved closer to the window. "Sammy, her lips are blue. Something's wrong. It's super-hot in the display. There is no reason her lips should be blue. I promise you. It's not even remotely cold inside there . . . I near roasted to death."

Heidi began to tap on the window lightly, and then Sammy banged her closed fist on the glass. Heidi grabbed Sammy's wrist and the two rushed indoors. They flung open the black velvet curtain, and Sammy began yelling, "Wanda!"

Heidi's nursing skills sprang to action. She jumped inside the window and checked the woman's neck for a pulse. Heidi looked at her cousin and shook her head. "Sammy, I think she's dead."

Chapter Three

No. This can't be happening. No . . . not tonight . . . not Wanda.

Sammy had to blink several times to focus, because she couldn't rationalize the distorted image of what was taking place in front of her.

Her cousin.

Dressed in an Ice Princess costume.

Performing CPR on Wanda inside the display window of her beloved shop.

As much as Sammy wanted people to stop gawking in horror at the scene playing out before them, the shock in her own body wouldn't allow her to move a muscle or look away either.

"She's gone, Sammy." Heidi finally looked up at her cousin, breathless. "Did you call 911?"

Sammy numbly nodded her head in acknowledgment.

"They should be here by now!"

"I'm sure, with the crowds in town and the snow . . ." Sammy let the words fall numbly from her tongue as Ellie came up behind her and tapped her lightly on the shoulder, interrupting her reverie. "Do you mind if I tell everyone to leave the store?

Due to the circumstances, don't you think you should close up shop tonight?"

"Yes. Of course." Sammy shook her head and breathed deep to try to clear the sudden whoosh of thoughts.

"Heidi, the ambulance is here." Ellie shoved Sammy to one side to make room for the bodies pushing past them.

Heidi looked at Sammy. "Go ahead and take care of evacuating the store, and move some of your merchandise racks so we can get a stretcher as close as we can to the window."

Sammy felt her head bob in agreement, but her legs still refused to move until her sister looped her by the arm and turned her to face the other direction. "Come on, help me move this rack." Ellie had already pushed the handmade soap display to one side, using the side of her body for leverage.

Sammy stood erect and cupped her hands to her mouth. "Attention, customers, we're closing the store immediately. Please drop your merchandise and head through the back exit to keep the front open for emergency personnel. Thank you!"

Customers with stricken faces turned to stare at what was happening before they made their way toward the back of the store. Many looked on with horror as one of the ambulance attendants placed a sheet over Wanda's lifeless body.

Sammy knew she had to snap out of it. Everyone was doing their part, and here she was standing numbly, trying to focus on what to do next. She reached for the jars of handmade cinnamon-orange–scented candles and began to rapidly pull them off the shelves so she could move the wooden display rack completely out of the way. After the shelf was moved, a stretcher should have enough clearance to push through.

Wanda dead. Dead in my storefront window!

Suddenly Sammy's dog galloped toward her, her nephew and brother-in-law, Randy, lagging not too far behind. Sammy noticed her sister blocking the horrific scene from Tyler's view and advising her husband to take their son home. Ellie's mumbling words all seemed to jumble together, and Sammy wondered if she might faint. She took an even, calculated deep breath to prevent herself from falling.

The sudden surprise of Bara shaking the snow off his fluffy fur brought Sammy back to planet earth despite her woozy head. She leaned down to stroke his wet back and was enormously thankful for the rush of unexpected comfort.

Deborah Morris, Sammy's part-time employee, appeared in front of her from behind a merchandise rack. "I'm sorry I'm late. Danny was late plowing the driveway and I couldn't get out. And then I had to park way down the road." She removed her gloves, stuffed them in her coat pocket, and then waved an arm dramatically to show how far she must have walked. "Parking is ludicrous tonight. There were absolutely zero spots left out back." Her long black hair was covered with a snow-covered newsboy cap that was now dripping into her eyes. "And *then* I tried to come in the back door, and it's like a mad dash to get out of here. What scared everyone off? What's going on in here?" Deborah finally caught a visual of the front window, and her dark eyes narrowed in question.

"Well . . . it seems . . . Wanda has passed away." Sammy could barely get the words out before Deborah interrupted.

"*Wanda*? You mean my-yoga-instructor-from-the-rec-center Wanda?" Deborah covered her mouth with a dainty manicured hand. Her fingernails were painted light blue with white snowflakes. The design made her nails look like expensive foiled wrapping paper.

Sammy's expression softened.

"That's *impossible*!" Deborah continued. "We just had yoga this morning!"

Sammy watched as a look of confusion washed over her coworker's face. "She must have had a heart attack or something."

"But how? She's so healthy! She's vegan, she works out several times a week, she teaches *yo-gaaa*! She doesn't even eat *sugar*!" Deborah's soprano voice lifted to an unusual octave, even for her normally feminine voice.

"I know. I can't believe it either."

"It's impossible! Incomprehensible!" Deborah's breaths were coming out fast, as if she were panting like a dog. "Now what do we do?" she asked sullenly, her face turning a deathly shade of white in direct contrast to her deep-black hair.

Sammy thought Deborah would need a few more minutes to adjust to the horror they were now facing. "Maybe you should take a seat in the office and catch your breath. There are water bottles in the fridge too, if you need something to drink."

"No. I mean . . . who's going to lead my yoga classes now?"

Sammy knew her coworker was in shock. Her friend wasn't being flippant in her remark, merely trying to come to grips with what had happened and the abrupt change brought by the finality of death. She reached for Deborah's arm and nudged her tiny frame in the direction of the office.

"Wanda did mention that she wasn't feeling well this morning. She thought maybe she was catching some type of bug,"

Deborah said over her shoulder, as she was now a few feet ahead of Sammy and heading behind the register into the private office. "But she still went on with the class, so she couldn't have been that sick. Could she? Isn't an upset stomach a sign for heart attacks in women?"

"Yeah, honestly, I don't know. That's a good question, though, one that Heidi might know the answer to. Sounds like the flu might be coming early this year also; I keep hearing about illness everywhere I go."

Just as Sammy was going to follow her coworker inside the office, she was stopped by Heartsford's only detective on the local police force: Liam Nash. She closed the office door so Deborah could have a private moment and held her hand to the doorknob in case she too needed an easy escape.

Liam Nash stood tall and his steady frame moved closer. His demeanor filled the room with an aura of control that unnerved her. How could someone be so consistently poised in these types of situations? Sammy hated that the scent of his cologne had such power over her, too. Even in horrible circumstances, her body seemed to react in a way that was grossly inappropriate. She could feel her defenses going up to shield herself from her body's treachery.

"Have you missed me?"

Sammy refused to acknowledge out loud that the detective had been noticeably absent and therefore remained tight-lipped. Sammy wasn't even sure if he had stayed in Heartsford during the holiday season. She had no idea where he'd been.

"Do you *really* have mistletoe hanging above your cash register? Or is that some weird random plant hanging from the ceiling?" Detective Nash combed his hand through his thick dark wavy hair peppered with random flecks of white, releasing the snow that clung there. His dark eyes were fixated on the mistletoe.

Sammy could feel her defenses kicking into overdrive. She had yet to kiss the detective. And even with mistletoe, she didn't think she'd ever amass the courage to make the first move. How could she have missed removing it when she had worked so hard on all the decorations? She had meant to take it down and had gotten distracted by a phone call. Heidi would probably mysteriously claim she had left it up on purpose—hoping for a kiss, perhaps. Sammy jumped to remove it, but to no avail; she was a few feet too short. "Maybe I was hoping you'd stop by during the holidays and I could use it on you," she huffed under her breath.

"What's that?" He cupped a hand to his ear.

"*Nothing.*"

Detective Nash reached up and with one hand plucked down the mistletoe, dangling from the ceiling with fishing line, and handed it to her. Sammy tossed it atop the cash register, and instead it fell to the ground, where she kicked it underneath the polished wooden counter.

Feeling a sudden flush on her cheeks, Sammy quickly changed the subject. "An empty store, emergency personnel; I'm guessing you caught the latest news over the police scanner." Sammy was miffed at Liam Nash. Since he hadn't been around lately like he usually was, she felt slighted by his recent detachment. *The detective just strolls in like weeks haven't passed and then acts like that's normal in a relationship.* Or friendship. Just *friendship*, not a relationship, she inwardly corrected herself.

Her tone must have been a dead giveaway to her irritation, because the detective replied, "What's wrong with you? Why are you already snipping at me? I've barely stepped in your shop, and you're already biting." His dark brows came together in a frown.

He was right. Sammy hated that he was right.

Sammy breathed deep and crossed her arms across her chest. "I'm sorry. I had such high expectations for tonight. Everything was going so well . . . and then Wanda goes and dies inside my shop. Forgive me for trying to process." Sammy blew her breath out with a huff, sending her auburn bangs to fly off her forehead. "I shouldn't take my stress out on you, though. That's not fair. But you're an easy target," she teased, trying to lighten the mood. "Cookie?" she offered, uncrossing her arms and pointing a finger. Ellie must have filled the cookie plate that she had neglected to put out on the counter. Bless her heart.

The detective reached out to take the peace offering. "I understand. I'm starting to see the pattern."

"Pattern?"

"Yeah. Pattern."

Sammy's eyebrows were now the ones to narrow in question.

"You get all stressed out in these situations and then you take it out on me. I think I'm actually getting used to it." His lips formed a lopsided smile that caused a shiver of electricity to shoot down Sammy's back. He then took a bite of the cookie, sending crumbs to the ground. He wiped a lingering morsel by licking the glittered sugar from his lips. "Oooh . . . these are good. I'm guessing that you picked these up from the Sweet Tooth?"

Sammy forced a smile. She wanted to be that cookie. *Again.* This was not the time for her body to be reacting in this fashion.

"What do you think happened to Wanda?"

"Honestly? I have no idea. I'm guessing she had a heart attack. But no one, including me, can wrap *that* theory around my head." Sammy pressed her fingers into her forehead. She was feeling a sudden tension headache coming on.

"Why not?"

"Well, from what I hear, she's a health nut, for one . . . *was* a health nut," Sammy added, correcting herself.

The detective wolfed down the rest of the cookie and, after wiping his mouth with the back of his hand, reached for another and said, "What do you mean, a health nut?" He cocked his head to one side and shifted his weight to lean against a nearby wooden rack that housed recipe books from local authors and mason jars full of fruits and veggies lovingly canned by nearby farmers hoping to cash in from the summer's abundance.

"Apparently Wanda didn't eat sugar."

"Ah."

"Be careful there," Sammy warned as she pointed a finger toward the shelf. "I don't need you knocking off a full jar of strawberry jam and causing a mess in the store. I think I have enough to contend with at the moment." Yes. Her head was beginning to throb right between her eyes.

The detective leaned over and plucked a small jar off the shelf. "Thanks for the reminder. I'm almost out." He smiled as he tossed the jar up in the air and caught it with one hand. Sammy thought he was trying to show off. She wished he'd dropped it. Then he wouldn't look so cool, smearing jam everywhere, now, would he?

"So, why *are* you here exactly? Is there something I can help you with?" Sammy's eyes drifted from the detective's dreamy dark-chocolate eyes to the front of the store, where Wanda's lifeless body was being wheeled out of Community Craft.

Heidi was close behind the stretcher with a snow shovel in hand, apparently preparing to remove snow from the walkway so the emergency personnel could get through. Sammy didn't wait for the detective to reply. She walked briskly past him to the storage room door located at the back of the store, stepped inside, and grabbed another shovel that had been leaning against an inside wall.

Detective Nash abandoned the mason jar of jam on the polished wood counter by the plate of cookies and proceeded to follow close behind her like a lost child. He then removed the shovel from her grasp.

"What are you doing?"

"I'm helping. Besides, I want to make sure nothing seems amiss." The detective smiled, showing the tooth slightly jutting from his lower jaw that Sammy had come to love when he grinned. She released her grip. "Fine. I'll grab another one."

As Detective Nash maneuvered the aisles to the front of the store, Sammy retreated to the storage room, and Deborah stepped out of the office and found her. "Anything I can do?" Deborah asked with a sniffle.

"Nah. Go home. We're officially closed." Sammy's eyes traveled the store and scanned items that had been abandoned and left in disarray in the rush of customers frantic to exit the horror scene. "What a mess," she uttered under her breath.

Deborah's shoulders slumped, and she sniffed again. "Are you sure?" It was obvious she'd been crying inside the office.

Sammy reached out and gave her coworker a hug. "Yeah, I'm sure. Try and get some rest tonight. I know these things have a way of keeping the mind active long past when we want them too. I don't mean to be insensitive, but is there any chance you can come in tomorrow? Bright and early before opening at nine, to clean up this mess? I could really use your help, but I understand if you need to take some time."

"Totally. You can count on me. It'll be best if we're together tomorrow, Sammy. Maybe by then we'll be able to comprehend all of this." Deborah wiped her nose with a tissue she had crumpled and hidden in her hand.

"All righty then," Sammy affirmed with a weak smile. "I'm heading out front to help plow out the rescue personnel; snow's piling up. I'll see you tomorrow. Safe driving, Deborah."

"Yeah, okay. See you tomorrow, then."

Sammy headed to the front entrance, where the ambulance was now pulling away from the curb. The lack of a siren didn't hide the bright-red neon flashing lights that sent an eerie reflection into the stone-cold snowy night.

Chapter Four

The next morning dawned bright as Sammy rolled onto her side and noted that the corners of her bedroom window were frosted inside her rented Cape Cod. The window sashes in her old rental were ancient and warped and, judging by the snow on the interior, desperately needed replacing. The sunniest days were always the coldest in Wisconsin, as the clouds seemed to have a way of blocking the arctic air.

Bara bounded into the bedroom and jumped onto her bed, encouraging her to lift her weary body from the comfort of her red-and-white star-patterned quilt. The handmade blanket was the only holiday adornment she had resurrected from the attic after Thanksgiving, as decorating Community Craft always took precedence. Sammy had pieced the quilt the previous year with wool batting that draped beautifully and was surprisingly cozy and warm despite its lack of thickness. The star-patterned quilt was the first she had attempted on her own, and as intricate as it looked, it had been surprisingly easy to piece together. Owning and running the craft shop hadn't given her a lot of extra time to work on her own handmade projects. Therefore, she'd sewn a seasonal design and decided to display the labor of love on her bed only for the duration of the holiday season. And now her dog was trampling the labor of love before she'd had a chance to put it back in storage for the following holiday season.

Sammy shooed Bara from the quilt, swung her legs to the side of the bed, and placed her feet on the cold hardwood. The icy floor jolted her awake, and she bent at the waist to peek under the bed for her missing slippers, which of course were nowhere to be found. Instead, a handful of dust bunnies stared back at her. Her lip curled in disgust. She fumbled her way to the long white bureau tucked against the wall and dug out a pair of blue fuzzy socks and immediately covered her feet.

As she made her way down the oak staircase, the horror of the previous night's events flooded her mind. She had looked forward to the Fire and Ice event for well over a month, and now, in a flash, it was over. A feeling of dread swept over her as she thought about how Wanda's family would move forward without her.

Sammy reached her tiny kitchen and mechanically filled the coffee machine. Before she knew it, the smell of brew tickled her nose and brought a hint of comfort. She hadn't slept well. Wanda's untimely death had kept her tossing and turning until the wee hours of the morning. Her phone, sitting on the center island, which was too oversized for the cramped space, beeped a text. This sent instant alarm through her, as the clock on the microwave showed it wasn't even seven AM.

It was Heidi. *Are you up? Wanda's husband MIA.*

Although Heidi preferred text as her main line of communication, Sammy did not. Sammy dialed her cousin, and Heidi picked up on the third ring.

"You're up," Heidi said in a clipped tone. "Hang on."

Sammy set the phone to speaker and poured herself a cup of coffee. She reached into the refrigerator, topped off the mug with French vanilla creamer, and took a welcome sip, all before Heidi returned to the phone. She still had coffee in her mouth when she heard, "You still there?"

Sammy swallowed. "Yeah. What are you doing?"

"I'm getting dressed for work. I have to be at the hospital soon. Did you get any sleep last night?"

"Barely." Sammy stifled a yawn.

"Yeah. I hear you. Me either."

"What did you mean with your cryptic text? Wanda's husband is missing?"

"Tim spent the night at my place, and this morning he received an early call from the police department. It seems they still can't reach Wanda's husband to tell him the news of her death. He never came to the hospital to say goodbye, pay respects, *nothing*. The police don't know if he even received the news that she passed away yet."

"That's odd."

"You're telling me!"

"Does he travel for business or something?"

"Nope; that's the same thing I asked Tim. He mentioned Marty travels locally around the state, but his neighbors insist he's usually home by dinnertime during the winter months. Sometimes he spends an overnight here or there, mostly during the summer, but this time of year he'd supposedly be home by now. Of course, the police department contacted his work. They're keeping tabs to see if he'll show up there on Monday. His cell keeps going to voice mail."

"That's odd. I can't believe they haven't found him yet." Sammy blew atop her mug and then took another sip. The hotter the liquid, the better.

"And get this, it gets even more interesting. The coroner doesn't think Wanda died from a heart attack. Apparently, her death is starting to look suspicious."

"You're kidding."

"Nope. So now Marty's absence is really looking a bit shady, don't ya think? Have you ever met him?"

"A few random times when he's popped into the shop with Wanda. Other than that, I don't really know Marty. You?"

"Ah, yeah, about the same. I'd know him if I saw him; that's about it."

"Do you think the police are under the impression Marty left of his own accord? As if he's trying to hide a guilty conscience or something? I'm assuming he's looking like a suspect now in their eyes. His wife ends up mysteriously dying, and now suddenly he's nowhere to be found? It does seem a bit suspicious, no?"

"I dunno for sure what's going on with the police. Tim's tight-lipped about the details when I pump him for info, but this latest development definitely left me curious. I've just overheard a few things that I thought I'd pass on to you. Obviously, I've been thinking the same thing you are—*suspicious*. Why should I be the only one wondering?" Heidi laughed.

"Well, my dear, I have to get to the hospital. I heard the ER has been busy too, with all the minor traffic accidents due to the snow overnight. I'll keep you posted if I hear the police find him."

"Yeah, keep me posted. Definitely. Thanks, Heidi. Have a good day."

"Yeah, you too. I hope you have time to shovel. Looks like we got about another foot of snow out there."

Sammy groaned.

"Sorry to be the bearer of bad news," Heidi added in a teasing tone. "Love you."

"Love you too."

Sammy clicked off the phone and then kneaded her forehead with her fingers. *Missing.* Where the heck had Wanda's husband disappeared to? Incredibly odd.

Sammy's eyes traveled to the back door, where Bara was patiently waiting. "Oh, I'm sorry, pup. I didn't mean to keep you waiting." She set down her mug and rushed to open the back door, which was blocked with snow. Yesterday she had welcomed the weather. Today she loathed it. How the mood could be so fickle! After a few good shoves, the door opened enough for her to make a pass with the shovel leaning by the back door big enough for her dog to squeeze through. Bara looked at her as if to say, *You really want me to jump over that snowbank to get outside and do my business?* But after a few minutes of sniffing, he pushed his paws through the cold stuff and barely made it outside the door before turning the snow yellow.

Sammy remembered she had asked Deborah to return to Community Craft earlier than their nine AM opening time so they could clean up the previous night's mess. She hurried her morning along with a quick shower and speedy breakfast. A slice of toast lathered in peanut butter and a second cup of tepid coffee did the trick. She breathed a huge sigh of relief when she peeked out the front window and noted that her driveway had been halfway cleared. The heavy stuff, where the plow often left a huge icy heap at the edge of the driveway, was gone. Her landlord, Ralph, must have stopped by to do a quick sweep and brush off her car while she was in the shower. She mentally calculated whether her car could roll over the rest and decided she would force it. She added to her mental list: *Pick up something special at Sweet Tooth Bakery for Ralph as an act of appreciation for plowing me out.* Or maybe, if she was lucky, she still had a full box of Marilyn's cookies left over from the previous night she could pass along. Now that the new year had hit, she was bound and determined to lose the extra holiday weight, and Marilyn's cookies sure wouldn't help with that.

The snow was surprisingly light and fluffy and blew like glittered dust when Sammy opened the back door of her car for Bara to jump inside. Her dog was wearing a blue tartan scarf that one of her talented seamstresses had sewn from a soft flannel material especially for him. Bara looked adorable wearing it, sending the first smile of the day to her lips.

"My customers are going to love you today, my handsome boy," she said to her dog as she patted his head and tucked him safely into the back seat, then closed the door. She waved her gloved hand over the front of the windshield and decided the wipers could blow off the rest that had fallen since Ralph had cleared her car.

Even though she had only a few blocks to drive to reach Community Craft, the ride to town was slow going. Every year, it seemed, people forgot how to drive in the white stuff, and the first major accumulating snow (not just a mere dusting here or there) had everyone readjusting to the change, causing a backup on Main Street. Sammy looked out the frosty car window at Heartsford Credit Union and the park square behind it and wondered if the bonfire had gone off without a hitch. She had missed it. The first year in a very long time that she had missed the traditional community gathering.

A heaviness filled her heart as her mind wandered back to Wanda. What had happened to her? And where was her husband?

After missing the stoplight again due to the slowed traffic, Sammy made a last-minute decision and flicked the blinker to turn right. She knew Wanda lived not far off Main Street and decided an impromptu drive past her house to see if her husband Marty had finally returned home wouldn't be a bad idea.

The quilting group had gathered at Wanda's home just a few weeks prior for a holiday party, and although Sammy hadn't been able to make it that night, she still had the invitation stashed in her glove compartment. She reached inside to locate it, then opened the card to reveal the address. Only a few blocks to go. She buzzed the washer fluid and turned the wipers on full speed to clear the windshield and find her way. When she reached Wanda's house, she was surprised to see a *For Sale* sign dusted with snow displayed on the front lawn. "Huh . . ." she said aloud.

Sammy pulled alongside the curb as close as she could without parking herself into a large snowdrift and set her emergency blinkers on so a snowplow wouldn't come behind her unexpectedly and plow her in. She gazed up at the stately white Victorian. The path of snow from the sidewalk to the house had not been cleared, but footprints littered the front walk, as if the police had come again for a return visit. The house windows were dark despite the curtains being pushed aside, showing no signs of life. And the large wraparound porch had also not been cleared of snow. Where could Marty be? Before the day was through, Sammy was sure she would have to find out.

Chapter Five

Townspeople were multiplying in front of Liquid Joy, the local coffee shop across the street from Community Craft, and Sammy silently wondered what the group was discussing among themselves. There had to be something keeping their attention in the bone-chilling cold. Were they talking about the Fire and Ice event from the previous night? Or were they talking about Wanda? Or had word hit the streets that Wanda's husband seemed noticeably absent? She pondered this as she flipped the sign on the glass front door to *Open*.

Deborah was adjusting jars of local honey on a nearby shelf and turned to Sammy. "I hate to bring this up, but we really ought to put a new display in the window, don't you think? The longer we leave the gaping hole in the storefront, the longer people are going to walk by and remember why it's vacant . . ." Deborah let the words hang in the air like a heavy, dense fog, clouding them in.

"I agree. We've both been avoiding the inevitable all morning." Sammy turned from the front door and regarded her coworker. "Let's turn it into a cozy winter scene, shall we? We already have the artificial fireplace in the corner and the fake snow. I'll walk around the store and see what would fit well with the theme out there." Sammy was about to step away when she saw Deborah frown. "What's wrong?"

"I just feel so out of sorts, you know? I normally go to yoga early every Sunday morning while Danny watches the kids. Wanda called it church yoga because many of us would head to church right after and meet up with our families. Wanda even came with me to church the last few Sundays. Honestly, I just can't believe she's gone."

Sammy reached an arm out to comfort her friend. "I know, it's crazy, right? I can't even imagine what her family will have to go through; such a loss. I'm also sorry to have taken you away from church this morning and encouraged you to work instead. I hope God doesn't hold that against me." Sammy looked to the ceiling, placing her hands together in a prayerlike position, and then her eyes returned to her coworker. Sammy's idea of church was loving people, not necessarily meeting and worshiping in a building—although her sister and family nudged her at times to attend. "Unfortunately, Ellie couldn't get here early today. Her in-laws came into town to enjoy the festivities last night and didn't want to drive back to Milwaukee in the snowstorm."

"Oh, that's okay. And I'm pretty sure this is where God would want me. Right here helping you." Deborah smiled. "Plus, I don't mind working early, and I know you only keep the store open on Sundays through Fire and Ice. The rest of the winter, Community Craft will remain closed on Sundays, right?"

Sammy nodded in agreement. "Yes, that's true. Unless someone in the community needs the doors opened for use of the craft room—then we'll make special arrangements to open up on a Sunday."

Deborah rubbed at her eyelid. "Not to mention, everything was left in such disarray last night. I would've felt horrible leaving you hanging to clean this mess yourself."

"Did her husband go along? To church, I mean?" Sammy swiped at her bangs, which desperately needed a trim. She needed to pay a visit to Lizzy at Live and Let Dye hair salon real soon, or she'd impatiently chop them off crookedly herself. It wouldn't be the first time poor Lizzy had needed to "fix" her hair.

"No. Wanda said church wasn't Marty's sort of thing. Honestly, she had only just started attending herself. I begged her for months before she finally acquiesced." Deborah sighed. "And anyway, a guy she used to work with at her old job before she started teaching yoga at the rec center goes to our church, and I guess Marty has issues with that."

"Oh? A little possessive, huh?" Sammy wanted to mention that Wanda's husband seemed to be MIA, but she figured Heidi had shared that in confidence, so she held her tongue.

"I feel so stiff without practicing this morning. Yoga is so good for you. You should try it, Sammy," Deborah suggested. "The stretching just eases all the tension from your body. It really helps with my mood too."

"I'm afraid I'm not very flexible." Sammy chuckled. "Besides, I get enough exercise around here." She widened her eyes and gazed around the shop. "I just need to stay away from the Sweet Tooth Bakery," she added as she tapped her stomach with her hands. "Hey, have you ever considered leading a yoga class? It's not like you don't have the background. I would think that would be a good fit for you, being a former ballerina and all. Besides, you teach the glass painting here—you also have amazing teaching skills. I mean, who else can teach someone to paint a rose when it initially looked like a cabbage?" She laughed.

Sammy could see Deborah contemplating the idea, so she added, "You should think about it."

"Maybe. Yeah . . . I'll definitely think about that."

"All righty, you think about it. Meanwhile, let's get back to work." Sammy turned, then stopped herself. "Hey, by the way, did you know Wanda's house is up for sale?"

"Yeah, she told us at the holiday party that she wanted to downsize. I wish you hadn't had to miss the party; she had the most beautiful Christmas decorations this year. Honestly, the house looked like something out of a storybook. Anyhow, she claimed the older Victorian was drafty, cost an arm and a leg to heat, and was way too much work. She said she wanted to live simpler."

"And how did Marty feel about the potential move?"

Deborah stared at her palms. "Dunno. But as Wanda pointed out, he apparently doesn't have to clean it. Which I could totally relate to; her husband sounds exactly like my Danny when it comes to cleaning."

"I guess she doesn't have to worry about that now," Sammy said gloomily as she hung her head in sadness.

Deborah mirrored her action.

Sammy could see their mood was going downhill. She needed to change that before customers entered the store. "We'd better split up and look for items to fill that empty display window."

Sammy left Deborah and began to peruse the racks, walls, and shelves of Community Craft. She moved into the storage room and removed an aged wooden five-foot ladder that closely matched her own height and lugged it to the front of the store.

Deborah almost collided with her between the narrow racks of knit scarves and then turned and paused with a questioning look. "I'm guessing you want to hang a few quilted items off of that?"

"You got it; that's exactly my thought. After working closely together this past year, I think you finally know how to read my mind." Sammy winked.

Deborah returned the smile, then moved in the direction of the shelves where the quilted items were on display as Sammy stepped inside the window.

While Sammy was adjusting the ladder in the perfect spot and gathering the artificial snow along the wooden legs, something caught the corner of her eye. Bunched in the corner beneath the artificial snow lay Wanda's hand-sewn lap quilt. A pang hit her heart. She bent at the waist and retrieved the heirloom off the display floor. She'd have to return this special keepsake to Wanda's family sometime soon. She wondered who had pieced it together, if not Wanda herself. Sammy folded the quilt neatly and stepped out of the window so she could tuck the blanket safely inside the drawer of her office desk. After making sure the lap quilt was placed inside a plastic bag and put away, she returned and began hanging various table runners that Deborah had left in a heap beside the entrance to the window.

As Sammy was draping the runners over the ladder, she felt that itchy feeling one got when it seemed like someone was watching. She lifted her eyes and looked through the glass and noted the crowd had dissipated in front of Liquid Joy, but

Detective Liam Nash was lingering with a steaming coffee in his hand. She should've known he'd be watching her.

When the detective noticed her gaze, he looked both ways across Main Street and then stepped off the sidewalk and headed in the direction of Community Craft.

Sammy breathed deep. She wished it wasn't only tragedy that brought that man around. She stepped out of the display window and met the officer by the front door.

"Good morning, Detective. What brings you out this frosty morning?" Sammy held the door while he stepped inside the shop. She hoped he noticed the lightness in her tone and greeting to make up for her agitation the previous night.

Liam wiped his feet on the welcome mat and then took a sip from his Liquid Joy cup before he answered. "I'm retracing Wanda's steps from yesterday. Seems her husband is missing, and things aren't setting right in my mind. Actually, I'm anxious to hear what the medical examiner has to say about her autopsy." The detective scrutinized Sammy as if he already knew she had information and was waiting for her to crack. Could he read the deep parts of her mind? She hoped not.

"*Really?* Well, that sure is interesting news," Sammy said, a little too enthusiastically. She'd tried to act surprised and had overshot. She didn't want the detective to know Heidi had confided in her about Wanda's missing husband. Otherwise, her cousin might never share info with her again, and she could lose her best inside source within the police department.

"Yeah. *Really.*" The detective studied her.

Sammy shrugged innocently. "Beats me. I don't really know the guy." Her eyes left his penetrating gaze.

"You don't?"

"Uh-uh, not really." Sammy lifted her shoulders innocently. "He's only stepped inside Community Craft maybe a handful of times, and when he has, Wanda's always been with him."

"Can you help me retrace Wanda's steps yesterday while she was here in the store?" Detective Nash lifted his coffee and took another sip.

"Sure, come on in." Sammy encouraged the detective to leave the front entrance mat, where he was still dripping snow despite wiping his feet. She led him to the glass-encased craft room within the store.

"I came in here to go over the details with the first group of people who were going to take a turn in the window," Sammy said over her shoulder as she stepped over the threshold. "And Wanda was one of them."

"Take a turn in the window?" The detective's eyes narrowed in question.

Sammy turned to face him fully. "Oh. I guess I'm surprised you didn't hear what we were doing during the Fire and Ice event. I was hosting a live-mannequin contest in the storefront display window. Which is why Wanda was inside the window when you arrived. Or had she already been moved to the ambulance when you got here? I'm sorry; that part is a bit of a blur." Sammy breathed deep, reliving the horrible memory of Heidi, dressed in costume, administering CPR. "Must be all the stress that's leaving me with a blank. Anyhow, let me think . . ." Sammy's eyes pinballed within the glass room, trying to remember where everyone had been seated around the table. "Wanda was here." Sammy laid her hand atop the back of the chair closest to the door. "Cheryl, Miles, Lynn,

Mary, and someone else . . . Wait. I can check the clipboard!" She turned to retrieve her clipboard with the list of participants that she had left on the countertop that lined the craft room wall, but she couldn't find it. What she did come across was Wanda's travel mug filled with peppermint tea. "Oh nooo." She blew out of her mouth and nodded her head grimly.

"What is it?" The detective moved closer and peered over her shoulder.

"Wanda left her peppermint tea. She asked me to guard it with my life, and now her life is over." Without warning, Sammy burst into tears.

"I know, this has to be a tough shock. I'm so sorry." Detective Nash laid a comforting hand on her shoulder. Sammy turned to him and allowed herself to fall into his protective, solid arms. It felt good to fold into him willingly, and she breathed in his manly scent mixed with a faint whiff of musky cologne.

"Oh . . . Gosh . . . Oh boy . . . I'm sorry to interrupt," Deborah said as she entered the craft room, her face immediately flushing red, as if she had walked in on the two of them getting frisky on the craft room floor.

Sammy quickly jerked back from the detective. "No. No interruption," she stuttered as she wiped her wet eyes with the back of her hand and awkwardly backed away from him.

"Oh Sammy! You're crying!" Deborah reached to comfort her as well, and then the two embraced until Deborah's eyes also began to mist.

The detective stood waiting for their tears to subside and then filled the glass room with the empty echo of his words. "I'm really sorry, ladies." Sammy secretly wondered if the detective felt awkward about Deborah walking in on their embrace. Did he feel something too? Or was she overthinking? She was *always* overthinking.

Sammy stepped back from Deborah and encouraged her coworker with an outstretched hand. "Maybe you can help answer a few questions Liam might have."

"Questions? Why are you asking questions? About what?"

"About Wanda."

"Why are there questions about Wanda? Isn't it pretty self-explanatory?" Deborah placed her manicured hands to her heart. "Didn't I see you in here last night, Detective Nash? Why are you here now?" Deborah's face furrowed in confusion. "What am I missing here?"

The detective cleared his throat. "Just standard protocol. I'm just clarifying a few things and making sure I'm being thorough. It's common practice in these types of situations."

"But I thought she had a heart attack." Deborah dropped her hands from her heart and placed them on her delicate hips. Her eyes bounced between Sammy and the detective.

"We're not sure yet. Especially now that her husband is missing, things are a bit weird," Sammy interjected.

The detective sent a warning glare to Sammy to not overdisclose. "Her husband's whereabouts have raised a few flags. I'm just being cautious."

Sammy grimaced in response to the detective's warning. It seemed, as per usual, she was already getting on his bad side by opening her mouth too soon. *Why can't I keep my mouth shut?* she berated herself inwardly. It seemed he was the only one around town she had to walk on eggshells with before she spoke.

"Whaaat?" Deborah shrieked. "Marty is *missing*?"

"We have yet to locate him to inform him of his wife's death, I'd appreciate it if you keep this information under wraps." He lifted an eyebrow and eyed Sammy as if to say, *See what you've done now?*

To defend herself, Sammy said, "I'm sorry to say, but if you're looking to hold down gossip, it may be a bit late for that. A crowd was outside Liquid Joy this morning eyeing my store. I'm sure Wanda's sudden passing is all people are talking about here in Heartsford."

"That's true," Deborah agreed. "The whole town was out for the event last night. And let me say, it was kinda difficult not to notice the ambulance parked out front, and of course everyone wants to know *why*. My husband Danny said everyone was asking and wondering why Marty wasn't around for Fire and Ice before Wanda . . . well . . . you know . . ."

The detective cleared his throat. "In any event, I'd appreciate it if this part of the conversation remains between us three."

"Absolutely, Detective. You have my word," Deborah answered, locking an imaginary key by her mouth.

Sammy remained silent. She figured it was her best option, based on Liam's growing irritation.

"But where could he possibly be?" Deborah asked.

"That's what we'd like to know. So, if you happen to come upon any further information or hear any rumblings, here's my card." The detective dug into his winter coat, plucked out a business card, and held it out with two fingers.

"Well, I know Wanda wasn't feeling well during yoga class yesterday morning, and didn't you say she still wasn't feeling the best last night?" Deborah turned to Sammy.

"Yeah, I don't think she was feeling well emotionally either. Cheryl was giving her a hard time about wanting to sit on a chair instead of striking a yoga pose," Sammy agreed.

"Cheryl hates her . . . I mean, hated her. I'm sorry, I keep forgetting she's gone . . ." Deborah placed her hand to her heart again. Her face looked stricken.

"Go on," Sammy encouraged. "Can you explain to the detective what you mean?"

"You didn't know? Haven't you heard the talk around town? Cheryl wanted to sue the rec center because she slipped a disk in her back and wanted to blame Wanda for it. She expected Wanda to pay all her medical bills—and then some—from what I heard. Which, personally, I think is completely ridiculous."

"Cheryl was a bit wound up last night," Sammy agreed. "She and Craig also had words inside the store, but it ended rather abruptly when they saw me coming. I'm sure it was just a marital spat. However, to be honest, I didn't hear what they were arguing about."

Sammy watched as the detective took that information in like a sponge. He pointed to Wanda's travel mug of peppermint tea. "I'll take that with me."

"Sure." Sammy handed him the stainless thermos, which he took custody of with a gloved hand.

"Was there anything else Wanda might have left behind?"

Sammy held her tongue. Was it necessary to tell him about the lap quilt? She doubted it. The last thing she wanted was for a special heirloom to be locked up in police custody, never to be seen by the family again.

"I can't believe everything that's happened," Deborah said, interrupting Sammy's thoughts. "I can ask Danny again if he's heard anything new or if he's heard if anyone else might have seen Marty since Fire and Ice. Sometimes Danny runs into a few of Marty's friends at a bar just outside town. What do you think, Detective?"

"Why don't you give me Danny's number, and I'll call him myself."

"Sure," Deborah agreed as she reached for a nearby drawer to pluck out a yellow sticky note and a pen. She wrote her husband's number on the pad and handed the slip of paper to the detective.

"If you ladies think of anything else, be sure and call me," Detective Nash said in an official manner, stepping over the threshold of the craft room.

Sammy wondered if Liam was suddenly acting formal because of Deborah catching their embrace. Or perhaps because of her own standoffish behavior the previous night? Or maybe he really didn't have any interest in pursuing her. Either way, it seemed that fate continued to bring them together. Why couldn't fate work a little less gruesomely and in her favor for once? She felt awful for the fleeting thought, because it was more important to get to the bottom of why Marty Wadsworth was missing and what had caused Wanda's sudden passing. She felt a hot rush in her cheeks. It was *not* important whether there was or *wasn't* a possibility of a romantic connection for her with Detective Liam Nash.

An unexpected rattling sound from the closed cabinet beneath the sink seized the attention of all three of them.

Deborah looked on with revulsion. "Please tell me we don't have mice again," she said as she moved across the threshold of the craft room to hide behind the safety of the detective, who responded with a smile and a protective arm block.

"I wouldn't be surprised. As cold as it is, those little fellas need to find someplace to get warm. Although Bara is usually pretty good about catching them." Sammy snapped open the cabinet door to release the creature, but instead of finding a mouse, her eyes fell upon Wanda's oversized quilt bag. Judging by the clatter coming from it, a cell phone was on high vibration inside it. "Wanda must've tucked this in here last night after her visit to the restroom. I didn't see her come back before she went inside the window, but I was a little preoccupied. I didn't even think about where her bag would have gone until now," Sammy easily admitted, hoping the detective believed she wasn't purposely trying to hide anything in her cabinet. She instantly handed the bag to the detective, and he reached inside to fish out the phone. "Fifteen missed calls," he said aloud as he scrolled through the phone. He then placed the cell phone on the table, because the call had ended and the phone's vibrating had abruptly stopped. "And it looks like they're all from her husband," he added as he pointed a lean finger at the abandoned phone.

Sammy moved closer to the table, and the phone instantly came to life again, glaring the name *Martin* across the screen.

"Answer it and pretend you're Wanda. I want to hear how he's going to respond. Don't give him any details; just tell him he needs to come home." The detective pointed to the phone bouncing across the table.

"*Me?*" Sammy shook her head, confused.

"Yes. Hurry! I don't want to tip him off; I'll write down what I want you to say." He plucked a small pad of paper and pen from his pocket. "But put it on speaker so we all can hear."

Sammy picked up the phone, hit the speaker button, and said, "Hello?"

"Help! Help! You gotta help me!" a voice on the other end pleaded. There was a loud, raucous sound, and then the phone fell eerily silent.

Chapter Six

Sammy found it nearly impossible to drop the frantic call from Marty and the passing of Wanda Wadsworth from the forefront of her mind. The vision of Heidi administering CPR inside the display window of Community Craft also replayed in her head like a horror movie on repeat. Her thoughts swayed again to the panic in Marty's voice bellowing from Wanda's cell phone.

Her anxiety morphed to curiosity as she drove toward her sister's house for dinner. What had happened to Marty? Was he hurt? Had he been in a car accident due to the inclement weather? Where was he? Did he know his wife was gone? She wished she could peek behind the curtain of the Wadsworths' relationship and see what she was missing. Unfortunately, she really didn't know a lot about Wanda's personal life. Although Wanda had participated in classes and spent time at Community Craft, talk of her home life had been unusually private, and now Sammy wished she'd paid closer attention.

Sammy's nephew, Tyler, was turning four years old, and a small family gathering had been planned. If not for her deep love of her nephew, Sammy would easily have canceled her dinner plans and instead tried to dig for more information about the whereabouts of Marty Wadsworth. The fact that Wanda had her husband's name listed as Martin and not Marty as her phone contact was an interesting tidbit. Did that mean anything? Sammy thought it rather formal when everyone else in Heartsford seemed to refer to him as Marty. She smiled as she reflected on her own cell phone contacts. Liam Nash wasn't listed by his name, either; he was simply *Detective N* in her phone. She wished he were *Liam* . . .

She hated that her mind diverted to longing for the aloof detective. It annoyed her that he was never far from her mind.

Was it really Wanda's husband who had been calling? Or another person named Martin? It wasn't as if Sammy recognized the voice. She'd even asked Deborah if she could distinguish Marty's voice on the phone, but her coworker couldn't tell. Everything had happened so fast. They had all been left stunned.

Detective Nash had promptly left her and Deborah in a cloud of confusion to return to the police station and have the call traced so he could hopefully locate Marty's whereabouts. Had he ever found him? Sammy didn't know. Before Liam's swift exit from Community Craft, she had begged him to please keep them posted. It was highly doubtful that he would share anything now. The remainder of the day had lagged on as she and Deborah waited patiently by the phone for a call that never arrived. Hadn't the police department been left with no choice other than to assume foul play? How could Wanda suddenly leave planet earth and her husband now apparently be in some sort of danger? The two incidents were obviously connected.

Leading her to believe health-conscious Wanda had *not* died from some hidden disease.

After pulling up the driveway in front of the familiar two-story white colonial, Sammy jammed the car in park. Bara stood in the back seat, eager for his escape. If she hadn't known better, she might have thought her dog was smiling. Bara, not normally welcome at her sister's house due to Ellie's neurotic cleaning habits, had been requested tonight. Ellie was making an exception, as Tyler had insisted that Bara be invited to his birthday party. How her sister would let that poor child grow up without a dog or a cuddly pet, she would never understand. A little extra work around the house—so what? For all the unconditional love a pet could bring to a family? Bara was more than worth it, in Sammy's opinion. This was just one of the few things she and her sister couldn't agree upon. She'd rallied on Tyler's behalf on several occasions to adopt a rescue, but Ellie wouldn't budge.

Sammy reached for the old faded towel beside her on the passenger seat so she could wipe Bara's paws. She wanted to be sure he didn't track snow inside. That was the least she could do to be considerate of her sister's feelings, despite the fact that they didn't agree that Tyler should have a dog of his own to love.

Bara bounded up the driveway just as the garage door was lifting with a large groan. Sammy quickly caught up with him and looped her finger around his collar to hold him back from leaping inside the garage. As soon as the door rose completely, she encouraged him to sit to wipe his paws. Before she had a chance to finish, Ellie swung the interior wooden door to her house open wide, and Bara leapt from her reach before she could wipe all four paws completely clean.

"Oh, it's okay, don't worry about it," Ellie said, tossing a dish towel over her shoulder as Bara shoved past her through the door with puppy-like excitement.

"Hey, I tried," Sammy said with a huff, sending her overlong bangs blowing from her forehead, reminding her again that she'd forgotten to call Lizzy and make a hair appointment.

"I know you did. But if Tyler had to wait one more second for his birthday party to begin, I don't think I could stand it. He's been hyper all afternoon waiting, and quite literally I'm the one now counting the minutes." Ellie smiled as she jammed a thumb toward her chest.

"Oh shoot. I forgot Tyler's birthday present in the trunk." Sammy turned in the direction of her car to retrieve the gift just as her nephew and Bara shoved past Ellie back inside the garage.

"Happy birthday, my sweet little Tyler!" Sammy said as she ruffled the boy's curly golden head and drew him in for a half hug. She simultaneously reached for Bara's collar and led him back in the direction of the house. "How about you bring puppy back inside so I can go get your present?"

Tyler jumped up and down excitedly and squealed, "Present, present, present!" as his hands clapped together like clanging cymbals. Pure delight raced across the little boy's face.

"Slow down there, Ty," Ellie said in a firm voice. "Bring the dog back inside and go settle him down. Otherwise your party will never get started, and I don't think you want that," she warned.

Tyler quickly heeded his mother's warning and darted back into the house, Bara galloping in close pursuit. Ellie closed the door to hold off a recurrence and followed her sister out into the garage in her moccasin slippers. "Boy, its freezing out here," Ellie said, shivering and running her hands up and down her arms.

"I hear you. The raw cold has definitely returned. Go ahead back inside where it's warm; I'll be right behind you," Sammy said over her shoulder as she moved toward her car.

She popped the trunk with her fob and carefully maneuvered patches of the icy pavement to retrieve Tyler's birthday present. The frigid day had turned everyone's driveway into a sheet of ice. She hoped she wouldn't fall and land flat on her ass.

"I can't. I have to talk to you."

Sammy eased back up the driveway, careful not to slip, a large wrapped box held tightly under her right arm. "What is it?"

"Wanda's husband is missing," Ellie said, wringing her hands and blowing into them for warmth.

"Yeah. I know. How'd you find out? Deborah and I were sworn to secrecy . . . don't tell Nash you heard it from me." Sammy didn't mention Heidi's call in the morning, as she didn't want to get in the middle of the two of them. "Who's the leak?"

"Wait. Detective Nash shared something with you?" Ellie flung an index finger in Sammy's direction. "That's a surprise," she teased, her eyes widening and dancing with amusement. "He's back, huh? No more disappearing act, twice in two days? Interesting . . ."

"Long story. One I'm not supposed to share, but I'm sure we'll be chatting about it anyhow, especially if Heidi's coming tonight. This is a real job for S.H.E.," Sammy said, invoking the childhood investigative club of three: *S* for Sammy, *H* for Heidi, and *E* for Ellie.

"No, no, no, Sammy. Not S.H.E." Ellie wagged a warning finger. "We're not involving ourselves in another investigation. Nope." She vigorously shook her head in disagreement.

Sammy smiled to lessen her sister's apprehension and hopefully warm her enough to dig for more intel. "Relax, I'm just teasing. No worries." She waved a casual hand to diffuse the anxiety. "How do *you* know Marty's missing, though? What've you heard?"

"Well, Randy is supposed to be co-listing the sale of Wanda's house. I can't believe his luck. His first genuine real-estate deal, and everything's now on hold. I'm so ticked off."

"He's co-listing? I didn't see his name on the sign."

"What were you doing in front of Wanda's house that you saw the sign?" Ellie plucked a loose hair off her sweater and then studied her. "That's not on your regular driving route. You're deeper in this than I thought. 'Fess up . . . you've been investigating already, haven't you? You little stinker!" Her frown transformed into a sly smile.

Sammy shrugged off the question and waved her sister off again, as if it were commonplace for her to drive a few blocks in the other direction from town on roads she rarely traveled.

Ellie shook her head and rolled her eyes disapprovingly, but then continued, "Randy doesn't have signs printed yet. They're still on order, but Regina was letting him co-list for his first trial run. Yes, Regina's name is technically on the sign, but my husband has been doing all the footwork, to be honest. The police department phoned him today, though, and halted all showings until further notice."

"Oh boy," Sammy said. "That's not good."

"Yeah. Not good at all. It's hard enough getting people to list their houses in the dead of winter without stuff like this happening. We really need the money. We're taking a huge risk here with this new 'hobby' of his." Ellie threw up her fingers in air quotes.

"I don't know if you should use the term *dead of winter* right now," Sammy suggested with a smile and a wink.

Ellie cringed. "Yeah. Oops . . . I didn't even think of that. I better think a little longer before I open my big mouth in public. What is it with us Kane girls?" she asked sheepishly. "I need to avoid that type of flippant talk right now!" She chuckled and nudged her sister playfully.

Heidi's car pulled into the driveway and her high beams blinded them both, prompting Sammy to shield them from the light with Tyler's present and Ellie to hide beneath her forearm. As soon as the lights dimmed, Sammy tucked the present under her right arm and Ellie dropped her arms to her side.

"Hey, *chicas*! What are you two doing out here in the cold? You're nuts to be standing out here." Heidi opened the rear door and pulled out a large present about the size of Sammy's. She hoped they hadn't purchased the same thing.

"Legos?" Sammy asked.

"Yeah, why?"

Sammy lifted the present tucked under her right arm for Heidi to view.

"That's okay. Boys can't get enough Legos—right, Ellie?"

Ellie nodded. "Although I bet neither one of you guys has ever stepped on one of those darn little plastic things. They're lethal," she added with a laugh and then a cringe.

"Speaking of lethal," Heidi interjected, "you guys heard they're running an autopsy on Wanda, right?"

"That doesn't surprise me," Sammy said.

"Yeah, Tim mentioned that you heard the frantic call."

Ellie's eyes bounced between the two, confused, and then she slapped her sister playfully with the back of her hand. "You're holdin' out on me?" she asked with an accusing tone. "I knew you were a stinker!"

"I was just about to tell you." Sammy's shoulders lifted in defense, and she almost dropped the package from beneath her arm.

The interior door swung open, and Randy popped his perfectly groomed platinum head outside. "Hurry up, you guys; Tyler and Bara are doing laps around the dining room! A little help here with the hyper party child?" Randy eyed Ellie, who quickly moved toward her husband.

"Duty calls, but I'm not done talking with you girls. Don't let me miss anything this time either, Sammy," Ellie said over her shoulder as she stepped inside the house.

Sammy caught Heidi by the arm to stop her from following Ellie into the house. "Wait. Did they find Marty? Nash was going to trace the cell phone and see if they could locate him."

"No, but the police department put out a BOLO."

"*Bolo*?"

"'Be on the lookout.'"

"Oh yeah, right. What do you think happened?"

"Dunno. But it's pretty crazy."

"I know, right? Nothing makes sense. I mean, there's no way Wanda had a heart attack. That woman was in the best shape and stuck very close to her vegan diet. Something fishy is going on here. Did you ever attend her yoga class?"

"Very seldom. She mostly led the later classes, which never really fit in my schedule due to my swing shifts at the hospital. But I heard a lot of the girls that used to take classes with her are talking about attending Joy's class now if there's room, so I'm guessing there isn't going to be much mat space."

"When is the next class?"

"*You* want to go to yoga? No offense, but this is a first!" Heidi smiled wide.

"No. I'd rather not contort my body in ways that seem utterly intolerable. However, I'll consider it if we can hear the chitchat about what was going on behind closed doors at the Wadsworth house. Which, by the way, is now for sale."

"That actually might be a good idea," Heidi said thoughtfully, rubbing her perfectly shaped chin. "Yeah, I heard it was for sale; did I forget to mention that this morning? Sorry, I was a bit distracted getting ready for work while we were talking."

"Any other intel from the police department that you want to share?"

"Not really. So far I've given you all the info Tim shared with me. One of these days he's really going to get in trouble for oversharing police information with me. But you know, I have my ways to get him to leak." Heidi batted her mascara-dipped lashes and puckered her lips.

"You're so naughty. But I love you!" Sammy pulled her cousin in for a half hug.

"We'd better get inside before we catch a cold." Heidi shivered.

"Yeah, maybe Randy can give a hint of insight as to what was going on behind closed doors at the Wadsworth house. He is one of the listing agents on the property, after all. He must know something."

Chapter Seven

Normally, the scent of dinner wafting from inside Ellie's house was one to tantalize the senses. Unfortunately, tonight was not one of those nights.

"Ellie, what are you cooking?" Sammy shadowed Heidi into the kitchen, where her sister stood in front of the large white farm sink. Ellie's hands gripped each side of a colander, and a plume of steam rose in the air.

Ellie laughed at her sister's remark, knowing full well Sammy wasn't a huge veggie lover. "Cauliflower. I'm making cauliflower mac and cheese. It's Tyler's absolute favorite, and this is what he requested for his birthday dinner."

"You've got to be kidding? *Cauliflower*?" Sammy wrinkled her nose. "No offense, but are you sure Ty-baby didn't request pizza or something else? You must be joking! Seriously? For a birthday dinner? What have you done to my poor nephew?" Sammy folded her arms across her chest. "You've got him on a diet now too?"

"Just wait until you try it before you judge. Trust me, you're going to love it. Have I ever cooked something you didn't like?"

Ellie asked over her shoulder as she dumped the steaming cauliflower florets into a large bowl lined with a towel to remove the excess water.

Sammy thought about it a moment. Her sister had a point there. But the pungent smell of cauliflower wasn't a very appetizing aroma and was most definitely conflicting with her belief system.

"I think it'll be fabulous!" Heidi said "And so low-cal! Way to go, Ellie, getting Tyler to love his veggies!"

"Shhhhh, keep it on the down-low," Ellie said, raising a finger to her lips. "Please don't tell him it's a vegetable; he still thinks it's really mac and cheese!" she laughed.

"Anything we can do to help? I'll do anything to hurry this along and get the smell outta this kitchen," Sammy said, waving a hand in front of her nose before pinching it shut.

Ellie encouraged her exit by directing a finger to the arched kitchen entryway. "You go help Randy with Tyler, then."

"Do you need me to set the dining room table?" Sammy asked.

"Already done," Ellie said, swishing her sister away with her hands. "Heidi, if you wouldn't mind sticking with me and grating the cheese over there?" She pointed to a large block of cheddar on the kitchen counter. "Meanwhile, I'll start the roux."

"No problem," Heidi said, reaching for the block of cheese and immediately starting to shred.

Sammy backed out of the kitchen, thankful for an escape from the pungent scent. When she arrived in the small living area, she noted Bara comfortably sprawled in front of the crackling fireplace and was instantly relieved that the horrid vegetable smell was replaced by the scent of smoky wood. Tyler stood with his hands behind his back, bouncing up and down on his toes, eyeing the side table that held his wrapped gifts. He dared not shake them, though, as his mother had previously warned that he wouldn't be able to open any of them if he didn't wait patiently. Sammy wondered how long Tyler would be able to hold out. A real test for sure. Randy was seated in a dark leather wingback chair reading the newspaper beneath a reading lamp. The room was cozy and welcoming on such a bitter January evening.

"Shall I pop another log on the fire?" Sammy suggested after moving closer and noticing the fire growing dim.

Randy's eyes lifted from the newspaper to regard the glowing embers. He folded the paper and set it aside on a nearby coffee table and then rose from the high-backed chair. "I can do it; no worries, have a seat and relax. I'm sure you've been busy on your feet all day." He gestured to the dark tweed sofa set along the wall. The sofa had a patchwork quilt draped over the arm and two matching quilted pillows, all purchased from Community Craft.

Sammy watched as Randy carefully sidestepped Bara, pulled back the fireplace screen, and stoked the fire with a metal poker before adding another log.

"Congratulations. Ellie tells me you're working on your first real-estate deal. That must be pretty exciting."

"Yeah. I'm sure she told you the current status, though. I mean, about the police now putting a hold on showings." Randy turned to face her, a blond eyebrow cocked in question.

"Well, hopefully the police will find Marty soon and all will be back to normal for you. I'm sure he won't want to keep that big old house alone, especially now . . ." Sammy chewed her lower lip to keep herself from saying what they both knew. Besides, Tyler had turned his attention to them, and she didn't think her nephew should hear such a conversation.

"Yeah. I hope so. Sure seems weird with what happened to Wanda, and then Marty disappearing?" Randy gazed in his son's direction and seemed to stop himself from saying too much also. "I just hope the police can get to the bottom of it soon."

Sammy agreed with a nod of her head. "No kidding. It's horrible," she said as she sank into the sofa and curled her feet beneath her.

"Open-present time?" Tyler moved over to Randy and tugged on his pant leg, looking up at his father with pleading crystal-blue eyes.

Tyler instantly knew by the shake of his father's head and a look of warning that he would have to continue to wait. So he slowly moved back to stand in front of the stack of gifts with longing eyes.

Randy returned his attention to Sammy. "The Wadsworths have only lived in the home for the last eight years. Initially they were going to restore it, but Wanda decided it was too much work with them both working full-time and Marty traveling during the summer months."

"What does Marty do for work? Do you know?"

"He sells seeds to farmers across Wisconsin. Mostly his territory runs from Heartsford along the southeast corner of the state, from what I understand."

"Oh."

"Anyhow," Randy continued, "their Queen Anne Victorian should be listed as one of Heartsford's historical properties. The house was built back in 1910 and still has many of the original features. I'm in the process of trying to make sure the new owner will choose to have it officially registered as a historical landmark, but it will take a very special buyer for sure. I may be able to encourage someone to go that route, as there can be some tax incentives or lower-interest loans if the buyer moves forward with that idea. I'm very lucky to be able to work on this type of project. Hopefully I can find a buyer who will respect the historical aspects of the property as much as I do. I'd hate to see someone come in there and destroy it by painting the woodwork." He shuddered at the thought.

Sammy knew her brother-in-law had been involved in the Heartsford Historical Society for the last few years, so she understood why this property would hold special meaning for him. She observed Tyler, who had moved away from the table of gifts and now knelt next to Bara to stroke his soft fur. If she could show Ellie the calming effect a dog had on Tyler, maybe her sister would reconsider having a pet? "You're being very gentle and kind, Ty-baby," she said to her nephew, who looked up and smiled. "Puppy loves when you pet him nice like that."

Tyler smiled shyly and continued to stroke his little hand tenderly along Bara's back.

Sammy returned her attention to Randy. "You know what . . ."

"Nope." Randy quickly held up a hand in defense. "We're not getting a dog. Ellie is pretty firm on that."

Sammy smiled and held back a chuckle. "That's not what I was going to say. Actually, I wanted to mention that I think I may know a potential buyer for your listing."

Randy cocked his head in surprise.

"You know Kendra, who leads the Beautification of Heartsford Committee? She was looking for a larger home a while back, and I think her lease is almost up. Now that I think of it, just recently she mentioned that she wants to get into the dry-floral business, and she needs the extra space to spread out to do that. Do you by chance have a listing sheet handy that I could give her? She pops in my shop at least once a week, and I'd be happy to pass it along. Maybe when this all settles down, you could take her for a showing. Do you know Kendra?"

"In passing. Our paths have definitely crossed a few times at different town events. Sure, I can print you off a sheet right now."

"Hey, when you pull up the listing on your laptop, would you mind if I peek at the online photos too? I'd love to see what the Victorian looks like inside since Wanda rewallpapered a few rooms. Unfortunately, I couldn't make it to her holiday party this year, as I was swamped stocking Community Craft for the last-minute holiday shoppers. You know how hard it is for me to attend all those parties during my busy season. Now I wish I'd made the time to go," Sammy said with melancholy. "Had I only known how important her last social gathering would be . . ."

"Yeah, sure, I'd be happy to, especially since you have so many connections with people at Community Craft. Maybe you can keep an ear open for those in the market to buy," Randy said with enthusiasm. "Let me just pull up the listing. I can print a listing sheet off too while I'm at it. It'll print in the office and then I can go grab it for you." He smiled wide, showing the deep dimple in his chin.

Evidently Sammy had struck the right chord with her brother-in-law. She watched him animatedly reach for the nearby laptop bag and pull out the computer. Randy's fingers flew over the keys after Sammy made room for him to join her on the sofa. As soon as he pulled up the listing photos, he placed the computer on her lap.

Heidi stepped into the room, held up a finger, and said, "Fifteen minutes until dinner."

This caused Tyler to jump to his feet—startling Bara—and make a mad dash toward the kitchen, where they all heard from the adjacent room a whine to his mother: "Mom-eee, I wanna open my presents nowwwww!"

"Whatcha doin'?" Heidi asked as she moved toward Sammy and Randy.

"Checking out the listing photos for Wanda's house."

"Oooh, can I see?" Heidi plopped between her and Randy, who was just rising from the sofa and jutted a thumb toward the nearby office.

"I'll go grab that listing sheet for you," Randy said, before leaving Heidi and Sammy alone in the living room.

Sammy readjusted herself on the sofa and planted her feet back on the carpeted floor. The two cousins huddled together as they perused the photos of Wanda's house, and Bara came over to sniff out the situation and stand nearby, looking for attention. As Sammy stroked her hand down Bara's back, his legs folded and he lay down atop her feet, keeping them warm.

"I knew you were in here digging for intel. Sneaky Samantha. I knew the second you started complaining about the cauliflower, it was just a ruse to corner Randy with questions without

Ellie present to stop you. You little instigator, you're in S.H.E. mode, aren't you?" Heidi said accusingly with a hint of teasing.

"Whaaat? Me? Come on now?" Sammy put a hand to her heart, and her eyes left the computer screen to regard her cousin innocently. "I was actually taking a peek for Kendra, but now that you mention it." She grinned. "Do you see anything in these photos that might help with the investigation?" She returned her eyes to the screen, hoping not to miss any minor detail.

"Pull them up one at a time so we can zoom in," Heidi suggested.

Sammy enlarged each photo and didn't initially see anything of interest. The home was well staged, meticulously clean, and perfectly photographed, as if no one lived there. She wondered how many hours Wanda must have spent in preparation before the photographs were taken. Personal items looked as if they'd been tucked away in storage, as the rooms were void of any clutter. Sammy wondered if Randy was the one who had taken the photos. She'd have to ask.

When they came to the photo of the Wadsworths' living room, Sammy enlarged the photo just as she had done with the previous ones. Something familiar caught her eye. She enlarged the photo to capacity. Her fingers scrolled over to a framed picture on the wall. "A barn-quilt picture; how pretty." The painted quilt block on the side of the barn looked a bit familiar, but Sammy didn't mention it. Instead she added, "What a lovely farm."

"I think that's a framed picture of Wanda's parents' farm," Heidi said. "Her parents were friends with mine back in the day, when my parents still had our family farm. I'm not sure how much they've kept in touch over the years, though, especially with Mom and Dad retired in Arizona."

"Oh?"

"Yeah, If I remember correctly, I think Wanda's brother Jackson still farms that old homestead. I'd have to ask my mother to be sure. I'm pretty sure the farm stayed in the family, long after their parents retired. I wonder how Jackson's doing with the loss of his sister. So sad." Heidi's smile faded.

"Do you know Jackson? Maybe we should bring him a casserole or something and pay our respects. I feel like Ellie and I should go with you. We can convince Ellie to prepare the meal and we'll deliver it," Sammy teased. "Just kidding. I have a few decent casserole recipes in my arsenal I think we could prepare. Why don't we?"

"Yeah, we probably should. I haven't seen Jackson in years, but I'm sure when I talk to Mom in Arizona and tell her what happened, she'd say the same thing. I was waiting to see what the police found out about Marty before I called my parents to tell them about Wanda, because I wanted to be sure she died from a heart attack before I shared the news with them. If I called them now, I'd just be peppered with unanswered questions like the rest of us seem to be wrestling with."

"Unfortunately, I'm sure Aunt Beatrice already knows. Because if Ellie has phoned our mother, that news will have traveled like wildfire." Sammy knew that, with Heidi's parents living close to her own in Arizona, there was no way they hadn't already heard the news. Ellie spoke with their mother almost daily.

"You're probably right about that," Heidi agreed with a nod. "Well, the farm community really looked out for each other back in the day. I'm sure when I talk to Mom, she'll want me to stop by and see Jackson on her behalf. I doubt if they can make it back from Arizona after just visiting Heartsford for Christmas. Besides, even if Jackson's farm is a bit outside the confines of our tight-knit community, he's still considered the outskirts of Heartsford. It's the right thing to do."

"And maybe we can ask a few questions?"

Heidi nudged Sammy playfully with her elbow and then rolled her eyes. "Yeah, maybe."

"Dinnertime!" Ellie hollered from a nearby room.

Sammy wiggled her toes, causing Bara to lift off her feet and saunter back to his original spot in front of the fireplace. "We'd better hurry up so Tyler can open his birthday presents. The poor kid is having a hard time being patient, and I can't half blame him." Sammy set the laptop carefully on the coffee table next to Tyler's stack of gifts.

Heidi took the lead into the dining room, and Sammy followed. The table was set with a colorful birthday-themed tablecloth and matching napkins. A set of red, yellow, and blue helium balloons were tied to the back of Tyler's chair, where the little boy sat at the head of the table. His cheeks were rosy, and he was grinning from ear to ear. Ellie set a large glass bowl filled with a salad onto the table, and Randy followed with a large steaming casserole dish.

"Have a seat," Ellie said, moving a red rooster trivet closer so Randy could place the hot dish on it. "Make yourselves at home."

Sammy took a seat at the long wooden farm table beside her cousin, and Ellie, instead of waiting for birthday cake, broke out in song: "*Happy birthday to you, happy birthday to you . . .*" By the second line, they all joined in and watched as Tyler clapped his hands, stretching his fingers to the max as if he were banging cymbals again.

"Happy fourth birthday, Tyler," Randy said when they all finished singing. "I hope you like this special dinner your mama made for you. She wanted to make sure the meal she prepared was something very special, just like you," he said as he ruffled the boy's golden head.

Tyler beamed.

Sammy hoped secretly she would like the "special dinner" as much as her nephew, but she wasn't so sure.

After the casserole dish was passed along and each scooped a portion, Sammy tentatively took her first bite of "cauliflower mac and cheese" and was pleasantly surprised. Ellie must have seen the acknowledgment on her sister's face, because she said, "Not bad, eh?"

Sammy smiled at Tyler, who was looking in her direction. "So, this is now your favorite, huh, Ty?"

The little boy nodded his head like a bobblehead with a mouthful of food, and Sammy said, "Yummy! Good pick!" and winked at her sister, who smiled with satisfaction.

The five talked amiably among themselves, keeping things light, and all focus remained on the newly appointed four-year-old.

After they finished their meal, Randy rose from the table, regarded his wife, and said, "I think we've held our boy back long enough. I'm going to go grab Tyler's first birthday present from the other room."

Ellie looked at her husband disapprovingly. "What about the cake?"

"Tyler." Randy looked at his son. "Do you want to open a present first or have a piece of cake?"

The little boy's eyes widened like saucers as he bellowed, "Present!" which made Sammy and Heidi laugh.

Ellie dropped her shoulders in defeat. "Don't you want me to clean off the table first?"

"Nah," Randy said as he left the room and quickly returned with a large box. He set the large wrapped package on the floor, and Tyler bolted from the dining room chair. Sammy watched as Tyler tore into the wrapping, revealing a large yellow dump truck that when pushed along the hardwood floor made rumbling noises. Tyler pitter-pattered his way out of the dining room, pushing the toy farther into the living room, leaving the adults alone. Randy was about to follow his son when Sammy stopped him.

"Hey, do you have that listing sheet? I'd like to put it in my purse before I forget."

Randy walked over to the dining room hutch, where he had abandoned the sheet of paper, and Sammy followed.

"Did you take the listing photos at the Wadsworths'?" Sammy asked. "They're very professional looking."

"Yeah, I did. Thanks," Randy said as he handed her the listing sheet. "It's been fun to get a real camera back in my hands to take some shots. I used to love photography, but my hobbies sort of took a back seat when Tyler was born. That's how it goes when you have kids." He rubbed the back of his neck as if to relieve the building tension.

"So, now knowing that there seems to be an ongoing investigation into the lives of the Wadsworths, can you think of anything out of the ordinary that might help the police?" Sammy placed her hands on her hips and waited expectantly.

"I'm not sure what you mean." Randy crossed his arms across his broad chest and tilted his head to the side.

"Well, the house has only been on the market a few weeks, right? I mean, it wasn't on the market over the holidays, because I was invited to Wanda's party and Deborah mentioned it wasn't for sale then. I'm just wondering what's been going on in their lives the last few weeks that might have caused Wanda's death and her husband to be seemingly in some sort of trouble too." Her tone changed to a whisper. "I didn't tell you earlier, but I was actually in the room when Detective Nash found Wanda's phone, and I heard Marty's cry for help."

"Oh, that's awful! No, I didn't hear that." Randy rubbed the side of his jaw hard as if trying to release some tension there. "The police just mentioned that Marty was still missing, they hadn't yet located him to inform him of his wife's death, and that I needed to put a hold on showings. Other than that, they didn't disclose any further details," he said with finality, seemingly trying to end the conversation.

"Oh."

"Yeah, I don't know what else to tell ya, Sammy."

"Well, you can see that something is amiss here, and I'm just trying to pick your brain to see if you thought anything was unusual when you were over at the house taking photos. Do you recall anything? Anything at all?" she pressed, hoping for a small detail he had potentially overlooked.

Randy folded his arms across his chest again and then rested his right fist underneath his chin to think. He held the pose thoughtfully before saying, "Huh. The only sort-of-weird thing . . . and it's probably nothing . . ." He brushed it off with a toss of his hand.

Sammy didn't dare interrupt. She waited patiently for her brother-in-law to internally review things, as if he were retrieving a file from the Rolodex of his mind. After a few moments, she couldn't hold it in any longer. "The one thing . . . Yeah? Go on . . ." She tapped him gently on the arm as if to wake him from his reverie.

"Well, it could be nothing—and probably is—but when I arrived to take the listing photos, I felt like I had just walked in on something. Like an argument between husband and wife. At first I thought it might have something to do with putting the house up for sale. Like maybe they were changing their mind or something along those lines. But then Wanda asked Marty to put some papers away that he was holding in his hand so they wouldn't get in the way of the pictures. I told him to just shove them inside the desk and assured him that it was no big deal, but instead he refused. It was like he didn't want me to know what was in his hand, like some big secret between them or something. I thought he was overreacting, because it's not like I was going to go through their desk drawers to take photos. I didn't care what the papers were about. Hey, none of my business." Randy lifted his hands in defense. "The reaction was just a bit over the top, in my opinion. But again, I'm learning people get anxious sometimes when listing their house. After all, it's a big decision. Maybe I just read the situation wrong. Hard to say," Randy added, dropping his arms to his sides and shifting his weight.

"Maybe that's something you should share with the police? Or maybe, since you have the lockbox number, you could sneak inside and try to find those papers he was so desperate to keep private? They might hold significant meaning that could get to the bottom of this tragedy."

"Oh no. The police made it perfectly clear they didn't want anyone over there. Don't be getting any hairbrained ideas there, Sammy," Randy warned, wagging a long finger.

"No, you're right," Sammy acquiesced. But in her mind, she couldn't help but go over potential combinations her brother-in-law might have chosen for the front-door lockbox on that historical Queen Anne Victorian.

Chapter Eight

The next day, Deborah provided a few hours' coverage in the afternoon at Community Craft, and Sammy jumped at the opportunity to join Ellie and Heidi on a house call to pay their respects to Wanda's brother Jackson. The three piled into Heidi's black Jeep and headed out on their errand. Ellie called shotgun and said it was because she held the prized lasagna on her lap. Sammy thought it was only fair. After all, Ellie had done all the heavy lifting by preparing the meal for delivery, so she guessed she should get the honored position up front. Sammy wished she could snag a bite, though, as the tantalizing scent permeated the vehicle and her stomach rolled from her serious cheese addiction and hunger pangs.

"Do you miss Scarlet?" Sammy asked, referring to Heidi's cherry-red Pontiac Solstice, as they bumpily drove along the back roads of Heartsford toward the outskirts of town. With every bounce of the Jeep, Sammy had to reach out and grip the side of the vehicle or the seat in front of her. She wondered if Ellie would be able to make it to Jackson's farm without a lapful of sauce.

"Nah, the convertible's in storage, where she ought to be. Don't worry, Scarlet will be back running the roads in the spring," Heidi said with a chuckle, regarding her in the rearview mirror. "Plus, this baby is great in the snow with the four-wheel drive. I'm glad I bought this one and not another car," she said as she tapped the dashboard approvingly.

Sammy gazed out the rear passenger window and noted that snow was beginning to fall again. Soft wispy flakes fell from a blindingly sunny sky, causing them to sparkle. Her attention was quickly diverted, though, when she heard Heidi say, "Oh boy, what's going on here . . . Ohhh nooo, this doesn't look good."

Sammy turned her eyes toward the front windshield, where she noticed flashing lights from a police vehicle ahead. Heidi slowed the Jeep on approach, and all three within the vehicle noticed a police officer's cruiser parked sideways, blocking the road and halting traffic.

"Is that Tim?" Ellie asked.

"Hard to tell with all that winter garb on, huh?" Sammy answered. The police officer was dressed in full uniform and wearing a dark hat and matching black neck warmer, so only his eyes were visible. It was so cold, visible steam rose from the officer's breath, penetrating the fleece as he adjusted it around his chin.

"Looks like it," Heidi said, as she pulled the Jeep to rest a few hundred feet in front of the officer. She immediately exited, and Sammy mirrored her and followed close on her heels. Ellie however, remained in the vehicle with the lasagna resting on a thick towel on her lap.

"What's going on?" Heidi asked as the two moved toward the officer, who was trudging through the recent snow, leaving fresh prints.

"You girls are going to have to make a U-turn," Tim said in an official tone, his dark-gloved finger making a lassoing motion around his head. "Road's blocked and tow truck is on the way. I'm going to need you to move outta here pretty quick." He then rested his gloved hands on his thick police belt.

Heidi reached to adjust the hat on her boyfriend's head. "You stay warm out here. Despite the sun, it's still freezing," she added with concern as she laid a gloved hand tenderly on his cheek. This melted the officer like butter in her hands, and his "officialness" immediately dropped back down a few pegs to casual Tim. He pulled his girl Heidi in for a half hug, then turned to her for a quick kiss after he adjusted his neck warmer again.

"What happened here? An accident?" Sammy swayed next to the officer to get a better view but didn't see a crashed vehicle anywhere on the road, leaving her perplexed.

"I just found Marty's abandoned car." Tim jutted a thumb down an embankment into the thick wooded pines behind him.

Sammy gasped.

"Where's Marty?" Heidi asked as her eyes darted around them.

"That's the problem. His whereabouts are still unknown at this time," Tim answered, all official again, as if he suddenly wanted to dismiss them *and* their questions. "You'd better get outta here before . . ." Tim huffed aloud. "Never mind. Too late." He threw up his hands in defeat.

Sammy turned her head to see Detective Liam Nash moving at a rapid pace toward them. Ah. That explained Tim's sudden rush back to official capacity.

"Please tell me they haven't already tainted my crime scene." The detective eyed Heidi's boyfriend and placed his hands firmly on his solid hips.

"Crime scene?"

Nash ignored Sammy's question and instead regarded the officer. "Tell me you didn't call them over here." He studied Tim as if he was looking for a slipup.

Tim shook his head. "No, sir. I can assure you I did not. They happened upon the scene, as they are headed . . ." Tim turned his attention to Heidi with a look of question. "Where *are* you headed, exactly?"

Sammy interjected, "We're on our way to pay our respects to Wanda's brother. We brought lasagna." She turned to point out Ellie in the front seat, who regarded the officers with a wave of her hand through the windshield.

"So you didn't call them over to come see this?" Nash said, utter confusion washing over his face.

"No, he wouldn't do that," Sammy defended Officer Maxwell, hoping this time she wouldn't get him in trouble yet again. She had a bad habit of causing angst, and if it continued, she could lose future intel within the police department. "Seriously. Why would we show up here with a lasagna? Go over and talk to Ellie. I promise you'll find we're telling you the truth." Sammy looked at the Jeep and waved her sister over to join them. Ellie took the cue, placed the lasagna on the driver's seat, and then opened the passenger door to join the group.

The detective threw up his hands in frustration and then rested them back on his hips defensively and hovered over Sammy, waiting for an answer. "Tell me you didn't approach the car, then?"

"Nope," Sammy replied innocently. "We've been standing here the entire time." She pointed a gloved finger to the frozen ground. "But what are you looking for? I mean, did Marty crash? Is he hurt? Is that why he was asking for help on Wanda's phone?" She couldn't help but ask.

The detective must have realized the group wouldn't retreat without a few answers, because he said, "After finally getting the trace back on the cell phone, we discovered the last tower Marty's phone pinged off was within a mile radius of this area. We've been searching ever since, but due to all the snow, we didn't find his car until now." Nash gestured his hand toward Tim. "Officer Maxwell just called dispatch to send me over here. I'm glad to hear you didn't actually disturb my scene," he added, puffing a sigh of relief.

"He's not in the car frozen . . . is he?" Heidi's face grimaced as if she had just sucked a sour lemon candy.

"No," Tim answered. "I've already been down to the car, and it's empty. Unfortunately, due to the snow, I can't tell if Marty left on foot or someone picked him up or what exactly happened here. If he was hurt, we would have found him at the hospital, and as you guys know, that isn't the case, because as far as *we* know"—Tim swung an imaginary lasso around the group with his finger—"he's not even aware of his wife's death. I've been waiting for Nash before I touched anything else so he can investigate, and then you three S.H.E.s came along."

"We'd be happy to provide any assistance if you'd like," Sammy suggested.

Nash replied with a lopsided grin. "Yeah, I bet you'd love that." He put up a hand of defense. "But it really won't be necessary. The best assistance you can provide is distance from my scene. Please, move along."

His hand of defense irked Sammy. "Hey, you were supposed to call Deborah and I to tell us what happened. Why didn't you? I was the one who answered the frantic call from Marty. The least you could do is keep me up to speed on what's happened to the guy! I find this out on my own because we were lucky enough to drive by? Don't you think you owe me at least that?"

"Oh boy, here we go. Now Sammy's gonna get all fired up . . . we're off to see her firecrackers explode," Tim said disapprovingly, shaking his head and then shooting pretend guns off with both hands.

Sammy turned to Tim. "Well, what do you expect? A woman dies in the window of my shop, her husband screams for help from Wanda's phone—which by the way, I was the one *holding*. Why wouldn't I be curious to know what's happened to the Wadsworths? Wouldn't you think I was a horrible person if I didn't care at all?" She bit the inside of her cheek to stop herself from saying anything else.

"It's okay, Sammy," Ellie soothed. "They're just trying to do their job, and we're evidently in the way here. Maybe we should go," she suggested.

"Maybe I should arrest you for poisoning her. You were the one responsible for holding on to her tea, weren't you?" Liam asked.

"What did you say?" Sammy's eyes lasered in on the detective.

"Sorry, bad joke on my part. I was wrong to instigate a reaction." The detective waved his hand casually. "Settle down, you're fine. I didn't think it was you anyway. Tox tested the tea; there was no indication of poison in the peppermint. Wanda had to have ingested the poison earlier in the day."

"Hang on, did you just say Wanda was poisoned? By what?" Sammy leaned in closer.

The detective looked at Officer Maxwell sheepishly. "You mean to tell me you didn't tell them already?"

Tim tucked his gloved hands around his police belt. He didn't say a word but shook his head no, a stoic look on his face.

"See what assuming does, Detective Nash? You assume Tim leaks things to us about the ongoing investigation, but he doesn't." Sammy grinned with satisfaction.

Nash continued without a flinch. "The preliminary results are back. Unfortunately, toxicology needs to run more tests. It wasn't the usual rat poison or cyanide or anything. They've never seen this before, so it's going to take some more time to try and isolate the type of poison that was used."

By this time, a look of confusion had washed across Ellie's face. "If you find out what kind of poison it was, maybe the substance will lead you back to your killer."

"Nice job, E!" Sammy smiled. "She has a valid point, don't you think, Detective?"

"What I think is that you girls ought to move along. I need to be sure you three will keep this information and this conversation private, or else you'll scare off our perp. Let us do our job here, and this time please respect the boundaries within the police department. We have enough on our plates."

"You have our word, we'll stay out of it," Heidi said, then added, "Looks like the tow truck has arrived too. We'd better hurry and get out of the way."

"I think that is a very good idea," Detective Nash said with finality. "I have a lot to accomplish before the tow truck can remove the car, so if you'll please excuse me." He turned on his heel, then quickly turned back around. "I'll talk to you later." He brought his fingers toward his eyes and then lasered them on Sammy's.

"Me?" Sammy jutted a thumb to her chest.

"Yes, you. Privately," he added, and then turned back in the direction of the embankment.

"What was that all about?" Ellie asked as the three made their way back toward the Jeep.

"Heck if I know," Sammy answered with an eye roll.

"It's *L-O-V-E*," Heidi sang out before opening the driver's side door, handing the lasagna to Ellie, and hopping back into the seat.

"Highly doubt it," Sammy said under her breath. But then she couldn't help but wonder. What did the detective want to talk to her about privately?

Chapter Nine

The snowdrifts blanketed a portion of the country road that led to Jackson's farm, making it nearly impossible to view the roadway. Evidently, the town must have run out of time in autumn and neglected to put up a snow fence before winter reared its ugly head. The wind whipping across the harvested open fields had wreaked havoc on any roads off the beaten path, and this one was no exception. Sammy was relieved Heidi was driving her four-wheel-drive Jeep through the snowbanks and they weren't in her old beater car, as they would've had to abandon their excursion out to the sticks a long time ago.

"Hold on to your lasagna, El!" Sammy chuckled from the back seat, gripping her seat belt tighter when the Jeep took a lunging dive through the white powder. "I'm not sure four wheel drive allows you to drive *through* snowbanks, Heidi. You may want to ease up on the gas pedal and quit pushing this Jeep to its very limits. Do you have a death wish or something? Maybe we should've turned around back there and waited for the plow to go through."

"I'm glad I was smart enough to wrap the towel underneath the lasagna, that's all I can say." Ellie joined in the laughter as they hit yet another bump in the road. "If this keeps up, I might toss my cookies; this ride is making me nauseous. Sammy's right, maybe we should wait for the plow."

"If we waited for the plow to go through, we'd have to wait days, maybe weeks. Hey, we made it this far. Don't worry, we're almost there," Heidi said, before her voice rose an octave and she shrilled, "What the heck was that?"

"I told ya, we need to slow down, my little race-car driver!" Sammy teased as she turned to look out the window. "Dunno . . . did we hit a rock or something?" A large, crusty boulder lay just to the side of the Jeep's freshly made tracks. "I think it was a huge chunk of ice left over from the last time the plow went through, which was probably not since the last storm blew through here. We're getting our adventure in today, that's for sure. No doubt about it! It's always an adventure when us S.H.E.s are together!" Sammy smiled wide.

The Jeep finally came to a clearing, and the three let out audible sighs of relief. Acres of open land revealed a brick farmhouse, scattered outbuildings, and a tall blue silo standing off in the distance with an American flag proudly stamped on its side.

Heidi turned the steering wheel in the direction of the recently plowed driveway.

Sammy recognized the familiar painted quilt block attached to the side of the barn a couple hundred yards from the farmhouse. She remembered viewing the very same quilt block depicted in the painting on Wanda's living room wall in the pictures from Randy's real-estate listing.

"What a gorgeous property," Heidi said with longing. "Man, I would love to live out here."

"I love the quilt block on the barn, don't you guys? It really adds a certain hominess to this place." The geometric star, painted blue, yellow, and green, matched the photo, its vivid colors starkly contrasting the deep red of the flaking barn. "It's stunning and really cool to see up close, firsthand," Sammy added. "I bet the quilting group from Community Craft would really appreciate the artwork too. Gosh, I should really organize a field trip and bring them out here to see it."

"Sammy, you know why they have that quilt block painted and attached to the barn, right?" Ellie asked.

"No. Why? Did Wanda paint it for her brother before she passed? She was one of our best quilters at Community Craft. Actually, I'd often suggested she publish a book with all the new patterns she'd come up with over the years. We lost a true artist." Sammy felt a lump form in her throat.

Ellie flung a gloved finger in the direction of the barn. "No, that quilt block on the barn doesn't have anything to do with Wanda's quilting."

"Okay, you lost me. I guess I'm not following. What do you mean?" Sammy asked. "If it doesn't have to do with Wanda's quilting, is it just to add pizazz or something? To be honest, it looks very Amish. Don't the Amish have quilt blocks on their barns? Wanda's family isn't Amish, are they?"

Heidi laughed aloud. "No. Wanda's family isn't Amish. And it's not just to add pizazz. How is it you're the last to know about this project?"

"Project? What project? You and I looked at the listing photos together, and you never mentioned any *project*. There was a picture of this barn in Wanda's living room, remember?"

"Sorry," Heidi said. "I thought with you working on Main Street, you were already up to speed on everything going on in and around this town."

"Well, first of all, it seems as if we're outside Heartsford on some country road which may or may not even be part of our county—or state, for that matter. Where the heck are we, anyway? I've never been out this way. But that's beside the point. How is it you guys know about some project that I'm not privy to?"

"It's not actually a project; it's more of a trail, to be honest," Ellie said. "Yeah, I agree with Heidi—I can't believe you haven't heard about it yet. Not only that, but Deborah has mentioned the painted quilt blocks to me on more than one occasion when we've worked together at Community Craft. I'm really amazed she hasn't mentioned it to you."

"Deborah knows about this project too?" Sammy was totally confused at this point. She broke free of her seat belt and tucked her body between the two front seats, her interest now officially piqued.

"Yes. Deborah was approached by one of the organizers to see if she wanted to head up the painting of these eight-by-eight quilt blocks, since the 4-H can't do them anymore, as more and more barns want to participate. There's a whole trail map that's being created. And it sounds like, from what you mentioned, Jackson's farm is going to be part of the map." Ellie gestured a hand toward the barn.

"Ohhh? A quilted trail map?" Sammy was finally coming to an understanding and nodded her head slowly. "That sounds like a very cool idea."

"Yeah, they're hoping to loop Heartsford and the rest of the county onto this Wisconsin quilt trail map, as it would be good for tourism in our area. I think it's a brilliant idea," Heidi said. "People come for miles for this sort of stuff."

"It really is brilliant," Ellie agreed. "It'll probably bring more business to Community Craft too; you know tourists love to shop." She turned to Sammy and winked.

"Do you miss the ol' farm?" Sammy turned her attention to her cousin, knowing full well Heidi was still contemplating purchasing a property of her own. She wondered if she'd buy acreage where, at the very least, she could raise chickens. Sammy hoped so; then she could snag some fresh eggs like she had when her aunt and uncle raised them.

"I do," Ellie interrupted, shifting the towel beneath the lasagna on her lap to keep the disposable metal pan from dripping onto her clothing. "We had so much fun at your family farm growing up, Heidi. I can't imagine our childhood without those fond memories. The freedom we had to explore out there. Sometimes I wish my Ty-baby had the same. I mean, I love my home, don't get me wrong, but our postage-size lot after having a childhood like ours, where we could roam free, just seems utterly unfair. Especially for a boy like Tyler, who absolutely loves to explore."

"Yeah, Ellie, he must take after his auntie. A curious mind and high energy. I just wish I wasn't feeling so old these days and still had the high-energy part," Sammy agreed with a giggle.

"I do miss the farm," Heidi said with a hint of nostalgia. "But I'm not sure, with my job at the hospital, if I'd have time for the upkeep. That's why it's taken me so long to commit to buying a property of my own. I just don't know what I really want, and I'm afraid to tie myself down to a thirty-year mortgage only to find out it's not where I want to be, you know?" Heidi said, unclicking her seat belt and opening the door of the Jeep. "Until I can stop waffling, I guess I'll have to remain a renter."

Sammy wondered secretly if Heidi was still waiting to see if Tim was finally going to pop the question—and if that was the real reason for waiting to purchase a home. She decided to remain quiet about that tidbit as she followed Heidi's lead and stepped out of the car.

A friendly black Labrador approached the Jeep and began to pace around the passenger door. Sammy stepped closer to the animal and patted the dog on the head, then reached into her thick coat pocket, dug for a piece of leftover Bara treat, and tossed it to the Lab. She then walked around to the passenger side to help Ellie negotiate transport of the lasagna. Ellie lifted the casserole from her lap, and Sammy removed the sauce-soiled towel, rolled it in a ball, and tucked it beneath Ellie's feet on the floor of the Jeep, then held the door so Ellie could step outside.

"That smells so good," Sammy said with longing, following the wafting scent. She was afraid that if she stood next to her sister much longer, she would dig into the lasagna with her own two hands. Her stomach rolled again with hunger. She hoped they wouldn't be long and have time to go out to a late lunch, as they'd planned earlier.

"Thanks," Ellie said, smiling. "I made two in case our visit ran a little late, so you'll have to come over for supper if we run out of time and don't get a chance to go to lunch."

"I'll take you up on that offer, no problem," Sammy admitted easily, returning the smile.

Heidi halted their pace before they stepped another foot forward and leaned toward her cousins conspiratorially. "Before we go and talk with Jackson, I think we should put our S.H.E. hats on," she suggested. "I mean, not literally—I trashed that baseball hat years ago," she added with a laugh. "However, I don't think we should tell him about Marty's abandoned car. Or the fact that Wanda was poisoned. Right? Let's not give away too much or share anything with him that the police department hasn't yet informed him or anyone else about. What do you guys think?"

"Totally agree. Marty is Jackson's bother-in-law, and we don't want to upset him regarding things that are completely unknown at this point. Let's play it cool. I think we'll find out more that way too. I'm interested to know his take on Wanda's death." Sammy zipped her lips with her fingers. They quickened their pace as a cold wind whipped up, sending glittering snow tornadoing around them.

The three approached the two-story brick farmhouse and climbed the few steps onto a modest front porch. Heidi knocked on the aged, sun-striped wooden door.

They stood waiting for what seemed to be an exorbitant amount of time, and Sammy grew restless, dancing from foot to foot to keep the blood pumping to her numbing feet. Despite the practical winter boots, her toes were freezing. She chastised herself inwardly for not wearing her wool socks. "Someone must be home. I can't imagine anyone would even consider leaving home if their dog was outdoors in this cold." She shivered.

"Can I help you?" The three turned their heads simultaneously at the sound of a male voice behind them. The man climbed the porch steps and stood before them.

Heidi reached her gloved hands out to touch the man's arm. "Jackson! It's me, Heidi Harrison. Remember me from our old 4-H days?"

The man towered over the three of them at about six foot two, if Sammy guessed correctly. He was wearing Carhartt winter overalls over a thick black sweatshirt, and his head was covered in a bright-orange hunting cap. His cheeks were rosy, as if he'd been out in the cold for some time. His expression morphed from confusion to recognition as he pulled Heidi in for a hug, still holding a bundle of mail in his other hand. "Well, for heaven's sake, I don't think we've seen each other since we were youngsters!" he said after he released her. "Look at you, all grown up now." He opened the front door. "Come in . . . please, let's get in out of the cold." He gestured with his large, work-gloved hand for them to step inside.

As soon as they stepped inside the modest entryway, Heidi grew serious. "Jackson, we're so very sorry for your loss," she said as she reached and touched the side of his arm again with her gloved hand. "This is my cousin, Sammy." Heidi dropped her hand from his arm, removed her gloves, and gestured toward Sammy. "Your sister Wanda often hung out at her shop—Community Craft on Main Street in Heartsford—and her sister Ellie works there part-time too. We're all going to miss your sister very much." Heidi pointed to the casserole. "Ellie made a lasagna for your family. If there is anything else we can do, anything at all . . ." she added in a sympathetic tone.

"Nice to meet you ladies. I'm sorry we're not meeting under better circumstances. Thank you," he said in a low, husky voice. He tucked the mail beneath his arm and removed his work gloves before wiping his dripping nose with the back of his hand. He hung his orange-capped head for a moment before raising his eyes again.

One of the letters beneath his arm fell to the floor, and Sammy reached to retrieve it.

"Where can I set this down?" Ellie asked, the lasagna obviously growing heavy in her arms.

Sammy wasn't surprised; knowing her sister, the thing probably weighed twenty pounds and could feed the U.S. Army. She licked her lips, knowing she'd be lucky enough to snag a piece of the other one waiting back at Ellie's house later for supper.

Jackson encouraged them to wipe their feet on the thick mat but leave on their winter boots, and Sammy was thankful. She thought a frozen toe might break off if she even attempted to remove them. He welcomed them into his clean, practical kitchen, which featured aged oak cabinets and dark vinyl flooring that was scratched in spots or had been ripped by a dog's long nails. This was a hardworking farm and the house had been well lived in, and Sammy was impressed by how neatly everything was set in its place. The toaster was tucked in the corner, and not a crumb lay on the aged Formica countertop. Loaves of quick breads and cookie plates lined the counters. Clearly the three women hadn't been the first to stop in and pay their respects.

"Are you hungry now? Or would you rather Ellie put this in the refrigerator for later?" Sammy asked, hoping to put the tantalizing meal as far away from her as humanly possible.

"It's so kind of you folks, really, so very kind. I do appreciate your kindness, but honestly, I haven't had much of an appetite lately," Jackson admitted. "I have to say, though, this meal might bring back my appetite, as it smells incredibly delicious." This comment caused Ellie to smile wide.

Jackson opened the refrigerator door, and Sammy noted that not only were the kitchen countertops filled with goodies, but the interior shelves of the refrigerator were lined with casserole dishes as well. He moved a few aside to make room, and Ellie slipped the large metal disposable pan inside.

"I'm sure the kids will want something when they come in from sledding, and they love lasagna, so thank you again . . . very much," he said. "We have a makeshift hill that I created on the back lot with the tractor before the snow hit, and the kids are loving playing in the white stuff. My wife's out there with them now. I just came in to drop the mail, as it was collecting in the box the last few days, and then I went and met the mail truck out on the road so he wouldn't have to trudge over here. How did you gals make it through? Impressive," he added with a slight smile, then wiped his weary eyes with his fingers.

"Jeep." Heidi smiled and then asked, "How many children do you have now, Jackson? I have to admit, I think I've lost count!" She pointed to the refrigerator, where there was a snapshot of the family standing in front of large, foggy mountains.

Jackson chuckled. "That was taken down south at the Smoky Mountains last summer when we went on a family road trip. Actually, Wanda took that picture, as she and Marty went along too." He regarded the photo with a nod of his head. "We're up to five now. Three girls and two boys. My wife's expecting again, and I'm hoping for more boys for farmhands," he added sheepishly.

"Come on now," Heidi teased. "Us girls can pull our weight around the farm too." She winked. "You remember all the work I did for 4-H. I think I even have a ribbon or two under my belt." She smiled wide, showing her dimples.

"Yes, that's very true, indeed. You were quite the winner back in the day." He paused a moment before admitting, "I think you may have beat me in a few contests." He placed his hand on his chin and rubbed hard. "Although, if I recall, much of your winnings came from your mother's cherry-pie recipes and not from the animals. Man, I miss those pies!" Jackson returned the wink. "How are your folks? Loving Arizona, I imagine? Especially this time of year."

"Yes, retirement is treating them well. They don't make it back to the frozen tundra much past Christmas anymore. They asked me to share their condolences as well. Unfortunately, they won't make it back when Wanda is laid to rest." Heidi's smile faded.

"Thank you, no worries," he said sincerely. "Good to hear they're well. Can't say I blame 'em. I wouldn't want to travel back either, especially this time of year when so many planes get stranded on the tarmac due to the bad weather. Please give them my regards the next time you talk with them. Your parents are great people. Great people indeed." He nodded his head.

Sammy was about to hand Jackson the letter he had dropped on the floor earlier when she glanced at the front of the envelope. It didn't have a stamp and was merely addressed to *Wanda's brother.* Sammy wondered who would make the drive out to the country only to deliver a sympathy note in the mailbox. She handed the letter to Jackson, still thinking how odd it was.

"What's this?" he asked, eyeing the envelope as he ripped the orange hat from his head, revealing sweaty, disheveled, dirty-blond hair.

"You dropped it by the door," Sammy answered, gesturing with her thumb behind her toward the foyer.

"No, I mean, there's no stamp. The mail carrier delivered it without a stamp?" Jackson's eyes narrowed. "Oh. This must be from the mail I collected in the box left over from the other day. Things have been building up around here. You know how grief goes . . . you forget to do the everyday things . . . our minds have been so distracted . . ." He blew out a breath, holding back his sorrow as he tore the envelope open. He pulled out a sheet of paper, and his eyes darted to the page before he gasped audibly and turned a deathly shade of white.

"What is it? Are you okay?" Heidi asked first. The nurse in her couldn't help it.

His hands were visibly trembling, and absently he handed the sheet of paper to Heidi as Sammy peeked over her cousin's shoulder. A printed sheet with cut-and-pasted letters in multiple fonts and of different sizes said the following: *$100,000. Or Marty DIES. Get the money. Wait for further instruction. Do NOT involve police. If you do—consider him dead.*

Chapter Ten

The three S.H.E.s gathered around Jackson's kitchen table while the tall farmer paced nervously around the room. They'd long since removed their winter coats and draped them behind themselves on the kitchen chairs. Evidently they were no longer here for a short visit, as the four of them, completely paralyzed by shock, remained assembled to analyze the situation.

"What are you going to do, Jackson?" Heidi asked finally.

"I don't want my wife and kids to come back inside this house before I figure out how to best handle this situation. My wife, Teyla, thought I was just coming back inside to drop off the mail. We didn't even know you all were here," Jackson stated, then began chewing the tough skin around his thumb. "Can one of you go outside and stall her? I need more time to think."

Ellie stood from the aged wooden chair. "I'll go," she said. Then she tucked the chair beneath the kitchen table, pulled on her hand-knit winter hat, and put on her coat. "Are you sure you don't want me to mention anything if I happen to get a quiet moment with her away from your children? I'm just here to drop a meal and pay respects? Mum's the word, right?" She zipped her mouth with her fingers.

"Right." Jackson nodded his head in agreement. "Please don't mention the ransom. I just need a few more minutes to think. Teyla is going to go absolutely ballistic. My wife and sister were very close. Teyla not only lost a sister-in-law, she lost her best friend. And now this? I know my wife enough to know she'll want to immediately alert authorities. I'm just not so sure that's the right call. I need a few more minutes to think." He took a deep breath and let it out slowly, wringing his cracked, hardworking hands together.

"Okay, I won't say a word, I'll just stall," Ellie said, then headed toward the front door.

Sammy heard the front door close softly behind her sister, and then she rose from her own chair and strode across the room to Jackson. "Can I get you a glass of water or something?"

The farmer gazed at her absently.

Sammy reached into a nearby cabinet above the large stainless farm sink and was lucky to find the glasses on her first attempt. She removed one and turned on the faucet. "Do you know anyone who would do this? Who would send you a ransom note? Obviously, it has to be someone who knows Marty is your brother-in-law."

"I have no idea. All I'm questioning right now is whether I should take the chance and involve the police." He scratched his head. "If I do, I could be putting Marty in even more danger. Is the note serious? Will whoever's behind all this follow through?"

Sammy handed Jackson the glass of water, and he immediately took a long drink. His hand was trembling as he set the glass onto the countertop.

Heidi rose from her chair and stood next to Jackson. She reached for his arm and patted it lightly as a sign of comfort. "I'm not sure if you're aware, but I'm dating an officer from the Heartsford Police Department. It's going to be kinda tough for me to keep this a secret," she admitted.

"Well, you might have to." Jackson gestured a hand toward the note, which lay open on the kitchen table. "Otherwise they'll kill him." He clenched his hands in fists at his sides and blew out a frustrated breath.

Heidi bit her lower lip. "I hate to even ask this question, but do you even have that kind of money laying around to pay a large ransom? I personally wouldn't."

"No, take a look around this place." He threw his hands to the air. "It's not like I'm rolling in dough here. Not to mention, I lost half my crop last year for reasons I can't yet explain. I'm broke!" He opened his palms and thrust them forward as if to prove the point. "Not to mention the baby on the way."

"Well, how would you come up with the money, then? You may have no other choice than to reach out to the authorities. I'm sure they have ways of handling these types of situations," Sammy interjected. Although Sammy couldn't think of anyone in Heartsford who'd ever been in this type of situation. She'd keep her mouth quiet on that one. It was definitely something Jackson didn't need to hear at this very moment.

Jackson's eyes darted around the room, as if his mind was working overtime and he would come up with a solution. He steepled his fingers and set them to his lips.

"What are you thinking?" Sammy asked.

"I'm thinking I'd rather this ransom note stay between us for now. Let *me* decide how I want to handle it with the authorities. Wanda gave me the combination to their gun safe at home for safekeeping. She mentioned that if anything ever happened to either one of them, a large amount of cash was tucked inside that safe. I just need to get inside my sister's house so I can see how much money they have stashed in there," Jackson said, pacing around the room once more. "Maybe they'll have enough."

"Heidi, may I have a moment?" Sammy beckoned her cousin to follow, then moved away from the kitchen toward the entryway. When the two were out of earshot, Sammy whispered, "You know, we have a way to get inside Wanda's house. We can steal the lockbox combination from Randy."

Heidi was aghast. "You're sounding a little crazy there, girlie. You might wanna rein that back in!" She shoved a pointed finger toward Sammy's chest.

"Heidi, I'm serious."

"I'm serious too," Heidi hissed. "That idea is ludicrous and borderline *insane*! What we need to do is encourage Jackson to call the police. This isn't a game, Sammy. Marty's life is at stake. This is a bit outside the S.H.E. wheelhouse!" Heidi's eyes were intense.

"Yeah, you're absolutely right, and whoever is behind this is gonna kill the guy. You read the note." Sammy bobbed her head in the direction of the kitchen. "You want Marty's blood on your hands if something bad goes down because we were the ones to encourage him to call the authorities? Then what? You seriously want that on your head?" Sammy circled an imaginary lasso over her head, mimicking Tim's earlier behavior, hoping to remind her cousin what they'd encountered on the drive over. "I certainly don't."

"Sammy. We *can't* . . ." Heidi's eyes were pleading now.

Sammy crossed her arms across her chest and paused, resting her chin on her fist. After a few seconds of pondering, she said, "How about this: what if we give Jackson our own deadline? What if we tell him we'll keep his secret for a few days, but after that we've got to share what we know with the police? Otherwise our own lives are at risk, as we're hampering an ongoing investigation, and we'll be slapped with obstruction of justice."

"Now I know you've officially lost your mind. What about Randy? You know full well he's not going to share the lockbox information with us, especially now, with a hold on real-estate showings. What about Ellie? Now you're putting her husband's new job on the line? She'll never go for it, not in a million years. Nope. Not going to happen." Heidi shook her head firmly and folded her arms across her chest.

"That's why we're not going to tell her."

Heidi threw up her hands in frustration, and her eyes popped to twice their usual size. "Come on now, you've got to be kidding me! You want to leave out E?" Her voice left the whisper stage and was now audible to anyone within a five-mile radius. This caused Jackson to cast a look in their direction and approach them from the next room.

Before he arrived, Sammy said, "We don't have much of a choice, Heidi. There's got to be a way we can figure out the code on the lockbox on that old Victorian. Maybe we'll get lucky and Randy left the manufacturer's combination on there and didn't change it. I've heard that realtors sometimes make that mistake and the house is pretty easy to break into." Sammy chewed nervously on her nail.

"What's going on with you two?" Jackson asked when he finally appeared in front of them.

Sammy headed Jackson off at the pass and suggested they all return to the small kitchen. Her eyes couldn't help but fall on the ransom note. "What are you thinking, Jackson?" she asked finally as she took her seat at the table. "What are you going to do?"

"I'm thinking of doing exactly what the ransom note says. I just wish I had a key to my sister's house to see if I can even gather that kind of funds. Unfortunately for me, that's not something she left behind. The keys, I mean . . ." He looked down in defeat.

Sammy's eyes left the ransom note to meet her cousin's to plead with her on Jackson's behalf. Heidi sank into the kitchen chair, rejoining her at the table.

"What makes you think Wanda and Marty had that much money in their gun safe, anyway?" Heidi turned her gaze on Jackson, who stopped pacing for a second to look in their direction.

"I shouldn't really be sharing this, but since my sister is gone now, I suppose keeping her family secrets doesn't really matter at this point." He breathed deep and looked to the ceiling for a moment. "Wanda confided in me before she passed that my brother-in-law has a bit of a problem hanging out and playing too much poker with his friends. Except instead of losing money, Marty's been on a serious winning streak, according to Wanda. My sister didn't like that much money showing up in her bank account, and she made a deal with Marty that as long as he kept the card money separate and didn't dip into their personal savings or checking accounts at Heartsford Credit Union, then she wouldn't have anything to say about what he was up to with his buddies. The minute the funds were gone, though, if he lost it all, she said she refused to let him have any extra to spend. That was their deal. Personally, I don't think that much money came from just playing cards. I think he's into something else—he has to be," Jackson said. "It's not like it's the World Series of Poker out here in the Midwest. I think my sister is just oblivious to his lies. Or chose to look at the world through rose-colored glasses."

"So . . . you're saying everything in their gun safe was 'play money' won from poker?" Sammy drew air quotes with her fingers.

"Exactly." Jackson threw up his hands at the absurd notion the money had come from playing cards.

"And you think he'd had a big win recently?" Heidi asked. "Enough to cover a hundred grand? That's quite a payout!"

"Hey, I'm just reiterating what my sister shared with me. That's what Wanda mentioned to me a few days before she died, and she seemed to believe her husband—she trusted him. According to her, he'd gone up north with some buddies on a weekend ice-fishing trip and they hit some big game up there. Apparently, Marty hit a jackpot."

"Which game?" Heidi asked. "At a casino? I mean, could you verify the win?"

"No, nothing like that. I know it wasn't a win from a casino. He's not into slots or anything like that. More like some midwestern underground group of card players, I think," he answered with a dismissive wave of his hand.

"Do you think it's a possibility that one of Marty's buddies that went on his ice-fishing trip might be up to all this? Maybe since one of them knew he had a lot of money tucked away at home? Is it possible one of them thought he could score big?" Sammy asked thoughtfully. "Who else would've known Marty had won that much money?"

"Yeah, I don't know." Jackson breathed deep, causing his nostrils to widen. "Do you remember Adam Boyd?" He directed his question to Heidi.

She quickly replied, "Yeah, from 4-H, right? The swine kid." She chucked. "I remember him. Why?"

"Yeah, I guess he's part of that group of guys that hangs out with Marty. I just can't believe the nonsense my brother-in-law has dragged my sister through over the years, and now it looks as if he was the very one to put Wanda in danger. Or even worse, possibly the one to put her in her grave." His hands picked at the suspenders on his Carhartt heavyweight bibs nervously.

Sammy looked at Heidi for confirmation. She wondered if Jackson had been notified that his sister had been poisoned. Or were they the only ones privy to this insider information? She remained quiet.

Heidi looked at Jackson and asked, "Was it common knowledge that the Wadsworths kept large amounts of cash in a safe inside their home?"

"Or do you think very few people knew? Like . . . *only* his fishing buddies?" Sammy interjected, and then looked at Jackson to gauge his answer.

"I'm not sure how many people they shared their private information with, but now that their house is on the market, anyone who looked at the property is sure to have seen the gun safe. They didn't put it away in storage before they put the house up for sale like I suggested. They couldn't move the darn thing. It's a huge piece of furniture—it takes up half the wall. The realtor has access to the home; he probably knows there's money in there too. It's pretty common for hunters to hide stuff in their gun safe—everyone knows that."

"Actually, I didn't know that," Heidi said with a slight shrug.

Sammy interjected, "The realtor you're referring to is Randy—my brother-in-law—and I assure you he's not trying to extort money from you. I'm also pretty sure that anyone he took on a listing appointment wouldn't have been left alone, even for a second. I'm sure he would've kept a close eye on anyone who stepped foot on their property. No one would've been able to toy with their gun safe."

"Are you sure about that?" Jackson forced his hands into the pockets of his Carhartts.

"Yes, I'm positive," Sammy answered, but she wasn't so sure Jackson felt the same.

Chapter Eleven

Sammy reached across the table for Heidi's hand to wordlessly gain her cousin's attention after Jackson left them alone for a moment within the confines of the kitchen. The farmer had excused himself to use a nearby restroom, and Sammy wondered if the highly stressed man might be ill.

Sammy leaned across the table and whispered, "Heidi, we have to do something. Didn't you see the look on Jackson's face? I can't believe I'm going to say this, but I get the impression he thinks Randy could be capable of stealing or extorting money from him. Don't you? You wanna talk ludicrous!" Sammy jutted a thumb to her chest. "This is *my* brother-in-law we're talking about now. Talk about going ballistic! Just wait until Ellie catches wind of this one. I think if we decided to help Jackson find a way inside Wanda's house, that'd be the least of our problems."

"Honestly, I don't know what to do." Heidi's green eyes rose to the large clock shaped like an apple above the stove, attached to the kitchen wall. "I know one thing; I'm running out of time. I've gotta get to the hospital soon. I don't want to be late for my shift, and you need to get back to Community Craft to close up too." Heidi lowered her voice. "I guess we don't have much of a choice at this point. We can't really force Jackson's hand, can we? Quite honestly, it's not our call to make. We're going to have to respect his wishes, I guess, and not tell the authorities just yet. But I'm not holding on to this information for long. Tim's not going to be very happy with me when the truth comes out that we were withholding pertinent information. Not happy at all." She blew out a frustrated breath as she gathered her long blonde hair over her right shoulder and combed her fingers through it.

The front door opened, and the sound of someone knocking the snow off their winter boots followed. Ellie returned to the kitchen soon after. "I did my best, but I couldn't hold them out there a minute longer—the kids are getting cold and hungry. I near killed myself trying to run ahead of them in the snow to give you guys a heads-up. They're all on their way back to the house now. Trust me, they're not too far behind. Where's Jackson?" Ellie's eyes pinballed around the kitchen, looking for the farmer.

"In the bathroom," Heidi said as she rose from the kitchen chair. "I've gotta hurry home and get into my scrubs for work. Otherwise I'm gonna be late for my shift."

"Okay." Ellie's face was strained. "Do we just leave, then?"

"Looks like that's our only option at this point." Sammy stood and threw up her hands in defeat before sliding her arms into her winter coat and slipping on her gloves.

"We can't just leave," Ellie said. "This feels wrong . . . what about Wanda?" she whispered. "Now that Jackson understands that Marty's absence and his sister's death must be somehow connected, should we tell him about her poisoning? Obviously, whoever is behind all this is most definitely capable of murder."

"We'll fill you in on the ride back," Sammy suggested. "Let's give this family some alone time to figure out their next move. We were only here to pay our respects and bring your famous lasagna. That is it." Sammy waved her gloved hands in front of her as if she were the umpire calling safe in a ball game and this call was final.

After Jackson returned to the kitchen, the three S.H.E.s bid him goodbye and assured him that he had a little time before any of them would share news of the ransom note. They explained that eventually they'd have no choice but to alert the authorities. With heavy hearts, they then made their way back to the Jeep.

When all three were safely tucked inside the vehicle, had clicked on their respective seat belts, and were halfway out of the driveway, Ellie said, "Okay, what'd I miss?"

"Well, thank goodness it looks like the plow went through," Sammy said, completely dodging her sister's question as she glanced out the rear passenger window of the Jeep. The sun was slipping into the western sky, and she was thankful they wouldn't have a repeat ride through rough terrain on the return trip home in the dark.

"Come on, you guys! Someone needs to bring me up to speed. You can't leave me hanging like that. What'd I miss? Tell me now." Ellie's voice reminded Sammy of her nephew begging to open his gifts at his birthday dinner.

"I'm not sure you want to know, E, but I can tell you this much: Wanda's poisoning must connect with something Marty's got himself involved in. It sounds to me like the guy's in way over his head. Right, Heidi?"

"Yeah, it's kinda hard to ignore that Wanda ended up dead due to poisoning and now her husband's MIA. Marty's car is found in the ditch, and now there's a ransom on the guy's head? *Seriously?* It's a lot to take in at this point." Heidi sighed heavily.

The three remained quiet, allowing the details to settle in their minds. After they drove several miles and passed the site where Marty's car had been located, Sammy broke the silence. "Looks like they've finished up the investigation over here." The tow truck had removed the vehicle, and the police cars, including Tim's patrol car, were apparently long gone, as snow was beginning to erase the most recent tire tracks.

"So, you both think holding out and not telling anyone about the ransom is a good idea?" Ellie asked again. "I'm not so sure this is the kind of secret I want to keep." She twirled her auburn hair nervously through her fingers. "I don't think this is the best idea, not at all."

"None of us do, but seriously, what other choice do we have?" Sammy said, then reached to the seat in front of her to tap her cousin lightly on the shoulder. "Heidi, would you mind dropping me off at Community Craft first? I didn't realize how much time we'd spent over there, and Deborah has already worked way past her assigned hours. I just received a text from her, and she's literally waiting by the door."

Sammy returned a text to Deborah after she'd removed her hands from her touch-screen gloves. She sometimes grew frustrated that the gloves didn't work properly and she couldn't move her fingers to text fast enough.

"Sure, no problem," Heidi said as they made their way through town.

"Are you coming over for lasagna after you close up?" Ellie asked.

"Honestly, as much as I appreciate the offer, I think I'd better take Bara for a quick walk after work. I know it'll be cold and dark, but my puppy needs his exercise. I've neglected his legs the last few days."

"Are you sure?"

"Uh-huh."

"So that's your final answer? We're not telling anyone?" Ellie confirmed as she adjusted her body in the seat to face her sister. When she remained shifted in her seat for several moments, waiting for an answer, Sammy sighed.

"Ellie, there's potentially a lot of money hidden inside the Wadsworths' house," she grudgingly revealed. "Possibly in the thousands of dollars, and Jackson alluded to the fact that the realtor might have known about it."

"What's *that* supposed to mean?"

"It means that Jackson is under the impression that either (a) your husband might have something to do with this, or (b) someone that he brought through on a listing appointment might be involved somehow. That's what it means."

"Why didn't you tell me this before? You're bringing this up now? Right before we drop you off?" The growing irritation in her sister's voice was hard to ignore.

"Because I didn't want to peak your anxiety, which I might have done by opening my big mouth."

"Heidi?" Ellie shifted in her seat and turned toward her cousin. Her tone was pleading now.

"We didn't want to alarm you, Ellie. Jackson's understandably upset. People say a lot of things when distressed. Try to see this whole situation from his point of view." Heidi's eyes left the windshield momentarily to console Ellie.

"Wait. He's insinuating my husband could have something to do with this! And you want me to take his point of view?" Ellie's voice rose an octave. "Maybe I should go right to the police then!"

Heidi eyed Sammy in the rearview mirror, waiting for her response.

"See, Ellie, this is how we thought you'd react. It's been a very stressful day. I think we all need to go home tonight and sleep on it. Things have a way of looking different in the morning. Do you think maybe you can do that? We'll regroup in the morning, I promise," Sammy suggested, although she herself wasn't sure that would change anything from her own perspective.

"Easy for you to say. It's not your husband under suspicion." Ellie readjusted in her seat and turned her attention out the windshield, shutting them both out.

Heidi reached out to her cousin, laying a comforting hand on her arm. "El, Jackson was just trying to figure out who had access to his sister's house. Randy's name was only brought up as a person that would have spent time over there. I'm sure he was just brainstorming who would possibly know about Marty's gun safe and if there was money inside. I'm also pretty sure if Randy knew there was that much cash left inside the Wadsworths' house, he would've insisted they put the money elsewhere while showing the property. Not to worry." Heidi fluttered a hand of dismissal. "Seriously, he just mentioned Randy in passing, like it was nothing. Right, Sammy?" Heidi looked in the rearview mirror to set her eyes again on her cousin.

Sammy knew Heidi was downplaying the whole scenario. Because what she had witnessed back at the farm was the complete opposite. It was her impression that Jackson very much thought Randy might have something to do with Marty's disappearance *and* potentially his sister's death, but she remained silent.

The Jeep pulled up in front of Community Craft, and Sammy knew she'd have to climb a pile of snow left over from the plow to navigate her way to the sidewalk. "Heidi, can you just pull back out into the road and double-park? I'll hop out fast. I don't think I can get the door open in this snowbank."

"Oh yeah, sure. Sorry about that," Heidi said, and then moved the Jeep forward as requested.

Sammy opened the door, quickly said her goodbyes, and hopped out of the Jeep. She moved quickly so that Heidi's vehicle wouldn't be hit from behind on Main Street. Then she returned a quick wave to Heidi and Ellie before trudging across the wet pavement to the safety of the sidewalk.

Deborah opened the front entrance to Community Craft, and Sammy stepped into the welcome warmth of her shop. "Sorry to keep you waiting. Thanks for holding down the fort."

Deborah dropped her purse to the floor and put on the winter coat that had been draped over her arm. "No worries at all. Sorry, I can't stay to chat though. I need to run to the supermarket on the way home for last-minute ingredients for supper. Seems the boys and Danny have broken limbs when it comes to preparing food for themselves. They rely on me far too much." Deborah adjusted the winter newsboy hat on her head. "That's something I really need to work on."

"You're a great mom." Sammy smiled.

"Yeah, well . . . it's either that or we starve," she said, laughing. "Did I ever tell you about the time I had to have minor surgery? I swear, the only meal Danny prepared for the kids during my recovery was ramen noodles. To this day, my boys won't touch those noodles. I was hoping one of my boys would take an interest in cooking, but they seem to be following in their dad's footsteps. I can't get either of them to step foot in the kitchen."

"All right, get going then. I'll see you tomorrow." Sammy smiled and encouraged Deborah's exit by gesturing a hand toward the door. "Thanks again for staying late."

"Oh, and by the way, Bara's been sleeping all afternoon. Just to let you know, he's had a few treats today from customers. Have a good night, Sammy," Deborah said, before disappearing out the front door.

Sammy sighed heavily. She loved that her customers were so loving to her dog, but sometimes they were almost too loving. She was afraid she might have to address the issue or her dog would end up getting sick. She maneuvered her way through the racks of merchandise and didn't see a single customer lingering throughout the shop. She went to give her dog a pat on the head before returning to her office to drop off her coat and hat. Bara followed her inside, where she said to him, "No more treats for you today." She wagged a finger and rolled her eyes. Bara sagged his head, and she could only imagine that, if it were possible, her dog would've rolled his eyes right back at her.

Business was slow the rest of the day, which was common after they'd passed the Fire and Ice event on the calendar. It was rare for customers to venture out past dark on bitter-cold evenings. Most wanted to be home cuddled by the fire reading a book, which, if Sammy was being honest, was exactly where she would like to be too. She wondered why she kept the store open as late as she did, but then remembered the evening classes were really what kept her business going during the long winter months. She was thankful there was no class that night, however, and wondered if she should just close early. The quilting group was meeting the following evening because they were working on piecing quilts for local hospice patients, so she'd have to remain open then.

As her stomach rumbled again, Sammy's eyes bounced around her office, looking for a snack. She reached into her desk and pulled open the bottom drawer, where she often hid a candy bar or small bag of chips, but her eyes stopped suddenly when they landed on Wanda's quilt, folded and tucked within the plastic bag. She reached for the quilt and unfolded it to glance at the artistry of the lap blanket. She laid it carefully on her desk to fully view the pattern and wondered if Wanda had designed the blocks herself. Her eyes moved from left to right to take in each quilted block, as if she were reading, and immediately stopped at the block four squares over. The block was an exact replica of the one painted on Jackson's farm—right down to the colors. A geometric star in hues of blue, yellow, and green.

"Huh? That's interesting," she said aloud, even though, aside from Bara, she was alone in the office. Wanda must have designed the quilt. How else would Jackson's star be part of the design? Had the quilt been made first? Or had the barn been painted first?

Bara walked over to the blanket and sniffed the corner that had fallen next to the desk. Without warning, her dog sank his teeth into the quilt and gave a rough tug, pulling it off her desk and dragging it onto the floor.

"Bara!" Sammy tried to get her dog to release his grip by reaching for the blanket, but he refused.

"Bara, drop it!" she said a bit sternly, even to her own ears. Finally, her dog dropped it to the floor, leaving wet drool on the corner's edge.

"Oh, Bara, what have you done?" Sammy bent at the waist and reached for the blanket to retrieve it from the floor. Although the blocks were machine-pieced, the quilt layers had been painstakingly hand-sewn together, and she was afraid there would be damage. And there was. A few of the hand stitches had come undone where Bara had inserted his teeth. She shook her head disapprovingly at her dog, and Bara hung his head in response, turned out the office door, and headed in the direction of his dog bed. She really needed to leave work and take him for a walk. With all the commotion in the last few days, her dog had been neglected, and his behavior was showing her that he needed to let go of some pent-up energy.

Sammy sighed heavily as she left the office with Wanda's lap blanket in hand. When she arrived inside the craft room, she placed the quilt on the craft table and rustled through a few cabinet drawers until she found what she was looking for: a seam ripper, white thread, a needle, and scissors. She cut a long thread, moistened the end in her mouth, and then threaded the needle.

Sammy pulled a newly painted wooden chair away from the long craft table and took a seat. She was happy with the new chairs that had been donated to Community Craft just a few short months ago. The library had taken on an interior remodel, and the library director had donated the unwanted old chairs to her shop. To revive them, Ellie had taken her painting skills to them and had painted each chair a different color. Deborah had also hand-painted a flower detail to the back of each one, adding even more flair. They gave the room a cheery, eclectic look and feel, which made Sammy smile as she took a seat.

Sammy picked up the corner of the quilt where Bara had chewed on it. She carefully removed the broken stiches with the seam ripper so she could find a place to knot the thread tight and repair the hole. While fingering the fabric loosely, she felt something stiff within the batting—something that didn't belong. She attempted to smooth out the layers so that when she stitched the quilt back together, it wouldn't be noticeable that anything had gone awry. She slid her finger inside to smooth the thick batting, but when she pulled out her finger, she was surprised by a paper cut.

"Ouch!" she said, and then she popped her finger into her mouth.

After she plucked her finger from her mouth, she noticed it had begun to bleed. "What the heck?" she said aloud. Once she stopped her finger from bleeding, she continued her attempts to patch the quilt back together.

But while smoothing the quilt layers together to prepare it for stitching, she dug her fingers around inside and fished out a small piece of paper lodged beneath the batting. It read: *The blocks pieced on this quilt release me of guilt.*

Chapter Twelve

Sammy's mouth hung agape as she reread, for the third time, the perplexing rhyme clutched in her hands: *The blocks pieced on this quilt release me of guilt.*

What in the world? It was as if Wanda were reaching out from the grave, testing Sammy's curious nature.

Sammy placed the note back on the table with trembling fingers, as if she could will it away. Now she was utterly incapable of piecing the ripped seam of the quilt back together. Her mind had run amuck. She lifted herself from the chair, abandoning the quilt, needle and thread atop the craft table, and began to pace within the confines of the craft room, trying to piece together this new revelation and make sense of it.

Why would Wanda have stitched this note within the batting of her quilt? Who had she intended to see it? What guilt had she been carrying? And what did the quilt blocks have to do with releasing her of guilt?

The bell on the front door alerted Sammy that a customer had entered Community Craft. She swiftly retrieved the rhyme off the table, stuffed the note deep into the front pocket of her faded blue jeans, and then stepped out of the craft room. She was surprised to see Detective Nash navigating the front door with a pizza box in his hand, which she instantly recognized as being from the Corner Grill. The box emitted a tantalizing scent, and her stomach leapt in a hungry response to the smell.

"Is that for me?" Sammy placed a hand to her heart as she approached him. The man either knew how much she loved pizza from the familiar restaurant, or he was completely mean hearted and was walking through her store to tease her.

"For us," Liam said as he looked around the store, noting it was empty of customers. "Looks like I picked the perfect time. No? Isn't it almost closing time around here? I figured you probably hadn't had a chance to eat yet, or did you beat me to it?"

"Not for another hour, although I'll admit I was contemplating closing early. And now I think you've helped finalize that decision." Sammy's eyes rose to the clock on the wall above the cash register and then back to the detective. "To what do I owe this surprise?" she asked as she tailed him into her office behind the register counter.

"Don't you remember I mentioned I needed to speak privately with you when we connected at the crime scene? I've learned from the past that you can get a little hangry if you haven't had time to eat. Am I right?" he said over his shoulder with a teasing voice.

Of course he was right. Unfortunately, under the current circumstances, he was more than right. She was starving, but how did he know that? He turned to her as soon as they were both within the confines of her office. "Tim?" She eyed him for confirmation.

"Yep, he was on the phone with Heidi and mentioned you three hadn't stopped for a late lunch like you had originally planned."

"Ah."

The way the detective's lips formed a lopsided smile solidified Sammy's suspicion that he had something on his agenda. The question was . . . what? Had Heidi confided in her boyfriend what they'd witnessed at Jackson's?

Sammy jutted a thumb behind her. "Excuse me for just a second; I'm going to go lock up. I haven't had anyone here in the last twenty minutes, and as cold as it is outside, I'd be shocked if someone stopped in at this point. I'd rather we not be interrupted if you have something you need to discuss with me in private. Besides, if anyone so much as sees you in here tonight, they're going to assume you're questioning me about Wanda. I'm guessing that's what you are here for. Am I right?"

Instead of answering her question, the detective placed the pizza box on her desk, flipped it open, and took a slice in his hand. He instantly took a bite, which made her mouth water.

Sammy left the detective alone in the office and proceeded to lock the front and back entrances. She wondered why he had shown up without advance notice and with a pizza bribe. He must want something, or he was digging for more intel. Sammy jammed the rhyme deeper into her jeans pocket. She wasn't ready to disclose Wanda's hidden note.

Not just yet. She wanted to probe the detective first and see how much information she could tap from him. Maybe she could learn something that might help Jackson figure out who was extorting money from him. If only she could keep her mouth shut about the ransom. Had Heidi already spilled to Tim the details of their visit to Jackson's farm? Did Liam already know, and had he now come to test her? She thought of this as she maneuvered through the merchandise racks back to the office. When she arrived, the detective was on his second slice.

"Are you sure that's for me to share too?" she teased.

"Hey, I haven't had time to stop and eat today either," he said between bites. "Haven't had a break all day."

"Here, why don't you go ahead and take a load off," Sammy suggested as she hauled a metal chair closer to her desk for him to take a seat. He immediately took the offer and sat down, all while continuing to consume the pizza slice still folded in his hand.

Sammy mirrored him by taking a seat behind her desk, reaching for the box, and taking a slice of pizza of her own. "Oooh, pepperoni my favorite," she said, before she sank her teeth deep into the slice.

"I know, I remember." He smiled, winked, and then took another bite.

"What brings you here with a food bribe?" She eyed him carefully, gauging his reaction.

"Bribe? No bribe. Just a meal between friends. We haven't exactly gotten off on the right foot again lately. Or am I missing something?"

Sammy thought for a moment. Something she rarely did before speaking her mind, but she was *really* trying. She weighed her words carefully and then said, "We missed you around the holidays. Seems you weren't around very much and didn't take part in the local festivities. I thought maybe I did or said something that hurt your feelings, to be honest. And the way you were acting, out by Marty's abandoned car. Forgive me, but I just assumed—"

The detective put up a hand of defense. "When it comes to work, you know I don't like anyone—I mean anyone, including you, Miss Kane—getting in the way of my investigations. But before we get into all of that, let me explain something." Liam took a breath and let it out slowly, as if debating with himself what to share with her. Then he surprised her by saying, "I'm not very fond of Christmas. It's not my favorite holiday."

Sammy cocked her head in question. "I'm not sure what you mean? Not very *fond* of Christmas?"

"Brenda passed away close to Christmastime, and every time I see a lighted tree, a wreath, or all the festive decorations . . . well, I tend to avoid it. All I see in my head are IV drips and machines with crappy decorations pathetically lighting up her hospital room, as if that could make it cheery. What a joke."

Sammy was surprised at his honesty. She nibbled on her pizza slice and didn't respond. She didn't want to say the wrong thing, so instead she said nothing.

Finally, after a long pause between them, he said, "Well now. I guess I shouldn't have shared that much." He tossed the uneaten crust into the box and picked up another slice, seemingly to keep his mouth busy and avoid further conversation.

"No, I'm really glad you did . . . share that." Sammy set her pizza crust down and rubbed her hand along the desk absently. "I'm sad for you, though. Brenda's been gone a few years now, and it's sad that you can't reflect on the good memories you shared during the holidays with her instead of concentrating on the way she died and when. Which is what you seem to focus on now that she's gone . . . at least when you're talking to me about her."

The detective's face lit in surprise, as if he was hearing something profound for the first time. "You know what? I never really thought about it that way."

"I'm sorry to be so blunt." She reached out a hand to soften the blow.

"No. I actually think I needed blunt." He set his slice of pizza in the box and wiped his hands together to rid them of the crumbs.

"I'm sorry, did you want something to drink?" Sammy rose from the desk chair and moved over to the small refrigerator that hummed in the corner of the room.

The detective cleared his throat. "Sure, that'd be great."

She reached in and pulled out two bottles of water. "Sorry, this is all I can offer at the moment," she said as she handed him one.

He took a long drink, looked her straight in the eyes, and said, "Thank you."

"Oh, you're welcome. I should've fetched us drinks right away, but my stomach led the parade." She laughed as she reached into the box for a second slice.

"No. I'm not thanking you for the water, although I appreciate it. What I'm trying to say . . ." The detective put the water bottle on the corner of her desk and wiped his mouth with the back of his hand. "When you watch someone die . . . I mean, in the manner that Brenda died . . . Watching someone you love waste away with cancer . . . it does something to you." His eyes dropped to the floor. "The suffering . . . and no way for me to fix it. The helplessness. Look, I'm a fixer. I fix things. Brenda's illness . . . it couldn't be fixed." He looked at his hands as if he were helpless.

"I can't even imagine. And I'm sorry . . . it was not my intention to hurt you with my words."

"Wait, let me finish." He put up a hand, and his eyes rose to meet hers. "Thank you, Samantha. For reminding me to look at the good and not the bad. Which is exactly where my focus has remained all these years. You know, my work hasn't left me absent of scars. It's left me jaded—the way I look at things. Look," he continued, "I see the worst in people most of the time. People do heinous things to each other—unimaginable things. It's hard sometimes to not become cynical. I think I've let my professional life carry over into my personal life, which is a gross mistake on my part. I'm going to try and rethink the way I've been seeing the world," he concluded, then picked up his pizza slice and continued until he hit crust, which he tossed back into the box.

Sammy didn't know how to react. It was rare for the detective to show vulnerability, but when he did, her heart swelled.

"You know, I have to admit something to you." Sammy cleared her throat. "After you and I uncovered what happened to Kate"—she lifted her eyes to the ceiling and looked up, as if she could see a vison of her best friend who'd long passed—"the amazing friend who started all of this and created strong community bonds here in this place . . ." Her eyes dropped and landed on him. "It was hard for me. Hard not to focus on what I'd learned, what *we'd* uncovered." Sammy wagged a finger between them. "It stayed with me. I'll admit, I focused on it for many weeks, and the anger burned inside me. But one day, when I was standing out on the shop floor here at Community Craft and a stream of light came through the front window and rested on me"—Sammy paused and smiled—"I felt her presence like I hadn't in a long time. I could almost hear her laughter, and it suddenly dawned on me. The only one that was hurting was *me*. And Kate wouldn't want that. Not for a second. What I'm trying to say, Liam, is . . . I don't think Brenda would want it for you either. She'd want you to remember everything good, everything pure between you two. She wouldn't want you to miss out on the joy that life provides. That's all I'm going to say on that matter. I think I've already said too much." Sammy lifted her pizza to her mouth and took a big bite to stop herself from saying anything further.

The detective's eyes softened. "I'll try," he said in a rough voice. "I'm definitely going to try."

Sammy felt he had received the message, but she also felt him growing uncomfortable in the growing silence between them, so she said, "Are you going to eat those crusts?"

"Why? You want 'em? Nope, they're all yours." He smiled.

Sammy rose from her chair and called out to her dog. Within minutes Bara filled the room with his furry frame, and Sammy sat back in the chair, leaned over, and handed a crust to her dog, which he took willingly. Then he sank down with it held between his paws.

"Looks like he loves the Corner Grill too," Liam said as he leaned over and gave Bara a pat on the head.

"He sure does. I try not to give him too much, but occasionally I let him have it. Why don't you tell me the real reason you brought me my favorite pie? You want me to open up about something, don't you? My turn, is it?" She hoped her voice sounded teasing, but she seriously wondered about his underlying agenda after the way he had treated her on the side of the road by Marty's abandoned car. He always treated her differently in private, which was interesting for her to ponder. She'd think more about that later.

The detective cleared his voice. "I'm not going to share anything I think you don't already know. Wanda's death was due to poisoning, and now Marty is missing. Let's just say things are looking very suspicious. So, I've been doing some digging."

Sammy's eyes narrowed. "Do you think Marty took off of his own accord? From the sound of your voice, I get the impression you think he was the one who poisoned his wife. Am I right? Don't you always look at those closest to the victim first? Hey, I'm only going on what you've taught me from our previous experiences." She winked.

"I'm not ruling anything out at this point. I'm now in a full-on investigation, which leads me to why I'm here."

Sammy wiped her hands on her lap, then clasped her hands and held them across her full stomach. She leaned back in the chair, attempting to act casual, but she wondered if he already knew the secret she was keeping and was about to apply pressure like a tight squeeze. "Go on."

Instead he surprised her. "I'm going to need you to stand down. Something I'm about to tell you is going to upset you, and I need your cooperation to let me do my job. Do you think I can trust you to do that?"

"I'm not sure I'm following."

"It's about your brother-in-law."

Chapter Thirteen

"My brother-in-law? You mean *Randy*?" Sammy sat upright in her chair, her back turned as stiff as a two-by-four pine board. "What about him?" She hoped the detective and Jackson didn't have similar thoughts regarding Randy's so-called potential involvement.

Detective Nash reached across the desk and closed the pizza box to keep Bara's sniffing nose from digging into what was left—which wasn't much. "I'm sure you're very well aware that Randy is the listing agent on the Wadsworths' property, and as I've dug deeper into this investigation, some things have come to light."

"What *things*?" Sammy placed her hands flat on her desk to steady herself.

Detective Nash put up a defensive hand. "I'm not going to divulge that kind of information right now. But your brother-in-law will be brought in for questioning tomorrow, and I need your full cooperation. I need you to assure me that you'll stay out of this." His eyes turned from warm chocolate to piercing. "I know how much influence you have over the people of this town, and your reaction will either hinder or help my investigation. I'm hoping for the latter, despite the fact that he's your relative. I'm respecting you enough to share this information with you. I didn't have to, but I *chose* to." He held a finger upright to drive home the point.

Sammy's heart began to thunder in her chest. "Wait a second. A minute ago, you thought Marty disappeared of his own accord."

"No. I didn't say that." He put up a hand to stop her.

"But you implied it."

"No. You're reading into things. I clearly said I'm not ruling anything out at this point." The detective lifted himself from the chair, making a scraping sound on the floor, which caused Bara to shift and saunter closer to the door.

"Wait. Where are you going? Please sit back down," Sammy pleaded as she fluttered a hand to encourage him to stay.

"I'm not staying, Samantha. I can't divulge any information to you at this point. I'm asking you to stand down and trust me to do my work. And to do that, you're going to have to let things unfold as they should and not overinvolve yourself this time." He reached for his coat and tucked it over his arm. "Please. I need you to cooperate. Can I count on you to do that?"

His response was so vague, it drove her to rise from her own seat. "Wait. Please, I'm begging you. Tell me what you've got on Randy."

The detective gave Bara a pet on the head and then moved over the threshold. He briefly turned for a moment to face her and rested his hand casually on the doorjamb. "Can you get rid of the pizza box for me?" He bobbed his head toward the desk, where the mostly empty box sat.

"Sure. I appreciate you bringing supper to share." Although the pizza was beginning to churn in her stomach due to the recent news. "But are you sure you can't stay? Can we talk this through?"

Sammy's hands turned clammy from the conflict flip-flopping in her mind. *Should I tell him about the ransom note?* Maybe this would change everything in his investigation. Her heart began to beat faster. *Will Jackson understand if I spill the beans? Will Marty survive if I tell Liam what's really going on? Will it change anything regarding Randy?* While she debated which was the right decision to make, the detective made it for her.

"Good night, Samantha," he said, and turned out the office door. After his frame disappeared from view, she steadied herself on two wobbly legs. Yet her feet felt like they were buried in concrete.

After a moment, she moved to follow him. "Wait!"

But it was too late. The detective had already slipped out the back exit.

Sammy stared at the closed glass door and held a hand to her rapidly beating heart. Part of her wanted to chase after him into the parking lot. The other part won out. She needed to think. The first thing that sprang to her mind was to call an emergency S.H.E. meeting. There was no way she was going to allow this investigation to get out of hand and drag Randy smack-dab in the middle of it. She needed to do something fast to stop this investigation from snowballing, but she didn't want to make a rush decision on her own. She needed the team.

Sammy rushed back to her office, and her eyes pinballed around the room, seeking her cell phone. Once she found it, deep in the pocket of her winter coat, she group-texted her sister and Heidi and asked that they meet back at her house at eleven thirty PM, immediately after Heidi's shift, regarding Randy. It had already been a very long day, but they didn't have a choice. The three S.H.E.s were going to have to break into the Wadsworths' estate.

* * *

Sammy continued to pace the floor of her cozy Cape Cod until her sister arrived a few minutes past eleven o'clock. Bara was curled in front of the fireplace fast asleep, tuckered out from his earlier winter walk. She'd promised herself she wouldn't neglect her dog's exercise, and she hadn't. Immediately after closing the shop for the night, she had bundled out into the cold. Even the sting of the biting wind hadn't phased Sammy as she had replayed events in her conflicted mind while trudging Bara through the snow like a warrior preparing for battle. The preposterous idea that Nash was bringing Randy in for questioning the following day was almost too much to handle. How nervous Nellie Ellie would take that news, she had yet to discover.

"Ellie, I'm so glad you came." Sammy held the door as her sister knocked the snow off her boots before entering the small foyer.

"This had better be good. I can't imagine why you'd be dragging us three S.H.E.s out at this ungodly hour of the night. Care to explain?" Ellie eyed her with a frown as she slipped off her boots and closed the front door behind her.

"To be honest, I was glad you decided to come. I didn't think I'd be able to convince you." Sammy's brows knit together. "Why did you come?"

"I have my reasons. Not to mention the cryptic text message about my husband. You mind telling me why I'm here, so I'm not left wondering? I'm sure I'm blowing this waaaay out of proportion in my mind. At least I hope so?"

Bara lifted his head from his comfortable position in front of the fire, recognized Ellie, and then rested his head back down on his paws and closed his eyes. "Even your dog is too tired to come and greet me." She pointed to Bara before stepping inside the living room beside him. "It's nice and cozy in here," Ellie added as she stepped in front of the fire and rubbed her hands together to warm them. "Okay, you dragged me out into the cold, dark night. What gives?"

"Detective Nash came to see me at Community Craft."

"Yeah, so?" Ellie interrupted. "I thought you said you wanted to talk to us S.H.E.s about Randy and it was super important we talked 'in person.'" Ellie lifted her fingers in air quotes.

"I'm getting to that," Sammy said, before Ellie interrupted her again.

"Please. Don't tell me what you're about to say. You guys already informed me Jackson insinuated my husband is involved in this, and now Nash pays you a private visit? Wait. I'm not sure I can handle this."

"Maybe you should sit down." Sammy led her sister to a seat on the plush love seat she had purchased as a Christmas gift to herself, replacing the old worn-out sofa she'd used in her twenties. She curled her legs beneath her and then reached for her sister's hands to calm her. Despite Ellie's recent visit to the fireplace, her hands were cold to the touch.

"Tell me right now why Nash came to see you. He talked to you about Randy, didn't he?" Ellie's eyes were searching.

Sammy took a breath and blew her mouth up like a blowfish before revealing, "Yep."

"Why? I don't get it. Just because he's Wanda and Marty's realtor? Now my husband is accused of something shady to do with all of this?" Ellie's hands flew from her sister's grasp, and she flung them in the air dramatically. "What the heck. My husband can't catch a break. Ever since he started this stupid real-estate career, it's been one problem after the other. I wish he'd listened to Dad and just stuck with working at the mortgage company. It was a lot less stress on our family, that's for darn sure!"

Sammy let her sister unload. She knew Ellie had never been fully on board with Randy switching careers, when his past employment at the mortgage firm had been stable and he was their main source of income. Especially since Ellie didn't have a career to speak of and merely worked at Community Craft part-time for minimum wage. Sammy couldn't blame her for being upset about his career move.

Ellie rose from the love seat and headed toward the fireplace again, seeking comfort. Bara rose next to her, and she stroked him down his back. While Ellie faced the fireplace, her shoulders began to quake, and Sammy knew her sister was crying. She moved to wrap her arm around her, and Ellie rested her head on Sammy's shoulder while she wiped away tears. "I don't feel so good," Ellie said, then quickly ran toward the staircase and up the stairs, seemingly to use the bathroom.

Sammy heard a soft knock at the front door and yelled, "Come in," knowing her cousin would likely be on the other side.

"What's going on? You've had me worried ever since I received your text message." Heidi stepped inside and immediately removed her boots. "This is unlike you to ask me to come over after a long day and then a shift. It must be serious. But here I am," she added with her famous jazz hands, albeit with far less than her usual enthusiasm.

"I'm sorry I couldn't text it all, and I didn't want to bother you at the hospital, but thanks for coming. It's super important." Sammy leaned in to share a hug.

"Where's Ellie?" Heidi looked beyond her into the living room. "I saw her car out front. I know she beat me here."

"She just ran upstairs for a moment." Sammy closed the door behind her cousin, ushered her inside, and whispered, "I think I may have already upset her." She cringed. "It's about Randy. Nash is going to bring him in tomorrow for questioning, and the news really upset Ellie." Sammy's eyes traveled to the empty staircase. "You think I should go check on her?"

"Nah, give her a minute while you bring me up to speed. If she doesn't come back soon, we'll both go and check on her."

Sammy shared the information she'd learned thus far and then asked timidly, "Tim didn't share any of this with you? I'm kinda surprised, to be honest." Her brow rose in question.

Heidi unzipped her long wool coat to display her scrubs. "I've been a little busy."

"I know, I was just curious if maybe you'd already shared with Tim what happened over at Jackson's farm. You didn't, did you?"

Heidi removed her coat and tossed it on the nearby leather recliner. "Nope, I didn't. For one thing, I seriously didn't have time. I'm surprised Tim told Nash we hadn't had lunch. I barely had a chance to catch up with Tim on my way in to the hospital, and he dropped off food for me to nibble between patients. I swear that was it. Tim literally handed a boxed lunch to me like a football pass." She crossed her fingers and held them up for display. "I was busy workin', girlfriend."

"You and I both know how anxious Ellie can get in these types of situations." Sammy wagged a finger between them. "I just hope she can help us figure out the combination to that lockbox. We have no other choice but to break into the Wadsworths'. If the money is in the gun safe, maybe we can help get Marty back and clear up this mess and Randy will be off the chopping block."

"You know Tim is on patrol tonight and will be circling the Wadsworth property. The police are keeping a tight eye on the place, hoping either Marty will return or someone involved will show up there. I'm guessing you want me to distract him while you and Ellie sneak in?" Heidi asked conspiratorially.

"Exactly. I just hope my sister is up for the challenge. You know how nervous she gets." Sammy was about to share the perplexing rhyme she'd found inside Wanda's quilt with Heidi when Ellie descended the stairs. The two of them looked at her with compassion.

"Are you all right?" Heidi asked. "You look a bit pale."

Ellie shook her head. "No, I'm not all right . . . I'm pregnant."

"Whaaaat?" Sammy reached for her sister.

"You heard me. I'm pregnant. You asked me what my reasons are for joining you two hooligans tonight. Meet exhibit A. I need my husband now more than ever!" Ellie said, raising her shirt to display her tummy.

Sammy instantly pulled her sister in for a hug. Heidi wrapped her arms around the two of them, and they covered Ellie in squeals and giggles. "Congratulations!"

When they finally released their three-way hug, Sammy said, "I'm going to be an aunt again! What is it—a boy or a girl?" She leaned back, placed her hand on her sister's stomach, and held it there.

Ellie laughed. "It's a baby, you goof. I just found out and we're in the first trimester, so I have no idea what the sex is yet. I didn't want to share my news before I took the pregnancy test. I took it this afternoon after we got back from Jackson's because I was feeling so sick in the Jeep on the way home, and voilà!" Then Ellie's smile faded. "I can't have Randy mixed up in a murder investigation right now. We have enough instability in our lives with his new job, and now this?" Tears filled Ellie's eyes, and she blinked them back. "You guys have to help me clear him of this. I need my husband!" Her tone was desperate and laced with fear.

"It's going to be okay," Sammy soothed. "We're gonna figure this out. Don't worry . . . I promise." Her eyes met Heidi's pleadingly and then landed back on Ellie. "Us three S.H.E.s will get to the bottom of this, and soon all this will become a distant memory. Don't you worry about a thing."

But by the look on her sister's face, Sammy knew Ellie wasn't buying it.

Chapter Fourteen

Sammy was relieved the town of Heartsford was going to be blanketed with a coat of fresh snow overnight. With each falling snowflake, crucial evidence of their visit would be buried deep beneath the snow and long forgotten. The few inches expected would more than cover any prints the Kane sisters were making as they made their way up the front walk to the Wadsworths' Queen Anne Victorian. The grand wraparound porch was framed with decorated columns, and a snowcapped turret rose high above their heads. The freshly fallen flakes were sticking to Sammy's eyelashes, and she brushed them out of her eyes with a gloved hand.

The two sisters had no other choice but to enter via the front entrance, where the lockbox was attached to the brightly painted door. Sammy peeked over both shoulders before taking the first step onto the wraparound porch. The street was devoid of cars, and the neighboring houses were eerily quiet. Perfect. The three S.H.E.s had planned their incursion to happen after two AM, when most people would hopefully be in bed. Sammy really hoped that would be the case and they wouldn't get caught by a vigilant neighbor. "Do you think you know the combination to the lockbox?" Sammy whispered, even though there wasn't anyone within earshot besides her sister.

"Yes, I know the combination. I helped Randy set up the lock when he first brought it home from the broker's office. My goofy husband picked the letters *F-U-N*. He said this career would not be like his last—this one would be fun. Oh, it's fun all right, so flipping fun," she added with a huff. "Are we having fun yet? Just look where we are in the wee hours of the morning. Don't you remember Mom always said nothing good happens after midnight?" Ellie fumbled with the lock.

"Yeah, how could I forget. She used to say that all the time, especially during our curfew years. Please tell me you haven't called Mom and talked to her about all this. She'd be completely freaked if she heard how deep we're involved. You know she highly disapproves of our sleuthing and anything, in her words, as 'childish as S.H.E.,'" Sammy said.

Ellie didn't answer, which was never a good sign. She must've already informed their mother back in Arizona. Instead she dug the key out of the lockbox and opened the door, and the two slipped inside the Queen Anne Victorian. Sammy immediately closed the door behind them, and they removed their snow-covered boots before they went any farther. "Tell me you brought flashlights," Ellie said. "The last thing we want to do is turn the lights on and alert the entire neighborhood. I'm sure the neighbors are already all on high alert. Don't you think?"

"Yeah, I brought two of those pen ones the credit union was giving away at the town barbecue last summer. Here." Sammy left her gloves on but dug deep into her coat pocket, pulled out two pen flashlights, and handed one to her sister.

"Okay, what are we looking for exactly?" Ellie adjusted the hat on her head, which consequently dripped water in her eyes. Sammy reached into her sister's pocket, dug for a balled-up Kleenex she knew Ellie would have stashed inside, and handed it to her sister, which made Ellie smile.

"Two things on our agenda." Sammy held up two gloved fingers. "First, we want to check the gun safe to see how much money is in there and if there's indeed enough for Jackson to pay the ransom. Second, we're looking for some sort of important paperwork. Randy told me at Tyler's birthday party that Marty had something in his hand that Wanda was adamant he put away before Randy had a chance to see what it was. We need to find out what was so important that it had to remain hidden from your husband. Hopefully that might give us a clue as to how this couple got in way over their heads." Sammy adjusted her gloves tighter on her fingers. "Don't leave prints behind either. Make sure and keep your gloves on."

"Randy told you all that, huh? All this was happening right beneath my nose while I was slaving away in the kitchen making our son's birthday dinner, I suppose?" Ellie rolled her eyes and then readjusted the winter hat on her head. "Gosh, it's creepy being in a strange house, let alone in the dark. Have your eyes adjusted yet?" She grimaced, then flicked on the flashlight and sent a narrow beam along the floor. "Let's hurry this up. I'm feeling really nauseous, and I don't think it's due to pregnancy. I think it may be more due to anxiety and uncertainty at this point." She moved in the direction of her flashlight beam, but Sammy held her back by reaching for her shoulder.

"Speaking of your pregnancy, I was about to tell you something before you shared your big announcement. I'm so happy for you, by the way; I can't believe Tyler is going to have a sibling!" Sammy smiled, then let it fade. "I found something interesting belonging to Wanda." She removed her glove for a second to dig deep into her jeans pocket. She handed the rhyme to Ellie, who shone a light on the note and eagerly read it.

"What is this?"

"I haven't the slightest, but it was sewn between the batting of Wanda's quilt. What do you make of it?"

"Well, besides the fact it's incredibly odd, I haven't a clue. Maybe the quilting group can help you figure that out? Unless you don't think it's a good idea to share it with them?"

"Yeah, it seems rather personal to share. I'll hold off on that but maybe share it with Heidi to see what she thinks. The quilting group meets tomorrow at Community Craft. Hopefully I'll be awake enough to sit in on that meeting." Sammy stifled a yawn.

"Come on," Ellie said, beckoning her sister to follow the beam of light in front of her.

"I think we should split up to make this faster." Sammy lifted her stream of light to an interior staircase leading to the second floor and then followed the beam along the wide pine baseboard to finally land on the narrow strip of pine flooring on her left. "I'll go this way," Sammy said as she turned in the direction of the front room. Despite their stocking feet, the wood floor creaked, sending eerie sounds echoing off the wallpapered walls.

"Do we have to split up?" Ellie whined, before complying with Sammy's plan and following her own narrow beam away from her sister toward the back of the house.

The front room was dark, even with the low sash windows void of blinds and the curtains pulled aside. The full moon did little to illuminate the large, rounded space. Sammy was careful not to send her light out the window and instead followed the beam along the wide baseboard deeper into what appeared to be the parlor. The room was decorated in highly ornate damask furniture, fit for a tea party or to meet the queen herself. Sammy didn't think a gun cabinet would be found in this room, so she followed her flashlight along the narrow floorboards, over an intricately designed iron heating element flush with the floor, back to the narrow strip of pine boards, until she reached the next room. As Sammy's flashlight bounced within the confines of each room, it illuminated several deep nooks and crannies crafted with original woodwork. She now understood why her brother-in-law was interested in turning this home into a historical landmark. The woodwork was old but remained in pristine condition.

She stumbled upon a rolltop desk, which she proceeded to try to open, but it was locked. *Darn it!* Her heart raced while she contemplated how she could explore the inside. She plucked a bobby pin from her hair that was holding back her overgrown auburn bangs beneath her winter hat, and bit off the rubber stoppers. She then used the pin to dig around inside the keyhole. It took several minutes, but she surprised herself by jimmying the inexpensive lock. She slowly rolled the desk open, releasing a groaning sound. She instinctively looked around to make sure no one was within earshot. She let out a nervous giggle, knowing full well she and Ellie were the only ones inside the grand Queen Anne Victorian.

She began rifling through the drawers with gloved fingers. The first drawer held a roll of stamps and bills that needed to be paid and junk mail stuffed away to be dealt with at a later time. The second drawer held nothing of importance either. Rubber bands, a stapler, an ungodly number of pens—*seriously, who keeps this many pens?* Scrap paper. Nothing. The third drawer held a stack of hanging file folders, which, if Sammy was being honest with herself, could take days to sift through. The labels seemed to indicate that most folders contained bill receipts and papers pertaining to home improvement.

The sound of a door creaking as it slowly opened made the hairs stand up on the back of Sammy's neck. She froze for a moment and held her breath. The sound seemed to be coming from the back of the house. She craned her neck for a better visual but then heard that the heating element had recently kicked in. The slope of the old wood floors along with the clanging radiators must've caused the door to move. Either that or it was her sister nearby.

"Ellie?" Sammy whispered. "Ellie, is that you?"

Sammy heard no response. She waited a moment, huffed a nervous breath, and continued with her search.

A laptop sat open atop the desk, and Sammy clicked the button and powered it to life, sending a glow into the dark room. Her fingers worked the keys to seek the last Google search. *Dicamba* was the most recent search on the computer.

Dicamba?

Sammy secretly wondered if this was the name of the poison that had killed Wanda. She followed the search to investigate. Upon further reading, she found that dicamba was a chemical weed killer used on farm crops. This search didn't initially surprise Sammy and felt like a dead end, as Marty sold seeds to farmers. But as she dug deeper, she learned that dicamba was a newer chemical used because Roundup seemed to no longer be working on the farm fields due to new superweeds. A superweed was a weed extremely resistant to herbicides, especially one created by the transfer of genes from genetically modified crops into wild plants. These new superweeds were popping up everywhere as they became resistant to Roundup, causing farmers to seek a new solution. Dicamba, according to the article, was controversial, as proper testing hadn't been done. In addition, the company selling the new herbicide also confirmed that farmers would have to buy genetically modified seed exclusively from them, as theirs was the only seed that could survive the harsh chemicals.

Sammy fished her cell phone from her pocket and snapped a photo so she could research this further, just as a chiming grandfather clock in the distance reminded her that time was ticking. She needed to hurry.

She next clicked on an Excel spreadsheet on the desktop and noted a ledger of potential seed customers. She snapped another quick photo with her cell. Maybe one of these farmers could provide insight on Marty's whereabouts?

"Sammy!" Her ears perked at the sound of her sister's muffled voice. She quickly powered down the computer and carefully rolled the desk closed. She followed the beam of light to where she thought she'd heard her sister's voice. "Ellie, I'm coming! Say something so I can find you!" She cuffed a hand to her ear and strained to listen.

When Sammy returned to the front of the house, she heard Ellie again. "Up here."

She followed the light and was surprised to see Ellie at the top of the ornate spindled staircase.

"Come up here." Ellie was summoning with a glove-covered hand. "You've gotta see this."

Sammy made the climb and met her sister at the top of the stairs. She was huffing and puffing by the time she reached the top, reminding her that her lack of exercise due to the cold winter was rearing its ugly head. "What's the matter?" she said when she finally caught her breath.

"I think I found what we're looking for." Ellie ushered her sister into a nearby room at the top of the stairs. There was only one problem. The gun cabinet in front of them was ajar, and very empty, with not even one rifle to be found. Someone had beat them there, and the gun cabinet was wiped clean.

Chapter Fifteen

"Whaddya think? You think Jackson found a key to his sister's house and beat us here. Or did someone else empty the cabinet? Randy would've said something to me if he had found it left ajar and empty like this. No doubt about it. He didn't mention a thing at Tyler's birthday dinner about this, not a thing." Sammy pointed to the solid oak cabinet with a deer etched in the glass that took up a better part of the wall. "It looks like whoever was in here searching was in a hurry and knew *exactly* what they were looking for. Maybe Marty found a way to escape his captor and came back here looking for his stash and guns to protect himself? What does your gut say?"

"My gut says I want to throw up," Ellie said sarcastically. "Don't worry, I'll hold back," she added as she placed the back of her gloved hand to cover her mouth. Her face scrunched as if she was tasting something nasty.

After a long pause, Ellie said, "What do we do now?"

"Well, it's not like we can phone Jackson at two thirty in the morning and see if he just happened to stop by." Sammy rolled her eyes. "I imagine if it was Jackson, though, he would've closed the doors and not left the cabinet wide open, in case Marty returned. Wouldn't you think? Maybe the police were here and left it open. Something's fishy."

"This sucks," Ellie huffed. "I feel like this was all a colossal waste of time. Did you happen to find anything of interest downstairs?"

Sammy scratched her jaw and sighed. "No. Not really. Nothing earth-shattering."

"How am I going to protect my husband now?" Worry riddled Ellie's face.

Sammy's cell phone chimed in her pocket. "That must be Heidi." She fished her cell out of her pocket and clicked on the screen with her text-messaging glove to read only two words: *Abort! Abort!*

Sammy's adrenaline immediately kicked into overdrive as if she'd had one too many caffeinated drinks from Liquid Joy, causing her heart to thunder in her chest. She took a calculated breath to steady herself.

Ellie peeked over Sammy's arm to see the message, and instantly her eyes bulged to twice their usual size. "Oh yeah, this night can't possibly get any better! Now this really sucks. We gotta get outta here . . . like now!" she said in a panicky voice, grabbing her sister by the arm—almost pulling it from the socket—and dragging her toward the staircase. The two ran like a train of cars, as quickly as they could without slipping, all the way down to the bottom.

When they reached the foyer, Sammy said, "Grab your boots!" She reached down and plucked her wet boots from the front mat and tucked them under her arm, leaving a path of drips in her wake. She turned to encourage her sister to do the same with her free hand. "Hurry! We'll have to escape out the back! We'll put our boots on back there. Come on!"

Sammy shone her penlight back on the narrow strip of pine floorboards, and they hurried to the back of the house, where they both instantly saw a shining beam of light traveling through the window, as if someone was already casing the joint from the outside. "This way," Sammy beckoned as they hid behind an inside kitchen wall, both breathing heavily but deathly silent. Neither dared utter a word. After no sign of further bouncing light within the confines of the house, they traveled cautiously room to room, looking for an escape. Every few feet they would hide, their backs firmly pressed against the interior walls. Finally, Sammy opened a door that led to a musty early-1900s cellar.

"Are you *crazy*? We're going to get caught locked in that dingy place!" Ellie backed away from the door and shook her head, covering her nose. "What is it with you and basements! Bad idea! Not a chance." Ellie dropped a boot from her grip, and her eyes bulged at the noise as if she had just given them away. She hurried to retrieve it from the floor.

"Ellie, come on! We have to go down there or potentially get arrested." Sammy's eyes darted with fear. "Your call . . . what do you want to do? Do you want to get thrown in the slammer next to your husband?" She hissed as her heart thundered in her chest, making it hard to breathe. She placed a hand to her heart and felt the rapid beat pulsating through her winter coat.

"Fine." Ellie shoved her way past her sister and headed down the cellar stairs in front of her, beaming the grossly inadequate penlight into the dark, damp old space. When they reached the bottom, Ellie turned to her sister and dropped her boots to the floor. "Now what? We're going to hide out here until we know it's safe to leave?"

"There's got to be an exit out of the cellar. These old homes usually have one. I hope I'm right. I say we wait until we hear footsteps inside the house, and then we make a run for it. If we try to escape now, we might get caught," Sammy said, moving next to her sister to balance herself and shoved on her winter boots.

"Okay, I guess we don't really have much of a choice. It's either that or hide out and sleep down here, which, I have to be honest, isn't on my short list," Ellie said hesitantly. She bent at the waist to follow suit and slipped her feet into her winter boots.

Sammy flashed the narrow beam along the large boulders that made up the basement wall until the light landed on a shelf of what appeared to be vintage wine bottles.

"If I weren't pregnant, I'd pop open one of those babies right here, right now, and take a swig!" Ellie whispered, pointing a finger at the wine.

"You? You'd steal someone else's property?" Sammy's eyes narrowed. This new revelation from her sister surprised her.

"Seriously? Are you *kidding* me?" Ellie flicked a finger toward her. "Coming from *you*, who has me locked inside a dead woman's basement!" She let out a nervous giggle, her voice rising to an unusual octave for a whisper.

Sammy held back a smile. She moved the flashlight away from the wine bottles and traveled the beam of light along the rock wall until it reached a steel cellar trapdoor.

"Bingo!" she said wildly.

She beckoned her sister to follow, and they stood by the few concrete steps that led upward to their potential escape. She placed a gloved finger to her lips for them to remain quiet. Within minutes the muffled sound of footsteps overhead alerted them that someone had entered the house and was inside above their heads. Sammy's finger left her lips and pointed upward. She then returned the gloved finger to her lips to signal Ellie to remain quiet.

Sammy waited for the muffled sound to dissipate and then whispered, "Now!"

The two made their way up three steps and before Sammy opened the bulkhead, she said, "make sure and drag your feet through the snow." We don't want the police to get a good image of the size boots running from the back. If we slide our prints into one continuous path, hopefully they won't lead back to us."

"Gosh, you're devious. Where'd you come up with that idea?" Ellie asked, horrified. "Who *are* you, anyway?"

"Hey, I watch a lot of crime shows. Don't judge me. And, anyhow, it may just save your Heineken! Now go!" Sammy gave her sister a nudge to urge her to prepare to exit.

Ellie's eyes were wide with fear as Sammy reached and pushed the heavy steel door with a great shove. Heavy falling snow greeted them as soon as they saw open sapphire sky. The cold wind whipped, sending sideways flakes to sting their eyes and cheeks. Sammy blinked them back as she held tight to the door.

"Hurry!" Sammy encouraged her sister to go first and then turned to close the bulkhead door. As soon as the door was secure, she followed Ellie into the backyard and heaved her feet through the snow. She attempted to follow her sister's jagged path to make it look as if there had been only one intruder leaving the premises. Doing so slowed the journey, and Sammy wondered if her idea had indeed been the right one when she heard a long-distance bellow in the form of Tim's voice from over her shoulder. "Stop! Police!"

Ellie ducked behind a shed and plucked Sammy by the coat, nearly knocking her from her feet to join her before she had a chance to run past.

"We can't outrun Tim! We might as well give it up right here and now," Ellie said between pants of heavy breathing. She threw up her gloved hands in defeat. "Cuff me now," she said dramatically as she held her hands out in front of her.

Sammy pushed her sister's hands down in one swift movement. "Not so fast." Her eyes darted across the backyard as they adjusted to the light of the wintry moonlit sky. "Over there." She pointed. The neighboring yard had a hard, plastic, blue sled leaning against the back side of a shed. "Let's make a run for it."

"You want to do *what*?"

Sammy didn't wait for her sister to agree. She grasped Ellie's coat, gave an encouraging tug of the arm, and aborted their one-path mission. Instead, the two made their way through the snow on separate paths as fast as they could. As soon as they reached the sled, Sammy set it down on top of the snow, grabbed hold of the string, and dragged it behind them as they continued to run as best they could through the deepening snowdrifts. The two kept a fair pace until they reached a small hill. "Get on." Sammy waved an encouraging hand for her sister to climb inside the sled.

"What hairbrained scheme have you gotten me into this time? *Seriously?* How old are we? We're going to go sledding now?

We may as well just give up." Ellie sounded resigned. "Do you have any idea the last time I sat on a sled?" Ellie looked at Sammy as if she had horns coming out of her head.

Sammy had to say only one word to convince her. "Arrested?"

Ellie glared at her before setting herself down and scooting her body on her backside toward the front to make room for her sister.

Sammy bent at the waist, took hold of the side rails of the sled, and began to run as fast as she could in the deep snow. She gave a shove as if she were running a bobsled in the Olympics before jumping onto the back. The icy wind bit at her face, but she knew Ellie was taking the brunt of it as she ducked behind the safety of her sister's body. The snow falling in swirly waves blinded them as they made their rapid escape, sliding down the snowcapped hill.

Chapter Sixteen

It didn't take long before a hard rapping sound reverberated on the front door of Sammy's Cape Cod in the wee hours of the morning. This caused three pairs of S.H.E. eyes to dart nervously among themselves and then out toward the banging coming from the front of the house. The three had recently removed their wet clothes and now stood within the heap of abandoned footwear in a panic.

"Someone had better get that," Ellie said with a resounding sigh. Sammy noted the exhaustion in her sister's voice and wondered how much longer she could remain upright and not collapse into the nearest bed. Ellie's face was pale, her eyes shadowed gray, and she looked as if she'd been awake for days, not just one very long night. Her cousin, on the other hand, who was comfortable with swinging shifts and working all hours of the night and day, looked like she'd just woken up and was still fresh as a morning cup of coffee.

Heidi cringed as she crept closest to the door and then uttered, "Oh no," after peeking through the peephole. Her shoulders sank, and she hung her head as she slowly opened the door to reveal her boyfriend standing on the other side. Officer Tim Maxwell stood at attention in official police capacity, dressed in his full uniform. His neck was bulging due to the clenching of his jaw, his eyes were blazing, and his navy-blue cap was covered in a blanket of white snow.

The officer removed his hat and jerked it downward, sending the snow flying to the ground with one swift angry movement. He stepped inside without saying a word. Sammy noticed his blond hair had been parted down the side, making him look more mature. When had he made that change? She wondered this as she studied his demeanor. He replaced the wet police cap on his head.

Immediately Tim's eyes regarded the welcome mat next to his feet, which was currently filled with an overgrown pile of wet boots and winter coats dripping with condensation. He ordered the three of them to take a seat in the living room. He needed to "talk with them." Sammy had never seen Tim conduct himself this way, and it scared her. She decided to refrain from any jokes, as the officer was clearly not in a joking mood.

As soon as the three were squeezed next to each other on Sammy's meager love seat, the officer stood in front of them in a military stance with his chest puffed, as if he were a drill sergeant. He took a calculated breath and eyed each of them individually before speaking, to set a very serious tone.

"You three have taken this little S.H.E. game of yours too far. This time you crossed the line." He lifted his index finger, pointed to the ceiling, and then flung it to the ground to draw an imaginary line between himself and the three women sitting in front of him.

Sammy was about to interrupt and ask what he was talking about to play coy, but after his eyes returned to their wet clothes and then traveled back to the three S.H.E.s, she knew he had potential evidence to bust them. She thought better of it and decided her best bet was to remain silent.

"I think I'm going to be sick," Ellie said, and made a run for the upstairs bathroom.

"Come back here," Tim said with a tone of warning. "I'm not finished with you three yet."

"I can't," Ellie said midstride. She covered her mouth with one hand and continued her journey upward.

When Ellie topped the stairs, the officer turned to them with thick brows furrowed and a shrug. "If she's that worked up already, just wait until I haul the three of you back to the precinct."

Sammy really hoped that was an empty threat. Her hands began to sweat.

"Did I upset her that bad? Or is she sick with the flu?" He turned his focus to rest directly on the two remaining women sitting in front of him.

"Pregnant," Sammy and Heidi said in unison.

The look of surprise on the officer's face did not go unnoted.

"*Pregnant*," he repeated under his breath. "Then what the heck is she doing out galivanting around with you two at this hour of the night? Or should I say morning." His eyes grew wider still as he digested the surprising revelation.

"Tim, please hear me out," Heidi said tentatively. "Ellie is very worried about her husband, and . . ."

Clearly Heidi's batting eyelashes and sensual voice weren't going to help them get out of this one, as Tim shut her down, interrupting her plea. "Stop. Just stop." His eyes lasered in on Heidi, causing her to recoil like an animal that had just been poked with a large stick.

The officer shifted his weight and placed one hand on his holster and the other on his thick police belt. "Ellie *should* be concerned for her husband," he said firmly. "And this little fiasco." He waved his hands in the air dramatically, as if he were a conductor for a professional orchestra about to direct the pinnacle of the song. "Well, you three aren't helping Randy's case one bit with these shenanigans."

He returned his hand to his holster and belt, his face washed crimson. "As a matter of fact, when I call Nash in on this one, I'm pretty sure it'll worsen Randy's case because it looks like you're all trying to tamper with evidence by covering something up. So, what is it? What are you mining for over at the Wadsworth place? Or what are you trying to cover up for Randy?" He smirked. "Which, by the way, I'm very close to making the call to Nash about. Give me one good reason not to." He wagged a warning finger.

Sammy didn't like the smug smile on Tim's face as he talked about her brother-in-law in a flippant manner, or the way he was bringing Nash's name into it. It set her off. Not to mention, a night without sleep had left her last nerves shot and raw. She tried as best she could to remain diplomatic, but the words spilled out like a waterfall. "You're barking up the wrong tree hauling Randy to the station today. You know the guy; he's not capable of any kind of crime." Sammy rolled her eyes. "You guys should be going after the real perps behind this case instead of wasting your time bringing my brother-in-law in for questioning. What a waste of taxpayer dollars." She added with a huff, "what's wrong with you people?"

"Oh, and I suppose you have it all figured out, do you?" Tim snapped as he pointedly moved his laser stare from Heidi to Sammy. "Tell us, oh wise one. I'm sure in your mind you have Wanda's death and our investigation into her missing husband in the bag, do you?"

"Well, at least I'm looking in the right direction and not barking up the wrong tree. I bet you don't have anything on Randy. What evidence do you people possibly have to even bring him in for questioning? Give me a break." Sammy's eyes left his pointed stare and she glanced at the staircase, hoping her sister wasn't within earshot for this.

"Randy's fingerprints are all over their house."

"Yeah, he's their *realtor*! What do you expect?"

"His fingerprints are in places they shouldn't be. And that's all I'm going to reveal on this matter," Tim said with finality, placing his lips together in a firm line.

"Just wait a minute here. Can you explain how Randy's fingerprints are even in the system?" Heidi interrupted. "How'd you get a match? He hasn't been questioned at the police station yet, nor has he had his prints taken—he hasn't yet, right?"

"Randy had a DWI when he turned twenty-one. According to our records, it was on his twenty-first birthday." Tim shifted his stance and crossed his arms across his broad chest.

"*What?*" This was news to Sammy. How could she not know this about her own brother-in-law? Did Ellie know that he'd had a DWI and kept it from the family all these years out of embarrassment? Or was Ellie not even privy to this bit of information?

Maybe there were things about Randy even her sister didn't know?

Sammy's rising voice caused Heidi to tap her on the leg, a signal to tone it down, but it was too late. "You don't know anything! There's a ransom on Marty's head, and you're looking at Randy?" Sammy spewed. And that's when she realized Heidi had *not* confided in her boyfriend, not for a second, because the shock on Officer Maxwell's face was priceless.

"Whoa." Tim's eyes narrowed, and he put up a hand of defense. "Back the train up. What did you say? You mind repeating that?" He cupped a hand to his ear.

Sammy felt a warm crimson climb from her neck to her face. The burning didn't stop until it hit the outer parts of her ears. Her heart began to thunder again.

Heidi slapped her leg with the back of her hand. "Way to go," she said out the side of her mouth.

"Wait a minute." Tim's eyes traveled between them and finally landed back on Sammy. "What exactly is going on here? Are you telling me there's more to this fiasco than you three taking me for a joy ride through the snow in the dead of night?"

Sammy cleared her throat. "Umm . . . I think we might have something to tell you . . ."

Heidi laid her hand on Sammy's lap to stop her from speaking and said, "Let me be the one to explain."

Tim planted his hands firmly on his hips and shook his head disapprovingly. "What did you three S.H.E.s get involved in this time? I can't even believe this nonsense! Do I really want to hear this from you?" His eyes rose to the ceiling as if he were prompting the Good Lord above to please have mercy upon him.

As Heidi began to explain all that had unfolded the previous day and what they had learned from their visit to Jackson's farm, Sammy noticed Ellie slowly making her way down the stairs, holding the oak railing to keep herself from falling. She couldn't remember a time Ellie had looked so frail. She knew her sister didn't handle stress well, and this level of stress was beyond insurmountable.

Sammy interrupted the officer by nodding her head in the direction of her sister. "I need to go tuck her into bed. Ellie's not going to be any good to anyone if she ends up in the hospital, or worse, loses the baby due to all this stress. Plus, with you taking her husband for questioning tomorrow . . . I mean today . . ." Sammy eyed the clock on the wall, which revealed the early morning hour. "She'll have no one to watch Tyler. She needs her rest. Please? Just a little bit while we straighten all this out?" She hoped Tim would have compassion on her sister and let her go to bed before she quite literally passed out in front of them.

One look at Ellie and he agreed. "Fine." His eyes lasered back to Heidi, who remained on the love seat. "Don't you move a muscle. I'm not finished with you yet."

Sammy had never heard Tim talk to Heidi in such a stern manner. He normally melted at anything she had to say. But not this time. Sammy walked quickly over to her sister and nudged her to turn around and head back in the direction of a warm bed. Ellie didn't argue and made the return climb. They entered the spare bedroom without flipping on the overhead light. Sammy rushed in front of Ellie, pulled back the worn comforter that lay atop the old twin bed from their youth, and waited for her sister to rip off her socks and slip into bed. She tucked the sheet and blanket up around her neck so only Ellie's head was visible and then sat on the edge of the bed next to her.

"Do you think you need a bucket by your bed? Or are you feeling better?" Sammy asked as she removed her sister's hair from her face and laid her hand aside her cheek, which was clammy to the touch.

"I think I just need sleep," Ellie said as her eyes drifted shut. "I'm so tired." She yawned.

"Okay, I'll be in to check on you later," Sammy said. She heard her sister grunt an acknowledgment as she rose from the bed and softly closed the door behind her, then held the doorknob and rested her head against the door.

She wished she could just walk across the hallway and crawl into her own bed, but that would be terribly unfair to Heidi. Besides, the way Tim was acting, she didn't think he'd allow it anyhow. For all she knew, they weren't out of the woods yet and might be spending the day behind solid metal.

Sammy could hear the muffled sounds of Heidi and Tim's rising and falling heated conversation but couldn't make out any specific words. She released the doorknob and wiped her grit-filled eyes with the back of her hand. Before retreating downstairs, Sammy stopped at the small bathroom at the top of the stairs, stood at the pedestal sink, and looked at the worn-out reflection staring back at her. The skin under her eyes was shadowed with gray, just like Ellie's, and her healthy rosy cheeks from traipsing around in the cold had now grown pale. She stifled a yawn, then splashed her face with cold water and dried off with a nearby towel. The cold water did little to revive her, so she reached into the bathroom cabinet for eye drops and dropped a few in each gritty eye, blinking them back to vision. She abandoned the eye drop bottle on the back of the toilet and then turned her body in the direction of the stairs.

As she began the descent, she saw Tim open her front door and Detective Nash step inside the foyer. Apparently, news of the ransom had caused Officer Maxwell to make the call after all. Actually, the call had probably been made long before Tim even showed up on her doorstep.

The detective's eyes traveled to meet her on the stairs, and he did not look amused. Sammy stopped midstep and slumped down on the stair. She rested her head in her arms and wished it all away. Liam came to greet her and, without words, encouraged her off the oak staircase to join the others in the living room.

Sammy noted her cousin's somber body language as Heidi sat quietly on the love seat with her eyes downcast and her hands tucked neatly in her lap. Her eyes rose when Sammy took a seat beside her, and a look of sadness swept across her face.

Meanwhile, the firing range of Officer Maxwell and Detective Nash stood before them, looking as if they were ready to fire off another barrage of questions.

Sammy broke the silence. "I'm guessing everyone is up to speed? And now that Jackson's ransom note was shared with you two, this might take Randy out of the hot seat, no?" Sammy almost felt relief. If telling Jackson's secret would take the pressure off her brother-in-law, maybe it was a good thing that the cat was out of the bag. She hoped for Ellie's sake that that was the case, at least.

The detective spoke first. "With this new development, we're going to hold off on bringing Randy in for questioning." He held up a hand of defense. "Not because we don't have reason to question him, but because it seems we're forced on to more pressing matters now. Let it be known Randy's not off the hook just yet. We will eventually bring him in because there are a few things that require answers. However, if what you're saying is true about a ransom note, it looks like the FBI will likely soon be involved." He stopped his speech to pause and eye them each directly. "Which means you three S.H.E.s need to stand down." He pointed a lean finger at them. "Let me make this perfectly clear: this is my last and *final* warning. It's one thing to involve yourselves locally. It's a whole other level when you mess with an investigation that the federal government is involved in. You will be arrested for obstruction of justice if you continue to meddle in this investigation. You three need to back off. *Now.*"

Tim interrupted. "And it won't just be breaking and entering, we'll slap you with a whole host of statutes as well. You three S.H.E.s aren't above the law."

"Breaking and entering?" The detective turned to his coworker, confusion riddling his face. Evidently Tim hadn't shared everything with Nash yet. Sammy wondered if he would or whether he'd keep that under wraps to save his own skin.

"Nothing." The officer waved a hand of deflection and then said, "Please continue." He gestured toward the two guilty parties, left to their own defenses, huddled on the love seat.

Nash turned back to face them. "Anyhow, if you three don't stay out if it, I'll have no way to stop a warrant on each of your heads."

The detective turned on his heel and headed toward the front door, but not before Bara came to greet him. He stopped, patted

Bara on the head, and then scratched under his jaw. Despite Liam's frustration, he was still loving toward her dog, Sammy noted. He summoned Sammy to the front door with a finger and said, "A private word, please."

Sammy quickly made alarmed eye contact with her cousin before she did the detective's bidding. Meanwhile, Heidi rose from the love seat, and she and Tim headed toward the kitchen, seemingly to have their own private moment.

When Sammy reached the detective, she stood defenseless, her shoulders slouched, and didn't say a word. He pinched the bridge of his nose, as if in doing so he could will away the frustration coursing through his head. It was quiet between them until he spoke. "Why didn't you tell me this earlier? You had every opportunity to share pertinent information about my case, and instead you chose to lie to me? What's that about?"

"I didn't lie . . . I just didn't tell you everything I knew." Her eyes left the floor to look directly into his, and what she witnessed was sheer disappointment. His dark eyes didn't show anger, just sadness. Sammy didn't know which was worse: him calling her out for not telling him everything or him being visibly disappointed in her. "What was I supposed to do? It wasn't my call to make! Jackson begged us not to say a word. I wanted to tell you. Really, I did!" Her words fell flat, even to her own ears. She reached out to touch him on the arm.

"Don't." He flung out his hand to avoid her touch and stepped back.

His reaction stung. It would have been better if he'd slapped her. She'd completely lost his trust. She saw it clearly in his demeanor.

"I came after you, but you left my office before I had the chance."

Her response fell on deaf ears. He looked away from her and said, "I don't have time for this nonsense." But his eyes met hers again, begging to understand, and his hands slipped onto his hips as he waited for an answer.

"I'm sorry," Sammy said. "I'm really sorry." Her lip quivered, and her eyes fell to the floor. "I should've told you everything that happened at Jackson's farm."

"I'm not sure if your apology is good enough this time," he said evenly, before turning toward the door. "Tell Officer Maxwell to meet me back at the station. We have a lot of work to do," he said over his shoulder, and then he was gone into the cold snowy night, leaving a chill deep within her heart.

Chapter Seventeen

Sammy awoke to Bara licking the side of her face and her left leg dangling off the love seat, causing her body to nearly roll onto the floor. Disoriented, she patted her dog on the head and then shook her own, trying to figure out what had happened. Her head pounded as if she were suffering from a bad hangover. The sad part was, she didn't recall dancing atop tables the previous night, nor a single sip of liquor. The gas fireplace was glowing, keeping the small living room comfortably warm, and the smell of coffee percolating tickled her senses. She noticed a chenille throw blanket tossed on the floor next to the recliner, where she assumed her cousin must've crashed for the night.

Heidi stepped cautiously into the room, navigating her way with two cups of steaming coffee without spilling a drop. She set one on a coaster on the end table next to the love seat.

"You're finally up. I was just about to wake you."

"Oh, don't tell me! What time is it? I have to open the store!" Sammy jerked upward, wiped her eyes with the back of her hand and blinked several times to focus.

"I wouldn't worry about it. Winter storm warnings were issued late this morning; the town is paralyzed. Nobody, I mean *nobody*, is going anywhere. I hope you have cereal. I didn't check the cupboard," Heidi said before slumping into the recliner, causing the leather to groan.

"Ellie?"

"Still completely zonked out. I think we should let her sleep; she needs it. Besides, it's not like any of us is going anywhere anytime soon." Heidi shifted in her seat and cupped the mug of coffee with both hands.

"Has Randy called looking for her?"

"Uh-uh, not yet." Heidi shook her head. "He probably would rather she stay put anyway, gauging by the roads out there. Especially now with a baby on board. I can't believe Ellie's having another baby!" She blew the steam emitting from her mug.

"I know. It hasn't sunk in for me yet either. I'm so happy for them, though. It'll be nice for Tyler to have a sibling too. I wonder how he's going to feel about being a big brother." Sammy silently realized that in about eight months, she'd have to hire additional staffing to pick up the loss of Ellie working at her shop. "Do you think I should post Community Craft's closing on Facebook?" She tossed aside the lap quilt currently hanging from her leg.

"Yeah, I guess so. But honestly, I really don't think it's necessary. I checked my phone earlier; everything is shut down, including the schools. Even the credit union is calling a late start. If they decide to open at all, it won't be until later this afternoon. I can't imagine anyone would expect you'd be open today."

"Crud . . . that's a real problem." Sammy lifted the mug off the side table and lifted it in cheers. "Bless you," she added before taking a slurping sip. Her mouth was like asbestos, and the coffee was scalding. The hotter, the better, and Heidi knew it.

"Why is it a problem? I figured you'd love the chance for a day off. Remember how much we loved snow days as kids? We'd spend the whole day building snow forts around the farm. We had so much fun, didn't we?" Heidi smiled wide, showing her dimples.

"Yes, I remember. Despite the weather, my parents would find a way to bring us over to your house. At the time, I thought they were just being nice, navigating the treacherous roads to drop us off. Now I know they just didn't want to get stuck home with two energetic daughters with nothing to do." Sammy returned the smile before getting serious. "The quilting group meets tonight. We're working on sewing quilts for hospice patients in our area. This way, not only are the patients comforted, but the families will have something to remember their loved ones by long after they pass away. And besides, I was really hoping I'd have a chance to talk to the quilters about Wanda. Maybe if the roads clear, I'll call everyone to see if they can still make it downtown."

Before Sammy had a chance to mention the odd rhyme she'd found between the seams of Wanda's lap quilt, Heidi interrupted her train of thought by swiveling the recliner to face the love seat directly. Her face grew serious. "I think we'd better drop the amateur sleuthing."

Sammy rolled her eyes. "You know I can't possibly do that. This is me we're talking about." She chuckled.

Heidi made sure she had Sammy's full attention before she stated, "I'm serious, Samantha. Listen to me clearly now. Tim suggested we take a break." The mug of coffee was cupped between Heidi's two hands as if she was warming them. But suddenly, after noting her cousin's demeanor, Sammy realized Heidi was looking for more than warm hands. She was looking for comfort.

"Wait. *Break?* What kind of break? You mean break from investigating, right?" Sammy leaned in closer as if sure she was mistaken in what she'd heard.

"Yeah, I'm sure he wants us to put the brakes on that too." Heidi paused and then added, "No. Break from our relationship." She raised the cup to her lips to blow on the steam again.

"Oh nooo." The sudden realization made Sammy sit upright. "Why didn't you tell me last night?" She shifted again on the love seat to place her mug down on the end table, then reached out her hands to touch her cousin's lap as a sign of empathy.

"We were a bit tired. Borderline delusional, actually. I figured last night was all just a bad dream, but it all came back to me when I woke up in your chair with a stiff neck." Heidi reached to the floor with one hand for the chenille throw and then draped it across her lap. Sammy helped her adjust it and then sank back into her seat.

"Are you okay? I mean, how do you feel about this?" Sammy reached for her mug and then settled in, tucking her legs beneath her.

"I dunno. It's not like I had much choice in the matter. He made his decision pretty clear."

"I'm so sorry, Heidi. This is all my fault. I dragged you into this." Sammy felt horrible. It was because of her that her cousin had agreed not to share the news of Marty's ransom note with the police right away. If it hadn't been for her, maybe her cousin would've made the opposite decision and the police would've gone straight to Jackson, looking for answers. Instead, out of her own selfish need to find the truth, she had again taken the sleuthing too far. This time to the detriment of her cousin's relationship with Tim.

"Don't be so silly." Heidi waved her off with a casual hand. "I'm responsible for my own decisions. I can't half blame him, though. If he manipulated me the way I did him . . ." She sighed heavily, leaving her words hanging in the air between them. "I guess I kinda deserve it, don't I?" She took a sip of coffee after blowing on the steam again.

"Now what? What are you going to do? Are you just going to let him walk out of your life? Just like that? Or are you going to fight for him?" Sammy was surprised at the casual ease with which her cousin was letting her boyfriend go.

"Not much I can do except try to regain his trust. I guess I'll just respect his time away from me and hopefully get the chance to repair things when he's cooled down a bit. Honestly, I'm still a little shocked. Since we've dated, we've never taken a break from each other. I'm sure after I replay everything in my head, I'll feel differently, but right now all I feel is confused and sort of terrible that we broke Jackson's trust by sharing the ransom note so quickly. But shouldn't my loyalty have rested more strongly with Tim than with Jackson? What's wrong with me? Perhaps that's a mirror into our relationship, if that's the case." Heidi breathed deep and then took another sip of coffee.

"What other choice did we have besides sharing Jackson's secret? Was it even our choice to make? I feel like we were caught between a rock and a hard place, to be honest."

"No, I know, I hear you. And in the long run, hopefully it helps Randy too. Boy, I'd love to know what they have on Randy, wouldn't you?" Heidi whispered after she glanced at the staircase to make sure they were still alone.

"Yeah, and I guess with you and Tim on a so-called break"—Sammy raised one finger to make air quotes while her other hand gripped her coffee—"we'll never know."

"You got that right. My intel within the Heartsford Police Department is officially cut off," Heidi said as she set her coffee on the end table and began to rub her shoulder muscle as if she were kneading a loaf of bread dough.

Sammy decided to refrain from telling Heidi about her private conversation with Liam Nash before he'd left during the wee hours of the morning. It was barely comparable. After all, as much as she might want it to be otherwise, they weren't technically in a relationship. She didn't dare bring up her relational issues in comparison with her cousin's loss of Tim. Instead she said, "I have an idea. Bacon always makes things better." She winked. "I think I may have some in the fridge and the fixings for my crustless quiche. How about I throw one together and we can refuel our minds after a really rough night?"

"Oooh, quiche, yes please!" Heidi batted her eyelashes. "Finally, speaking my love language," she teased. "I'm sure Ellie can use something in her stomach when she wakes too. Good idea."

The two plodded to the kitchen with Bara following closely behind. Sammy opened the back door to let her dog out and quickly realized the rising snow would soon be a factor. The wind whipped the cold wet flakes into the kitchen, and the path she'd shoveled earlier for her dog was already a distant memory. Heidi reached for the snow shovel by the back door to clear a new path for him. "Looks like we're gonna have to hunker down here for a while. It's wild out there!" she said after she made a short path and closed the door behind Bara for a private moment.

"Yeah, poor Bara won't last too long out there," Sammy said as she fished the breakfast fixings out of the refrigerator.

Before long, the bacon was sizzling on the stove, and Ellie made an appearance in the kitchen. "Smells good in here. Maybe this baby will be a bacon eater," she chuckled as she rubbed her abdomen. "Usually meat smells get to me, but the bacon actually smells delicious." She stifled a yawn.

"I'm surprised that cauliflower didn't get to you the other night. I'm sorry, but that vegetable smells horrid!" Sammy said as her face lit with a smile.

"Yeah, I know, right? But not so much. This pregnancy, only meat smells seem to get to me for some reason. Who knows? Maybe my little one will love cauli mac and cheese as much as her brother."

"Her?" Heidi questioned with a raised brow. "Did I just hear you say *her*?"

"A girl can dream. I'm hoping for a 'her' this time." Ellie smiled.

Sammy reached to give her sister a hug. "You look much better this morning. Feeling rested?"

Ellie sighed. "Yeah, I slept like a log. I guess I needed it. How can I help?"

Sammy laughed at her sister. "It doesn't surprise me that you want to take over in the kitchen, but why don't you just relax and let me handle it this morning? How does that sound?" She encouraged her sister to move out of the way with a nudge of her shoulder.

"It depends. What are you making?" Ellie eyed the fixings strewn atop the large kitchen island. The island was so massive, it took up the majority of the space, and Sammy had room for only a small table and two ladder-back chairs tucked into the far corner of the room.

"I have a new crustless quiche recipe I think you'll love. It's lower calorie because you skip the pie crust, but trust me, it's almost as good and you don't really miss the crust. The only real calories are in the bacon, but I'll try not to overload it."

"Well, you've piqued my interest for sure!" Ellie smiled. "But don't skimp on the bacon on my account," she winked. "Now that I'm eating for two, I have an excuse." She smiled and rubbed her abdomen again. "Bring it on."

At that moment Sammy knew her sister's constant weight management program was over for the next few months, now that she was pregnant.

"We have some good news and bad news, but I think you'll be happy to hear this," Heidi said as she plucked the chair from the corner table and brought it closer for Ellie to take a seat by the door. She then opened the door, letting Bara back inside, where he sauntered past them, back to the front room, seemingly to curl by the fireplace.

Sammy was shocked he didn't stop to try to snag some bacon first. He must've known it would be a losing proposition. She smiled as she watched her dog do exactly what she had imagined he would and go slump in front of the roaring fire.

"Okay, bad news first," Ellie said, before taking a seat in the chair.

"Bad news." Heidi held up a finger. "We had to tell the police about the ransom note Jackson received," she said, and then took the mushrooms from Sammy's grasp and began dusting them off with a paper towel over the sink.

"Oh, I kind of figured that would be the only thing preventing us three from being arrested." She swirled a finger between them. "I'm kinda glad that secret is out. The guilt was killing me. I don't know how much longer I would've lasted anyway. What's the good news, then?"

"The police are holding off on questioning your husband, as now they're busy with the ransom, and possibly the FBI might soon be involved. It seems the case is hopefully heading in a different direction. Far away from Randy—at least for now." Heidi yawned.

Ellie put a hand to her heart and sighed. "Oh, I'm so thankful to hear that."

"Not to scare you, E, but he's not completely out of the woods yet. We're going to have to solve this thing to get him completely in the clear," Sammy said as she cracked organic eggs she had purchased from a local farmer into a ceramic bowl and whisked them with a fork.

"With no help from Tim," Heidi piped up.

"I'm sure Tim's pretty hot with us, huh?" Ellie's face scrunched into a wince. "Boy, I've never seen him so ticked off."

"Oh, it's more than that," Sammy added. "He broke up with Heidi over it."

"What?" Ellie gasped, and her eyes flew to her cousin.

Heidi agreed with a sad nod of her head.

"Are you okay?" Ellie looked at Heidi with dismay.

"Honestly, I don't think it's sunk in yet," Heidi admitted. "Maybe after a few days of not speaking with him, I'll really believe he's actually broken up with me."

"Well, there's only one thing to do then," Ellie said as she rose to comfort her cousin with an arm around her shoulder.

"What's that?" Sammy and Heidi said in unison.

Ellie surprised them both by saying bravely, "Us three S.H.E.s must solve this crime."

Sammy's eyes widened in surprise.

"Well, now, this is a definite switch," Heidi said. She carried the cutting board covered with sliced mushrooms and met Sammy by the stove.

Sammy emptied the contents into the skillet and handed the cutting board back to her cousin.

"What do you mean?" Ellie asked.

"What she means is usually *you're* the one who wants us to back out of an investigation, and now you're front and center and Heidi wants to drop it," Sammy clarified. "Am I right?"

"Well," Heidi hesitated. "If I have any chance of regaining Tim's trust, I should stop all involvement. Otherwise, I may as well completely kiss my relationship goodbye."

"What if we just keep you behind the scenes? You can be the brains of the operation," Sammy said as she rinsed her hands in the sink and dried them off with a nearby towel. She reached for her phone, plucked it from the charge cord, and scrolled to her photos. "Look." She handed the phone to Heidi, whose eyes narrowed as she viewed the picture.

"What's this?"

"This is the last thing someone recently Googled on the Wadsworths' computer. Do you know anything about that chemical? Your parents farmed; did they ever happen to use it?"

"No. I know it's thought to be controversial, though." Heidi's eyes left the screen and darted around the room as if she was deep in thought. "Wait. Give me a minute." She steepled her fingers and placed them to her lips.

Sammy stood at the stove sautéing the mushrooms and onions in butter and filling the kitchen with a heavenly scent. She crushed a glove of garlic over the pan, then tossed in fresh spinach and continued to stir so it would wilt. "What do you mean, *controversial*?"

"Okay, the way I remember it, there are different ways to farm grain and soybean crops. There's the organic farm, which doesn't use any chemicals for weed control and meets or exceeds the high FDA standards to be labeled organic. And then you have farms that are considered Roundup ready, right?"

"No," Ellie interrupted. "I don't know what you mean by Roundup ready. I know what Roundup is, but I'm not following. Please explain."

"All right. Let me back up. A Roundup-ready farm means that the seeds that were planted will sustain the weed killer. Meaning, the crops won't be affected. The plants will grow, and the farmer will have a great yield or harvest minus the weeds completely taking over the field."

"Okay?" Sammy said over her shoulder. "So, what's the problem? What's that dicamba or whatever it's called have to do with it?"

"I'm getting to that," Heidi said. "So, what's happened over the years is now these superweeds are taking over. Roundup is no longer strong enough, as weeds have been popping up that can resist the weed killer farmers have been using for years. This is a real problem for farmers, as you can imagine. So they're trying to come up with a solution."

"And they think dicamba is a viable solution?" Sammy asked as she tossed grated cheddar cheese into the whisked eggs, then added the spinach mixture and crumbled bacon before pouring it all into a pie plate and placing it carefully in the oven.

"Well, yes and no. The problem with using dicamba is that certain seeds haven't gone through the proper testing channels."

"What do you mean?" Ellie asked. "I'm still a bit confused. And how have you become an expert on these chemicals?"

"There's been talk throughout the farm community on how best to fight the weed battle for years. My parents debated this over the dinner table countless times. The problem is that the levels of dicamba haven't been thoroughly tested. It takes a while to see how much of a chemical is needed without harming either the seeds or the nearby fields."

"Nearby fields?" Sammy asked. "How could it damage fields nearby?"

"If the wind blows onto a neighboring farm and they haven't used seeds that can withstand dicamba, they could lose their entire crop."

Sammy wiped her hands with the dishrag next to the stove, then turned to face them and crossed her arms across her chest. "What would this do to Marty's job?" Her eyes bounced between Heidi and Ellie. "Anything?"

"Didn't you mention that he sells farm seeds for a living or something along those lines?" Ellie asked.

"Yeah. So he's probably just researching work stuff. Although Wanda might have had a problem with it if her husband was selling seeds doused with heavy chemicals, as she shopped completely organic. I heard in a yoga class she was a fanatic about that with her whole vegan lifestyle," Heidi said. "What else did you uncover? Anything?"

"Not much else on my end. I was looking for hidden paperwork but didn't come across anything unusual. Ellie, did you?"

"No, just the empty gun cabinet. Hey, did you ask Heidi about the rhyme?"

"Rhyme?" Heidi reached for the dishrag and began to wipe the kitchen island top clean.

Sammy patted her jeans pocket. She was still wearing her clothes from the night before. What she'd really needed was a hot shower and some clean clothes. Instead they'd all collapsed after the heady night. She couldn't remember the last time she'd crashed wearing uncomfortable jeans to bed. She handed the note to Heidi. "What do you make of this?"

"What is it?" Heidi accepted the note in her hands, and her eyes darted to the paper. "Where did you get this?"

"I found it within the batting of the quilt Wanda was holding on her lap the night of Fire and Ice. And that's not all. When I looked carefully at the quilt blocks, one of the blocks was identical to the one painted on the side of Jackson's barn. I found that very interesting. Right down to an exact color match."

"*The blocks pieced on this quilt release me of guilt,*" Heidi said aloud. "Then what if the quilt isn't a quilt at all but instead it's a map? Like the trail maps we discussed in front of Jackson's?"

"A map?" Ellie's face scrunched in question.

"Heidi. You're a genius!" Suddenly, in Sammy's mind, it was all clear. She reached for her nearby phone and showed Heidi and Ellie the ledger, the photo of the Excel spreadsheet. "What if Marty's customers somehow coincide with Wanda's quilt?"

The quilt that had lain across Wanda's lap the night she died could potentially be a map that would enable them to sew together the clues of this mystery. Wanda was going to lead them to piece it all together into one astonishing quilt.

Chapter Eighteen

Sammy peeked outside the glass front door of Community Craft, willing the members of the quilting group to make an appearance. She turned her head and eyed the large clock on the wall above the cash register. They still had time to arrive; it was early. She couldn't half blame any of them for skipping, as the roads were still dicey. Especially the back roads, where the plows were having trouble keeping up with the most recent heap of fallen snow. If this was a prequel to the winter Heartsford was going to experience, it was sure to be one for the record books. She was thankful the three S.H.E.s had had a chance to nap that afternoon. Otherwise, she wasn't sure if she could've made an appearance herself. Not due to the weather, but due to lack of sleep.

She stifled a yawn and turned toward a rack of quilted pillows, noticing that they were askew. As she moved to rearrange them on the rack so they stood upright, Cheryl unexpectedly bounded through the door, eager for Sammy's attention. "Hey, is Jas here yet? Doesn't she usually come to the quilt meetings?"

"Oh, hey, Cheryl." Sammy turned in the direction of the voice over her shoulder. "No, she's missed the last couple due to some family stuff. I highly doubt she'll make this one, especially with this weather. I'll be lucky if anyone shows." Sammy faced her and shrugged.

"Well, if you see her, tell her I need to speak with her immediately. She's been ignoring my messages, but this is really important."

Sammy turned away momentarily to be sure all the pillows were aligned, and Cheryl grew annoyed. "Did you hear me?"

"Yeah, I'll definitely pass on the message if I see her."

Sammy's eyes returned to Main Street. Lynn was juggling her quilt bag and a large thermos as she stepped out of her car and shut the car door with her hip. Sammy opened the front door of Community Craft, and a bluster of cold air instantly hit her in the face, replacing her overtired condition with a jolt. Cheryl slipped back outside with a wave of her hand.

"You made it!" Sammy held the door wide so Lynn could step inside without dropping any of her gear.

"Yeah, and I hope everyone shows this evening, because I brought hot cocoa and homemade chocolate-chip cookies to share. Since the credit union was closed this morning and I didn't have to go in to work today, I needed something to keep me from getting cabin fever. It was sure nice to have a surprise day off and a rare chance to return to the kitchen and bake. Moderation is key." She grinned. "Keeping the sugar close in proximity will never do, though. I have zero discipline, so I brought them in to share." She lifted the bags to display the loot she'd brought.

Lynn had worked so hard on losing weight and exercising with the local Jazzercise group that she'd literally transformed into someone unrecognizable to her former self. Sammy could understand why she wouldn't want to leave tempting treats at home.

"That is so kind of you to bring homemade goodies to share. I'm sure we'll all enjoy the fruits of your labor." She returned the smile.

"Do you think it's okay to park there?" Lynn nodded her head in the direction of Main Street.

Sammy followed the direction of her gaze to see Lynn's car tucked into the side of the snowbank. "I think you're just fine there. The plow went through recently; it'll be a while before they do another sweep in town, I think."

Eleanor was next to arrive and bustled through the front door behind Lynn. She plucked the hand-knit hat that Sammy recognized as a hot seller from Community Craft off her head. She combed her hand though her thick short silver hair and said, "Oh, was I glad to get out of the house tonight! I was afraid you were going to cancel. If I'd had to spend the entire evening arguing with Paul about what program to watch on TV, I think I would've gone mad! I'm sick to death of his nature shows. Besides the fact that he's always asking me to bring him something." She made her voice deep and low and mimicked, "'Honey can you make popcorn? How about some Rice Krispy treats? What do we have to eat around here?' As if his own legs are broken, which I assure you they are not." Eleanor rolled her eyes. "Oh, I don't think you realize how this craft shop has saved my marriage.

Men and retirement. Not for the faint of heart," she laughed as she placed her quilt bag on the floor.

"Hey, guess what? I brought homemade treats! So instead of waiting on Paul, I've got something special for you tonight. How about that?" Lynn cajoled over her shoulder. "Come, let me pour you a cup of my rich hot cocoa."

The two headed off toward the interior craft room to settle in, and Sammy waited by the closed front door to see if others would show or if they'd have a skeleton crew. She was adjusting scarves on a nearby rack that'd been left in disarray when a man approached the door and gave it a hard tug. Apparently he had expected the door to be locked. He stepped inside, shadowing Sammy with his large frame.

"Oh good, you're open!" He stomped his wet boots on the welcome mat.

"Well, technically not; we're here for a quilt meeting." Sammy lifted a hand and gestured toward the interior craft room. "But is there something special you're looking for? I'd be happy to help you quickly, before we get started." Sammy abandoned the scarves and returned to the front door to greet him.

"I hear you sell local honey here. The wife's home with a sore throat, and she said Community Craft honey with a bit of lemon is the best cure. In her mind, everything from the pharmacy is lethal poison." He chuckled and threw up his hands in defeat.

Sammy led him to the shelf where she kept the jars of local honey, and supplies were pretty sparse. "Lucky for you, we have a few jars left. Otherwise, you'd have to wait for the restock, which won't be until next harvest."

"When would that be?" he asked, adjusting the winter cap on his head.

"Harvest is late summer, but sometimes my vendors don't bring it in to sell until early fall. Is that all you need?" Sammy asked, moving behind the cash register.

"That'd be it." He smiled, removing his winter gloves to reach in his back pocket for payment. He fished through his wallet and handed her a credit card.

Sammy ran the card through the machine and took a quick look at the name: *Adam Boyd*. Her heart skipped in her chest.

"Adam?" Her eyes narrowed in question as she handed him back the card and the printed receipt for him to sign.

"Ah, yeah?" he said as he took a nearby pen and quickly signed the receipt.

Sammy braced her hands and leaned into the counter. "You and Marty are friends, right? Do you know where he is?" she whispered. She looked down and noted the Smoky Mountains key chain dangling from his car keys.

Adam tossed the signed receipt across the counter and turned toward the exit. "I need to hurry; the wife's waiting in the car out front." He quickly grabbed his keys, strode toward the front door, and threw it open. Sammy followed him, her mouth agape, wishing she'd known just a few minutes earlier who it was who'd entered the shop so she could've asked him some pointed questions. Not to mention, she'd caught him in a lie. First he'd said his wife was waiting for him at home, and then suddenly she was outside waiting in the car? Why would he lie?

Soon more figures appeared, and she pushed the door open and held it wide as Mary, Gertie, and Barb trickled through the front door, chatter bubbling between them. So deep were the three in conversation, they barely acknowledged Sammy holding the door for them.

Sammy turned to gaze at the clock again. It was quarter past the hour, but she could understand why the last two might be late. She abandoned the front door momentarily and headed for the craft room to join the others.

This was the first time the group would be meeting since Wanda's passing. She shivered at the thought of how fleeting life could be and wondered how they'd all feel with an obviously missing person at their craft table. It would feel strange gathering without Wanda for sure.

When Sammy entered the craft room, she leaned her hands on the edge of the table, and when the group looked up at her expectantly, she met each of their eyes.

"How's everyone doing tonight?"

"It's going to take us a few more times getting together before we feel normal again," Eleanor admitted as all eyes turned to the empty chair beside her. Out of habit, each member of the quilt group always sat in the same place. For all of them, Wanda's chair had become an obvious hole.

"I know. Maybe we should all shift where we usually sit? Would that help if we change things up a bit?" Sammy suggested.

Gertie piped up. "I'm not moving. I've been sitting in this spot for the last three years, and this is where I'll stay," she said firmly. "Besides, when I croak, which could be any day now, I want you all to miss me taking up space in this ol' chair." She clicked her fingernail along the table as if to mark her spot.

This caused a light chuckle within the room.

Sammy knew Gertie was trying to be funny and lighten the mood within the glass walls. "Okay, Gertie, you can stay right there. Anyone else?" It seemed her suggestion fell on deaf ears. "How about we share a few Wanda memories for a minute. Maybe that will help us come to grips with our loss here." Sammy pointed to the empty chair. "Who wants to go first?"

"What really happened to her?" Eleanor asked as she fluffed her silver hair with her fingers. "She seemed, out of all of us, the one in the best shape," she added with a grunt. "I guess my shot of whiskey at night before bed is good for the old bod after all." She leaned back, rubbed her abdomen, made eye contact with Gertie, and winked. "Screw what the doctor suggests; he knows nothin'," she added out the side of her mouth.

No one answered the question of what had happened to Wanda, and Sammy was not going to be the one to spill the beans. She remained quiet.

Lynn raised a timid hand. "I just loved Wanda. Not only because she was in our quilt group, but she also helped me so much with my sciatica. She taught me exercises that really made a difference in my life. I sit so much behind a desk at work, some days my back pain became literally unbearable. She really helped me with that."

A few heads nodded sullenly in agreement.

"Can anyone think of any reason Wanda would feel a sense of guilt in her life?" Sammy had to ask. She didn't think she could wait another second to ask the question burning in her mind regarding the rhyme she had found within the batting of Wanda's quilt.

"Guilty?" Barb squished her nose as if she'd gotten a whiff of bad fish. "Over what?"

Sammy quickly recovered by saying, "You know, when someone as young as Wanda dies, it makes you take inventory of your own life. I guess I've been doing a lot of soul searching as of late . . . and well, I have a few regrets," she admitted.

That seemed to appease Barb, and she nodded her curly brown head in agreement as she removed her reading glasses from the case and put them on. "I know she didn't have reason to be guilty . . . but that husband of hers. What a jerk!" she said under her breath as she tucked the glasses case into her bag. "I never liked him for her. She was way too good for him, in my opinion."

All eyes landed on Barb, silently urging her to continue with the can of worms she had just opened.

"What? Don't look so surprised. Don't you all remember?" Barb asked, viewing them over the top of her reading glasses. "She almost had to stop coming to our meetings because her husband was accusing her of having an affair. Don't you remember, he came in here a few times to see for himself that there was really a quilt meeting going on? Give me a break." She uttered under her breath, "Way too controlling for me."

Gertie waved a hand of dismissal. "That was several years ago! I thought that was water under the bridge between them."

Barb leaned into the table and pushed her glasses up on her nose. "Wanda told me that was the reason why she no longer worked at the manufacturing plant off Sumner Street. She had a great job in the HR department and then took quite a financial hit to teach yoga. All for that jerk, because he thought she was cheating on him with someone at work, but she wasn't." Barb's face twisted in disgust. "Then she really depended on him financially. She couldn't get out of that marriage even if she wanted to."

"I hadn't heard that's why she started teaching yoga over at the rec center. She seemed pretty tight-lipped about her personal life around me," Sammy admitted.

Nods of agreement around the table made her feel like she wasn't alone in that regard.

"I'll be right back, ladies." Sammy decided to return to the front door to see if the last two in the group had arrived.

Instead, her attention was diverted by a familiar figure beneath the streetlamp across the street, causing her to do a double take. She peered out the glass for a better look and noted Detective Nash holding the door for a woman, who stepped into Liquid Joy in front of him. The image took her breath away. Who was this unknown woman? Were they together? Or had they just happened to walk into the coffee shop at the same time? Curiosity won out and she had to know. Sammy turned on her heel and moved with purpose back to the interior craft room. She took a step over the threshold and said, "I'm going across the street to grab a coffee. Anyone want anything?"

"But I brought cocoa." Lynn pointed to the large thermos. The banker was in the process of filling Styrofoam cups with a deliciously scented liquid chocolate.

"I didn't get much sleep last night. I think I need something a little stronger," Sammy admitted easily. "But I'll be sure to buy a large coffee and dump some so I can add your delicious hot chocolate to it. It smells heavenly, by the way."

Lynn smiled with satisfaction and continued to pour.

"Anyone?"

The group all waved her off as if she were crazy. And she might be. Why was she so desperate to find out who Liam was with? Her heart skipped a beat as a sudden rush of adrenaline pumped through her veins. They'd had words just a few short hours ago, and he was already keeping company with another woman? Didn't seem to take *him* long. Since the detective had moved to Heartsford, Sammy had never heard rumblings around town that he was keeping company with another woman or dating. She'd always assumed it was because he wasn't ready after losing Brenda. Well, by golly, he certainly seemed ready now!

Instead of retreating to her office for her coat, she decided on a mad dash across the street. She flung open the front door of Community Craft, stepped out into the rush of cold, and navigated the piled snow left over from the plow to make her way across the street.

Main Street looked like a ghost town. The street was devoid of cars, to the point of seeming eerie. It appeared as if the entire town was hunkered down for the evening—except, of course, for her quilting group, and evidently the lead detective of Heartsford with his new lady friend.

Sammy shivered as she stepped inside the warmth of Liquid Joy. Her eyes darted across the space until they landed on the owner, Douglas, standing behind the counter. He waved when he saw her.

"Good evening, Sam. What's got you out and about? I thought for sure Community Craft would be closed this evening. You're open?" He adjusted his dark-rimmed glasses and studied her.

"Quilting meeting tonight and no one wanted to cancel, including me. I guess the members were feeling a little cooped up and decided we should still meet." Sammy stifled another yawn. "Can I get a large coffee to go, but leave a little room on the top, will you?"

"Sure, coming right up."

The barista reached for the coffee machine, and Sammy turned from the counter to see Detective Nash seated by the window overlooking Main Street. He was sitting with the unidentified woman, whose back was to her. When the detective saw her studying them, he smiled and lifted a hand in greeting. At least he was mature enough not to ignore her after they'd had intense words. He'd officially broken the ice. Now she felt she had no choice. If she didn't approach the table and say hello, she'd be rude. But if she did approach the table, she'd be nosy. Either way, she didn't like the odds. She finally settled on nosy.

"Douglas, I'll be right back." She reached into her pocket for a five-dollar bill and placed it on the counter.

"Hello," Sammy said cautiously after she'd maneuvered her way around several empty tables to land at the edge of the detective's table seated with his unfamiliar guest.

"Samantha, what brings you out this blustery evening?" he said professionally, as if they'd never had an intimate conversation in their lives. The sudden stiffness surprised her. She hated that he was acting different with her in public. Only when they were alone did he seem to let down his guard and show himself. It irked her.

"Quilting meeting."

"Ah," he said, and then finally gestured his hand to the woman sitting across from him. "Ginger Davenport . . . meet Sammy Kane. The one I told you about."

The way he said *the one I told you about* officially set the tone. Sammy's eyes narrowed.

"Oh," Ginger said with a hint of amusement. "So you're the one."

"Am I missing something?" Sammy finally asked, after a long pause with four eyes on her. She looked closer at the woman, whose hair matched her name perfectly. Her deep russet hair was secured at the nape of her neck in a low ponytail, and her hazel eyes were penetrating.

"Ginger works with the FBI," Detective Nash said, returning Sammy's attention to him. She noted his eye flicker. Was that a hint of warning in his eye?

"Welcome to Heartsford," Sammy said dryly.

"Thank you. I wish I had a chance to peruse this charming town." Her eyes momentarily gazed out the window and then returned to Sammy. "Unfortunately, it looks like we'll be burning the midnight oil. Despite the circumstances, I'm happy Liam and I have a chance to reconnect," Ginger said as her eyes danced in his direction.

She reached across the table and touched his hand for a brief moment. Sammy's eyes darted to read his reaction, but he gave none. No surprise there.

"While I'm collaborating here with Detective Nash and the Heartsford PD on a case, I suggest you keep your distance and stay out of the way. I've heard you have a tendency to involve yourself." Ginger's tone turned a little sharp. "Do I have your word you'll stay out of the way?" She wrinkled her brow.

"Of course," Sammy said, and then took a step back from the table. "Enjoy your evening," she added, then turned to retrieve her coffee from the counter, snagged the change Douglas had left behind, and flew out the front door of Liquid Joy.

This time, she didn't feel the sudden rush of cold upon encountering the frigid outside air, possibly due to the fuming in her head. *You're the one? Great. Just great.* Sammy took a deep breath to steady herself before entering Community Craft. She didn't want the quilt members to sense her sudden mood change. Why did her interactions with Nash annoy her so much?

She absolutely knew why. But she dared not admit it to herself.

Since the first day detective Liam Nash had waltzed his way into Community Craft and into her life, she'd felt something for him. He was different somehow. He challenged her. He drove her nuts. And she loved it. When relationships with men she'd dated in the past had sailed along smoothly, it always seemed to eventually fizzle out, like a fleeting high school crush. Even her longest-lasting relationship with Brian had bored her to tears by comparison. He hadn't challenged her either, and that relationship had ended with a thud. Maybe that's why it bothered her so much to see Liam with Ginger. Sammy sensed their relationship was deeper than just work. Something about the way Ginger had looked at Liam and touched his arm seemed almost intimate. As if there was history between them. Sammy's expression turned sullen.

"Everything okay?" Lynn interrupted her reverie as she stepped over the threshold into the craft room.

Sammy shook her head to refocus. "Yes, of course." She smiled as she set her coffee cup down on the table. "Oh good, you're already getting started." She noted the scraps of fabric strewn across the craft table and each member deciding on quilt block patterns for their latest project.

"I know we talked about our next project being piecing quilts for those entering hospice, but we were talking while you were across the street and decided that we'd like to create something in memory of Wanda first," Eleanor said as she fingered a patch of calico fabric between her fingers. "A small memory quilt that maybe we could hang here in the craft room?"

"Or somewhere on the walls of Community Craft," Gertie added, her eyes bouncing within the glass room. Her hair was as white as the new-fallen snow, making her blue eyes sparkle against her pale complexion. "We spent so much time with her, we feel it's a way we can all come to grips with our loss too."

"I think that would be a lovely tribute," Sammy agreed.

They needed to do something for Wanda. After all, she'd spent countless hours piecing, sewing, and commiserating with the group as they made quilts for anyone in town who'd had a need. And now the sudden loss of her was a like an aching, visible hole.

Just then, the jingle on the front door alerted them that someone had entered Community Craft. Soon after, Jasmin stepped into the craft room. Jasmin was a stunning young woman whose dark skin shone year-round with a healthy glow. Her long black hair fell to her shoulders in long, shiny spiraled curls, which she'd admitted she'd inherited from her white mother. She'd even done some modeling as a teen, but later decided it wasn't for her, and instead was attending beauty school to become a stylist and hopefully rent a chair from Lizzy at Live and Let Dye. Sammy reached out to share a hug.

"Oh, Jasmin, so glad you could make it. It's been ages!" After they released their quick embrace, Sammy held her friend at arm's length, smiled, and searched her dark eyes. "Where've you been? We've missed you around here!" She turned from her for a moment and said, "Everyone look, Jas is here!"

The group of women gathered around the craft table all stopped chitchatting and regarded the missed member with smiles and *so glad you're heres*.

"I know, I've been away far too long. I've really missed you all too. But between a hectic school schedule and helping my mom during her recovery, I just didn't have time to step away." Jasmin began to unbutton her long wool coat.

Jasmin's mother had taken a bad fall when she'd slipped on a patch of ice in her driveway. The accident had occurred right before Christmas as her mother was lugging shopping bags into her house. Unfortunately, she'd broken her hip. It'd been a long recovery, and her daughter had supported her through it all.

"How is your mom?" Sammy asked with an empathetic grimace.

"You know? It's been a long road, but I think she's finally getting around a little better. At least now I can break away for a little respite to come and quilt again. Besides, I wanted to hear what happened to Wanda. What a shock. I can't get over it! I just felt I needed to be with you all tonight." Her smile faded, and her lip began to quiver.

"Oh, we totally understand. I'm not sure her passing has sunk in for any of us. As a matter of fact, I find myself looking toward the door, half expecting her to appear," Sammy admitted.

Lynn pulled out the chair closest to her and summoned Jasmin over. "Here, come take your usual spot by me. I've just finished pouring cocoa for everyone. Can I interest you in a cup?"

"I would love some cocoa." Jasmin rubbed her hands together to warm them after removing her coat and hanging it on a nearby peg rack with the others. "I don't think I've lost the chill yet from the walk over here."

"You walked?" Sammy asked with a hint of surprise.

"Yeah, Mom's condo is right behind the credit union. I figured it would be easier to walk than try to find a place to park if the parking lot out back wasn't plowed yet."

"I didn't know your mom lived over in those condos," Gertie said. "So, you must've had an incredible view of the bonfire for Fire and Ice, then. Did you attend this year? I was sorry to have missed it."

"I didn't make it either. I didn't want to make Mom feel bad by leaving her home alone, and I figured with the weather, it'd be too hard for her to navigate with a walker or cane, so we stayed home and watched movies instead. However, I did have an excellent view from my mother's window." Jasmin lowered her voice and looped her arm through Sammy's, turning her body toward the door so that only she could hear. "I had a view of something else that I can't get out of my mind. Can we talk in private?"

Chapter Nineteen

"Ladies, go ahead and get started brainstorming ideas for Wanda's commemorative quilt. Jas and I will be right back. Feel free to begin the conversation about what pattern you think you'd like to use. Or if everyone wants to go ahead and pick a different block to contribute, we can consider that idea too. We'll be just a few minutes, I promise. I just need to show her something in the office really quick." Sammy tugged Jasmin gently by the arm and encouraged her to follow her out of the room.

"But what about your cocoa, Jasmin? It'll get cold!" Lynn looked up to regard the young woman heading for the exit.

"No worries, I'll warm it in the microwave when we return. We'll only be a moment," Jasmin replied, forming deep dimples and a radiant beauty-queen smile.

Immediately the chitchat around the table resumed, and Sammy and Jasmin rushed out of the craft room and weaved between the merchandise racks on the shop floor to reach the other side, where the cash register stood unattended.

Sammy was barely over the threshold of the doorway leading to her office before she turned to Jasmin and blurted, "What is it? What did you see from your mother's window?" Curiosity coursed through her veins.

"Well, you'd have to live under a rock to not hear the gossip flying around town. I keep hearing that Marty was missing the night of Fire and Ice, but there's only one problem with that. I *saw* him with my own two eyes standing at the bonfire." Jasmin's dark eyes rounded like saucers.

"You saw him the night of Fire and Ice? Are you sure it was him? You're aware the police are trying to figure out the last time someone actually *saw* him to consider a timeline for his disappearance, right?"

"Yeah, I kinda figured, and that's why I'm worried, to be honest." Jasmin bit her lower lip. "It's hard not to assume something sinister is going on in this town."

"How so? Help me out; I'm a little confused. When did you see him?" Sammy laid a comforting hand on Jasmin's shoulder.

"I was standing at my mother's patio door, looking out at the snow. It was so pretty that night, wasn't it? The first real snowstorm of the year sort of had me captivated. I could see the snow falling because of the backdrop of the fire; otherwise it would've been too dark for me to see." Jasmin shrugged. "Anyhow, I remember it was toward the beginning of the event, because the fire marshal had just started the fire, and he'd tossed a few branches on top to get the blaze to take. Then it seemed he just up and left the fire unattended, which I thought was odd, because don't they always have someone in charge of watching the fire the entire event? You know, to ensure it doesn't get out of control?" Her face took on a look of confusion.

"Yeah, that's true." Sammy said. "Go on."

"Well, then as I'm watching the snow and seeing the wind blowing the embers, it occurred to me the fire shouldn't be left unattended. I was afraid my mother's entire condo complex was going to go up in a blaze—and not in a blaze of glory! I thought the flames were growing uncomfortably tall. They seemed as high as my mother's second-floor patio at one point. And to be left unattended like that? With the wind? A fire of that magnitude seemed very unsafe, especially so close to the condo complex. Sheesh!"

"No kidding." Sammy fingered her necklace and adjusted it so that the pendant faced forward. "That doesn't sound safe at all."

"Well, that's when I saw Marty appear all by himself. It seemed from my vantage point that the fire marshal must've left Marty in charge, which I thought was odd. I don't know, maybe he had to go get a backup hose or something in case the fire got more out of control. I don't know." Her gaze bounced to the wall and then back to Sammy. "Obviously I'm going by what I could see, not what I couldn't hear. Anyhow, Cheryl's husband Craig appeared out of nowhere and approached Marty, who was just standing there doing absolutely nothing but watching the flames grow bigger."

"Okay, so you're saying you saw just the two of them?" Sammy's eyes narrowed. She wondered if this was soon after Cheryl and Craig had started a ruckus inside her shop. The time frame might fit and would certainly explain why Cheryl hadn't been with Craig. And Wanda had most likely been in the display window at that time.

"Yeah, just the two of them. Based on their body language, it seemed neither one was happy with the other." Jasmin sucked in a breath. "That's why I'm so afraid of saying anything. I don't want to make Craig look bad to the authorities."

"What do you mean, make Craig look bad? Do you think he was up to something?"

"Well, arms were flailing, and then the two were standing pretty close to each other, like one of them could throw a punch at any second. To me it certainly looked like they had a pretty heated conversation. They both seemed angry. No question about it." Jasmin shifted her weight to one hip.

"That's it? Is that all you saw?"

"No. Not exactly." Jasmin hesitated before blurting, "Then Craig pulled a file folder or papers or something from inside his coat. Marty grabbed the file and tossed it into the fire!"

"Papers?"

"Yeah, like a manila folder or something. And then Craig tried desperately to grab the burning papers out of the fire, but it was too late. Then the fire marshal finally returned, and Marty stormed off and Craig followed him. That was it. I didn't see either of them any time I looked out the window later that night. And now Marty's *missing*? You don't think Cheryl's husband is the reason Marty's missing? Do you? My word, I certainly hope not."

Sammy couldn't reply, because she was too busy wondering if it was the same stack of papers her brother-in-law had said the Wadsworths were keeping hidden from him. Could it be the same? If so, clearly there was nothing left of them now but ashes and soot.

"Do you? Oh my gosh, you *do* think Craig kidnapped Marty!" Jasmin squealed and then covered her mouth in horror.

"No. Hold on a second, I didn't say that." Sammy tried to calm Jasmin, who seemed to be growing more nervous by the minute. "But Jas, have you shared this with the police?"

"No." Jasmin hesitated. "Cheryl is my friend, and I don't want to take the chance of getting her husband in trouble if it was nothing. I don't know what to do." Jasmin rolled the silver bangle on her wrist nervously. "I mean, I could only see; I couldn't hear a thing. What if I'm totally overreacting to what I saw? Each day that passes, I begin to think maybe what I saw was wrong," Jasmin said, desperately trying to backtrack.

"Well, now I know why Cheryl was in here earlier eager to talk with you. She mentioned you haven't been returning her messages. Did you talk to Cheryl yet about what you witnessed?"

"Uh-huh. She was in here looking for me? I think she's trying to keep me quiet," Jasmin said nervously. "She wouldn't tell me if she knew why the two men were together at the bonfire or what was in the folder, but she *begged* me not to say anything. She said it would only get Craig in trouble. It's eating me alive, Sammy! What do I do?" Jasmin's normally animated face fell. "I hate being in this position!"

Sammy took a calculated breath and carefully chose her words. "I don't know, Jas. What if that file that was tossed in the fire was the key to the entire investigation behind Marty's disappearance? I hate to admit it—I know you and Cheryl are close friends—but you can't keep this information to yourself. Clearly you can't—you just told *me*!"

"I told you because I thought you'd know what to do. Sammy, I hate this. The whole thing sickens me. Especially now . . ."

Jasmin's voice turned to a whisper. "I heard a rumor that Wanda didn't die from a heart attack," she murmured.

"I know, Jas." Sammy rubbed Jasmin's arm to comfort and encourage her. "That's why keeping this inside is going to wreak havoc on your mind. How is it fair of Cheryl to ask you to hide information that could be critical to the case?"

Sammy instantly felt a rush of heat suffuse her cheeks. *Didn't I just do the exact same thing? The very thing that disappointed someone I clearly can't keep out of the forefront of my mind? Someone very involved in solving this case?*

Liam.

Sammy pushed on. "Maybe their altercation really has nothing to do with Marty's disappearance and it'll clear everything up to have Cheryl's husband questioned. Either way, I don't think you have much choice in the matter. You have to go to the police and share everything you just shared with me," she said firmly.

"That's not exactly the advice I was hoping for." Jasmin's eyes dropped to the floor, defeated.

"I'm sorry." Sammy's shoulders rose in a defensive shrug. "You asked for my advice . . . Okay, let's switch gears for a moment. Can I ask you something? Do you know anything about any other quilts Wanda was piecing or working on? Besides the projects our group here at Community Craft have been sewing together? Or do you know if she was involved in the quilt barn trail project?"

"Trail project?" Jasmin placed her hands on her slender hips. "Nah. Not sure I'm following."

Sammy was relieved she wasn't the only one who hadn't heard of the trail project. She bent to one knee, pulled out the bottom drawer of her desk, and plucked out the plastic bag where she'd rewrapped Wanda's lap quilt for safekeeping. She carefully removed it from the bag and handed it to Jasmin to view. "Initially, I thought this was an heirloom quilt, but now I think she must've tea-stained it to make it appear old. I noticed that this block is identical to the block painted on the side of her brother Jackson's barn."

Sammy stood and pointed to the star pattern as she eyed Jasmin carefully.

"Which makes me wonder if this quilt has meaning. Do any of these quilt blocks look familiar to you? Do you know of anyone who may have one of these blocks painted on the side of their barn or garage?" Sammy picked up two corners of the quilt, and Jasmin mirrored her action by picking up the opposite two corners. Together they laid the blanket across Sammy's desk to view it fully.

Jasmin took a step back as if to adjust her vision, thought for a moment, and then said, "This one looks kinda familiar. I know I've seen this flying-geese pattern block somewhere. The colors seem familiar too." After a moment she snapped her slender fingers. "I know where I've seen it. North of town . . . driving toward Waupun on Highway Forty-Nine, I think. The farm up on the hill off the interstate. You know the one?" She looked to Sammy, who confirmed with a nod of her head. "Yeah, that's where I think I've seen this particular block."

Sammy's heart skipped a beat. "Any of the other blocks on this quilt look familiar?"

Jasmin scanned the lap quilt feverishly, looking for familiarity. "No. But I'm not sure what you mean or what this has to do with a trail. What's the trail project? Why do you ask?"

"I knew this blanket had more meaning then keeping someone warm and cozy," Sammy uttered under her breath. "It has to. Wanda had to be sending a message with all of this."

"Huh? I'm sorry, what did you say? I missed it." Jasmin placed a slender hand next to her ear.

"Nothing." Sammy waved her off and changed the subject. "This quilt is pretty, isn't it? Wanda was quite an artist. These blocks go together beautifully, despite the differing color palate," she added, taking the fabric of the quilt between her fingers and rubbing the soft muslin corner.

Jasmin hung her head sullenly. "Yeah, she was quite the seamstress too. Look at that design. She'll be missed around here, no doubt. Maybe we should show the others in the group? I'm sure everyone would love to see this work of art too. Don't you think?"

"Yeah, sure. Hey, do you know of anything Wanda felt guilty about or struggled with recently?"

"Uh-uh. Why do you ask?"

"No reason."

Sammy would hold back on sharing what she had found hidden within the batting. The meaning of the rhyme was still unclear. She'd keep tight-lipped about it as she silently continued to patch together a theory in her mind.

Chapter Twenty

The next day, Sammy stood by the front door of her shop, mentally willing people to stop in. She'd already been open for three hours, and not one measly customer had stepped inside the doors. The falling snow had subsided, but the temperatures had dipped dangerously below zero, causing even the local schools to call an early release. Sammy loathed January and February for this very reason. The gray sky and dirty snow from car exhaust were the same dingy color. The image out the window was depressing. She meandered over to where Bara lay beside the cash register. He rose from the dog bed and came close to her hand at her greeting.

"Let's just close for the day and get outta here," she said to her dog, which caused his fluffy ears to perk up at attention.

"No, we're not walking outside in that." She waved a disgruntled hand toward the door. "It's much too cold. But we're not staying here either."

As she walked toward the office, Bara followed. She thought about calling Ellie to ask her out to lunch, but then changed her mind. After her last conversation with her sister the previous night, she'd realized her sister and brother-in-law had some things to work out. Apparently, Ellie hadn't known about Randy's DWI from his youth. This bothered Ellie, as she'd thought she knew everything about her husband and, in her own words, "clearly did not."

Sammy logged on to her open laptop on the desk and posted the closing on Facebook before powering it down. She moved beyond the desk and reached for her winter coat hanging on a nearby rack, stuffed with her hat and gloves. While she dressed, she thought about stopping by the hospital to see if perhaps Heidi would like to go out to lunch. Then she thought about the recent flu outbreak and, due to her germophobic tendencies, decided that entering the hospital during flu season might not be a good idea either. Texting Heidi during the day wasn't an option either, as she likely wouldn't receive the text until her shift ended. Sammy sighed. The idea of heading to the grocery store was not an enticing one, as she'd have to bring Bara home first, because she couldn't leave him to wait inside a frigid car.

Sammy flicked the light off and was about to step over the threshold of the office when an abrupt feeling held her back. Something caused her to hesitate. She turned around and immediately bumped into Bara. "Sorry," she said as she gave him a quick pat on the head.

Sammy returned to her desk, removed the plastic bag containing Wanda's quilt, and tucked it under her arm. She decided to take it home and study it a while. Maybe Wanda could provide her with more clues if she took the time to study the quilt more closely.

"Come on, pup," she said as she tapped her leg for Bara to follow out the back entrance of Community Craft.

The rush to her car in the empty parking lot was almost unbearable. The bitter cold bit at her cheeks, causing them to sting. She hurried Bara to the back seat, where he immediately jumped inside and then jutted his head between the two front seats.

"What do you say we grab a burger?" Sammy said to her dog, after she slipped into the driver's seat and started the engine. As she waited for the car to warm and the windshield to clear of ice patches, she phoned the Corner Grill to place two orders: one plain burger for her dog and one loaded for herself. The owner, Colin, answered the phone and told her to stay in the warmth of her car and he would deliver it as soon as the food was ready. Sammy's mouth watered in response. Colin often provided this extra service for her during the winter months so she wouldn't have to leave Bara waiting alone in the cold car, which she appreciated immensely. When the windshield finally cleared, she eased her car out of the icy lot and around the corner to land back on Main Street, where she double-parked directly in front of the Corner Grill.

While Sammy waited for her food delivery, she flipped on the local radio station. Her favorite broadcaster, Dave, was sharing a weather update: "*Bitter-cold temperatures stay with us for the next few days, and wind chills dip to dangerous levels . . . another possibility for snow later this afternoon . . .*"

Sammy grunted at the thought and turned the radio off for fear of more bad news. Bara nuzzled her shoulder, and she reached around to snuggle his nose before she heard a knock at her driver's side window. Colin waited with a paper bag in hand, and Sammy reached into her purse for a twenty-dollar bill. It was almost double the cost of the meal, but she appreciated the extra service and compensated him well for it. "Keep the change," she said as she rolled the window down.

"Nah, that's too much. I'll keep a surplus tab for you on your next order," he said, the icy temperatures turning his breath to steam.

He quickly turned, running for the door, before Sammy had a chance to respond. She certainly understood his rush. Just dropping the window momentarily had sent a whoosh of cold air inside the car. She removed Wanda's quilt from the plastic bag and placed it in her lap to warm up.

Bara immediately sniffed the food bag, and instead of pulling away from the parking spot, Sammy reached into the bag, pulled out a hamburger patty, and broke it up into pieces for him. After her dog had a few bites, she took a few bites of her own burger. Once she felt satisfied, she tossed the other half of her burger back into the bag for later when she arrived home. Bara needed a bit more convincing that his meal was over, but finally settled into the back seat.

Sammy drove away from the restaurant with the food still lodged in her chest. She dug inside her oversized purse with one hand for a partially full water bottle she remembered she'd left inside. She uncapped the bottle, took a swig, and pounded her chest until the food slowly went down. That's what she got for not taking a proper lunch break and rushing to eat in her car. If she didn't let herself get so hungry, maybe this wouldn't constantly happen.

As she drove toward the comfort of home, she headed down Main Street and stopped at the one red light in town. She tapped her fingers along the steering wheel, impatiently waiting for the light to turn green. When the light turned, instead of driving straight and heading home, she instinctively flicked her directional left and followed the streets leading in the direction of Wanda's house.

It wouldn't hurt to do a quick drive-by, she thought.

When Sammy arrived in front of the Wadsworths' house, she did a double take when she noted a man exiting the back door of the Queen Anne Victorian, moving speedily toward the detached double garage. Her heart hammered in her chest. She squinted her eyes to confirm what she already knew. Her eyes were not playing tricks on her.

Marty!

Sammy jammed the car in park but blasted the heat and let the engine idle to keep Bara warm. She removed Wanda's quilt from her lap and tossed it aside to land on the passenger seat. She then leapt from her vehicle to try to catch up with him. Tripping her way through the snowdrifts and gasping for breath, she caught him by the arm just before he reached Wanda's car.

Marty startled to her touch. "Sammy Kane?" His dark-brown hair looked greasy and disheveled, as if he hadn't showered or shaved in days. A thick shadow outlined his mouth and cracked lips. "What are you doing here?"

"No! What are *you* doing here? The police have been looking for you! Your wife . . ."

"I know. Wanda's dead," Marty said with no hint of sadness.

The bluntness of his tone stunned her, and Sammy took a step back in disbelief.

"And I'm next if I don't hurry out of here, so please . . . excuse me!" He brushed her aside with the back of one hand, opened the driver's side door of his wife's Volkswagen, and flung a zipped duffle bag across the seat.

"You can't! You have to wait and talk to the authorities. They can help you!" Sammy pleaded. "Don't just take off—go and talk with them."

"No." His hazel eyes blazed wildly. "They can't help."

"Marty! Come on now, I'll have to tell *someone* I saw you. Where are you going? Tell me, please!"

"What are you, nuts? These people killed my wife, ran me off the road, threw a sack over my head, stuck me in an abandoned warehouse, and left me for dead. I'm not going to the authorities! They couldn't protect my wife—and they can't protect me!"

"Sure they can. I'll call them right now. My phone's in my car; I'll go get it." She jutted a thumb in the direction of her car parked out front.

Marty's sudden change in demeanor made the hairs stand up on Sammy's neck. Obviously, her words had struck a chord. "Get in the car," he ordered.

"What? No!" Sammy stepped back, and he swiftly grabbed her arm tightly, dragged her to the back door of his vehicle, opened it, and shoved her inside before she had a minute to think.

"What are you doing? Marty! No!" Sammy shook her head to refocus, her mind unable to comprehend what was happening.

"Give me your hands."

Sammy shook her head, her eyes wide, and recoiled into the seat.

"Give me your hands now!" he ordered.

Sammy backed farther into the seat, but his quick movements outpaced her.

Marty pulled the cord from his sweat shirt in one swift movement and wrapped it tightly around her wrists, then attached it to the passenger seat headrest to detain her. "Now behave, and I won't hurt you," he spat, spewing saliva from his mouth.

"What are you doing, Marty? You can't do this!" Sammy still couldn't come to grips with what was happening, even as Marty got behind the wheel and the Volkswagen pulled out of the driveway. "My dog! Bara is in my car! And my car . . . it's still running! If you leave it running in front of your house, someone will know I've been here! People who know me know I would *never* leave my dog behind." Sammy thought if she could get him to stop beside her car, she could try to make an escape. Though her hands were tied and attached to the headrest, it was her only hope.

Marty behaved exactly as she'd thought he would. He pulled his car alongside hers and hopped out. Before she had a chance to escape, he locked the doors to the Volkswagen. He tore the keys from the ignition of her car and threw them in the snow.

Between his movements, Sammy kicked at the door handle. In one mismanaged moment, she managed to pry the door open, but Marty slammed it back shut using his knee. Then he opened the back seat of Sammy's car and let Bara out into the cold. Before Sammy could manage an escape, he tore away from the curb, and she watched as the image of her dog moved farther and farther away.

Chapter Twenty-One

Sammy couldn't get past the shock coursing through her veins. Her body felt numb, as if her muscles were made of rubber. She tried to stay alert to the familiar landmarks rapidly drifting past her view from the car window. Walmart, the industrial park where the three S.H.E.s had played tag as kids, the local animal-feed store. The car was moving farther and farther west from Heartsford, and she wanted to be able to pinpoint exactly where Marty was taking her. The only thing giving her the least comfort was the fact that Bara was wearing dog tags. Surely *someone* would find him and take him in out of the cold. And then hopefully someone would know to look for her! A lump formed in her throat.

"Where are you taking me?" she asked finally. Her mouth was growing increasingly dry from the adrenaline rush that made her breathless with fear. She wished desperately for a sip of water.

"Sammy, I'm not going to hurt you. I just need to be sure you won't tell anyone you saw me. And right now, I'm not getting that type of certainty from you." He looked at her pleadingly, and she turned her head so as not to give him the satisfaction of their eyes meeting.

"You killed her, didn't you? You killed your wife . . . and now you're going to kill me too." Sammy figured she had nothing to lose at this point. She was most definitely in a losing proposition; she might as well dig for answers. Didn't she deserve at least that much before he chopped her into little pieces?

Marty snorted a nervous laugh. "You really do have a wild imagination, don't you? The answer is no. I did *not* kill my wife. However, the people who kidnapped me certainly led to her demise, and I need to get far away from them. Otherwise I'm going to be next on their list!"

"So, let me get this straight. You're telling me you escaped your so-called captors, and now you've decided it was a good idea to kidnap me?" Sammy huffed. "Isn't that just a brilliant idea."

Marty snorted again.

"Hey, you mind giving me a few pointers, then? How did you escape captivity? Maybe you can give me some tips on how to get away from *you*." She rolled her eyes.

"Like I'd share that kind of information with you." He regarded her again over his shoulder. "Don't blame your little situation here on me. You didn't leave me much choice with your needless meddling! In fact, cover your eyes or I'll do it for you. Your choice."

He unzipped his duffle bag, dug around with one hand, and then tossed a well-worn baseball hat to the back seat for her to block her own vision.

"Are you kidding me? How am I supposed to reach that?" Sammy couldn't believe the audacity. Marty made it sound as if it was her own fault that her hands were tied and she was stuffed in the back seat of his car. And now he wanted her to cover her eyes? Barb was right—what a jerk!

He removed a large zip tie from the seat and zipped her wrists together, then untied her from the headrest, all while balancing the steering wheel with his knee.

"Do it!" he ordered, then constantly rechecked the rearview mirror to see if she was cooperating.

"Do *what*?" she said mockingly. "Not much I *can* do locked in the back seat of your car with my hands tied, you moron!"

"Cover your eyes with that hat or I'll cover them for you. I do *not* want you to see where we're going!" His voice rose and grew angrier, which unnerved her.

Sammy held the cap with her two hands tied together and attempted to cover her eyes as best she could under the circumstances. "Don't you have anything else besides this smelly hat?" she asked dryly. "It stinks like old sweat!"

"How about duct tape? And keep it up, missy—don't tempt me to use it on your mouth too!" he warned.

Sammy thought through all the possibilities of escape. Her phone had been left inside her purse, which was now abandoned inside the glove box of her car. She had no way to make a call or send a text. Heck, she didn't even have a match to send up a smoke signal. Would someone find Bara loose and come to her aid? She dared not think of her dog left out in the cold. That last image of him standing in the road, stunned, as they drove farther away, was too much to handle. Bara was so good-natured, he hadn't even barked when he was let out of the car and abandoned.

Sammy thought maybe she could try to kick open the door when the car slowed, but what would happen to her then? She'd die out in the cold in mere minutes. Especially if Marty was taking her out on a low country road where there was very little or no traffic. Her winter hat was also back inside her car. Sammy groaned. The putrid smell of the cap filled her nostrils, and she tried desperately not to breathe it in.

"What are you moaning about? Shut up!" Marty cautioned. "You're making this much harder than it has to be!"

Really?

Sammy remained silent for fear that her captor would indeed cover her mouth with duct tape. She didn't know if it was a baseless threat or if he was even smart enough to keep a roll of the stuff in the trunk of his car. Did he have a make-shift kit back there to dispose of a body? A backpack filled with rope, knives, a gun? She watched far too much *Dateline*, she thought. She decided that from now on she'd watch only Hallmark or the Disney Channel with Tyler instead of any more crime shows. That is, if she made it out of this mess alive.

This line of thinking wasn't helping. Her heart began to beat faster, and she shuddered. Had he poisoned Wanda? Or had these so-called kidnappers done the deed as he claimed? She needed to calm down and ease her rapid heartbeat. If only she could clear her mind. She needed to focus on what she knew to be true.

She knew nothing.

Finally, after what seemed like an hour or more of endless driving, the car slowed and turned, allowing Sammy to shift the baseball hat from her eyes just enough to peek at their destination. They were pulling into the driveway of an abandoned farm, she quickly noted. It appeared there were no other vehicle tracks in the deep snow, causing the engine to sputter. When the Volkswagen hit the edge of a fluffy snowbank, the engine cut completely.

"Where are we?"

"Have you been here before?"

"How would I know?" she finally answered sharply. "I've had to smell this stinky hat the whole trip."

Marty turned to face her squarely in the back seat, ripped the hat from her grip, and tossed it aside onto the passenger seat. He then leaned over, reached for the glove box, and removed additional extra-long zip ties.

Sammy gulped with what remaining saliva she had, which wasn't much. She didn't want to surmise what those long ties would be used for.

If I go out, I'm going out blazing! Her eyes darted through the window to gauge her surroundings. "Where have you taken me? I don't have any idea where we are." Confusion riddled her thoughts. "Should I know where we are?" Neither the oversized red flaking barn nor the pale-yellow farmhouse off in the distance looked familiar.

"Good," Marty stated, then unlocked the doors. "Get out of the car."

"Here?"

"Yes, here!"

"But why here?"

"Do it!"

Sammy did her best to scoot her butt to the edge of the back seat. She hadn't realized how hard it was to maneuver around with one's hands tightly bound together. Marty opened the back door, noted her predicament, grabbed her tied hands, and yanked her outside the car, almost causing her to fall to her knees in the snow. Her ankle twisted, causing her to writhe in pain, and she let out a yelp. The biting wind whipped at her cheeks as he dragged her by the arm toward the old barn. There was no way she'd survive outdoors in the cold if she attempted an escape, especially now that she was limping. The temperature must've plummeted even further below zero. She began to shiver and her teeth chattered. She suddenly thought of Bara. The mere idea of him left out in the cold almost brought her to tears, so she pushed it away. Her eyes scanned the acreage for a nearby neighbor, but there was nothing but a sea of barren snow-covered land. Wherever they were, it was desolate.

Sammy looked up as they approached the barn and noted an eight-by-eight painted quilt block in a log-cabin pattern above her head. She smiled inwardly as she recognized the block as one of the blocks sewn on the corner of Wanda's quilt. It gave her instant hope.

This means something.

It had to.

Marty removed a key from his pants pocket and opened a padlock attached to the large barn door. He kicked at the snow that was hampering his ability to freely open the door. He then shoved the door open to reveal the dark, cold interior.

Inside, it was obvious that the farmer who owned the property was using the space for winter storage rentals to cash in on the long, cold Wisconsin winters. Three tarp-covered boats, one pontoon about twenty feet long, and two ski boats roughly seventeen feet long lined the wall. An older-model motor home was centered in the interior of the barn, and Marty pushed Sammy in the direction of it. When they arrived, he opened the small metal door and ordered her to go inside.

Sammy stepped into the motor home, and her eyes scanned the small, narrow space. Muted gray wallpaper covered the walls, and gray pleather seats with back pillows upholstered in a hideous pattern ran along the walls of the kitchenette.

"Is this your camper?" she asked.

"Yes."

Marty shoved her into one of the seats in the kitchenette. Before she had a minute to think, he was binding her ankles together with two long zip ties. After her ankles were secure, he proceeded to weave another zip tie in and out of her fingers in a way that made her hands virtually unusable.

"You really feel the need to secure my feet and hands this way? Where do you think I'm going?" She waved her tied hands animatedly. "And by the way, this is too tight! My ankle is throbbing!" She scowled.

His nonverbal answer was to add an additional zip tie and secure her legs tighter. A long pause ensued between them.

Sammy decided that acting ignorant and befriending him would be a better option for getting answers than her previous accusatory stance.

"Oh Marty, I'm very sorry about all of this. How awful to lose your wife and be running from these crazy people! Do you know who they are? Do you know why they chose you and Wanda to harass? Are they extorting money from you? What is this about? Do you know?" Her eyes searched him for answers.

"I don't know who they are. They ran my car into the ditch. When I got out to check and chew them out, instead of giving me an apology, the guy was wearing a ski mask. He covered my head with a potato sack so fast, I'd never recognize him in a lineup," he admitted. "Anyone would be able to get away with wearing all that winter garb with the kind of weather we have around here."

"And how did you get away from them? What did they want from you? Do you have a bad debt or something?"

"You really are incredibly nosy. Just like the rest of the Heartsford gossips," Marty spat. "You people think you know everything. Do you know how close to death I came? I could feel the barrel of a shotgun held to my head through the potato sack, and then someone must have come into the warehouse and interrupted the guy, because suddenly I was being dragged out of there, and for a few short minutes I was left alone . . . why am I even telling you this?" He huffed under his breath. "I'm done talking to you. I don't owe you any explanation."

Sammy had to know; it was her only chance. "Did it have something to do with the papers you took from Craig and tossed into the fire the night of Fire and Ice?" she blurted.

His head jerked in her direction and his eyes blazed. "What did you say?"

"What were those papers? Was Cheryl trying to serve you papers and sue you over her back pain? I know she slipped a disk and blamed Wanda for it. Was that what it was about?"

Marty moved so close she could smell his rancid breath. He stood in front of her and pointed a finger a few inches from her face. "No! What went on between me and Craig was a work issue, and it's nothing to concern yourself over, Little Miss Nosy, so why don't you just drop it?"

Sammy swallowed. "My mouth is so dry, I'm having a hard time speaking. I guess you'll get your wish," she admitted, turning her head from his breath.

"Good. Maybe you'll stop pestering me, then! Stay put," he warned, flicking her nose with his finger before leaving her to sit alone in the motor home.

She wanted to cry. She wanted to scream. She wanted relief from her parched mouth. But more than anything, she wished she was back home with Bara, cuddled in front of the fire with a cup of hot cocoa. She shivered again, missing the recent warmth of the Volkswagen, which was quickly becoming a distant memory.

Within minutes, Marty returned to the motor home, opened an upper cabinet, and began flipping dials.

"What are you doing?"

Sammy felt a rush of warmth into the small space, answering her question. She realized he must've turned on the propane. Gratitude overwhelmed her, as she wasn't ready to succumb to the cold. She watched as he continued to dig through random cabinets. He plucked out an old can of peanuts and shook it in his hand.

"You hungry?"

Sammy felt her stomach churn at the question. "No, but I'm dying of thirst," she admitted. "The least you could do is give me a drink before you kill me."

"Wait here." He exited and let the flimsy metal door slam behind him.

Like I have a choice? Sammy mentally responded, with a roll of her eyes.

After a few minutes, Marty returned with three frozen water bottles in his hands. He set one on the small table in front of her, and due to its expanded bottom, the bottle rolled to the floor. He leaned over, plucked it off the vinyl floor, and then handed it to her. She attempted to hold it in her bundled hands.

"That's all I had in my trunk. You're going to have to wait for it to melt a little," he added as he rifled through nearby cabinets and drawers.

"Can you at least open it?" She hoped he'd have mercy. She couldn't do anything the way her hands were tied together, and she was beginning to feel like Pavlov's dog. She could almost taste the water.

He leaned over, uncapped the bottle of frozen water, and then Sammy brought the bottle to her lips and attempted to melt the ice with her tongue. She sucked on it for as long as she could but barely defrosted enough to quench her thirst.

"Why are you being nice to me all of a sudden?" She licked the frozen water from her lips and looked at him.

"Sammy . . ." He slammed the last cabinet door after finding it empty and looked at her squarely. "This is the end of the road."

Chapter Twenty-Two

Marty had abandoned the camper, letting the metal door slam behind him. Leaving Sammy alone to stew over his parting words.

This is the end of the road.

The words hung in the air like a haunting mirage, ready to reappear at any moment.

The end of the road? Was Marty about to take her life? Her life flashed before her eyes. Images of Community Craft, downtown business neighbors, and the people she'd come to love and work beside filled her mind. Would she ever step inside the Sweet Tooth Bakery again? Indulge on Marilyn's sweet treats and hear her neighbor sharing the newest gossip swirling around town? Or step inside Liquid Joy and smell the rich dark java and chat with Douglas? What would happen to all the vendors at Community Craft? Would someone take over the shop as she had in memory of Kate? Would someone carry on their legacy?

And what about Bara? Who would take care of her dog? A lump filled her throat, threating to choke her. Would she ever see Heidi marry, and would she miss out on the birth of her new niece or nephew? And what about S.H.E.? The club of their youth? Would Heidi and Ellie be able to move on without her? Suddenly she realized how much she loved her little town of Heartsford, and she wasn't ready to leave it. Stamped on her own heart forever—Heartsford.

Then her mind filled with the image of Liam Nash. Would she ever feel the touch of his lips on hers? The warmth of his embrace?

Sammy's heart thundered as she eyed the door, anticipating Marty's return. Was he retrieving a loaded gun from the trunk of Wanda's Volkswagen? A knife? Would he kill her in a humane way? Would it be fast . . . or would he make her suffer? *Poison*? She still couldn't gauge whether Marty had told her the truth about not being responsible for Wanda's death. Was someone out there singling him out and targeting his family? For what reason? Was this about the financial windfall from the card games he'd once had stashed in his house? Or was he involved in something shady? Was it a deal gone bad between him and Cheryl's husband, Craig?

So many loose ends had her mind spinning for answers. Could she trip him up somehow to find out? She supposed it didn't matter. If he told her the truth and she never escaped, what good was it anyway? She shuddered. The rushing thoughts were only exacerbating her fear and not doing her any good. She dropped her head and noticed her hands trembling in her lap. She tucked them between her legs to try to make them stop. Instead, her entire body began to quake with terror. She needed to get herself together. This was *not* the way her life was going to end!

No!

Sammy was a S.H.E. And a S.H.E. would go out fighting, she resolved as she clenched her teeth hard. Her hazel eyes darted around the space, looking for a way to untangle her hands and feet. Her heart beat wildly. She maneuvered to her feet and hopped over to a nearby cabinet like a bouncing kangaroo, causing new pain in her swelling ankle. After lifting her frame as high as she could manage on her tippy-toes, she swatted the round metal knob with her knotted hands. A stack of Tupperware bowls shifted and fell out of the cabinet with a thud, nearly missing the top of her head. Sammy's eyes darted toward the door to be sure Marty hadn't heard the noise. She sucked in a breath. She was hoping for a pot or pan she could use to hit him on the head when he returned—not a *plastic* Tupperware container! She bent at the waist and slowly pulled out a lower drawer with her teeth. Her heart leapt with excitement as a serrated bread knife shone back at her.

Sammy eyed the door before she reached into the drawer with both bundled hands to retrieve the knife. Her fingers were woven so tightly together that merely grasping the utensil was difficult at best. She thought for a moment. Marty was at least a foot taller than her—maybe more. Could he overpower her and take the knife? She wrestled with the decision before maneuvering the knife clumsily into her hands. She hoped she wasn't making a grave mistake. But what other choice did she have?

A thumping sound stopped her in her tracks.

Thump. Thump. Thump.

She held her breath to distinguish the sound. Or was it more like a knock?

Knock. Knock. Knock.

A woodpecker, maybe? Off in the distance . . . out on the barn? Could it be?

Then a sudden loud bang hit the outside of the camper, as if someone had pounded the siding of the motor home with a large fist. Sammy looked at the knife trembling in her hands and wondered if she should quickly hide it or put it back before Marty returned, as she was ill prepared. Her objective was to release her hands and feet, not stab the man. But something in her will to live wouldn't allow her to let the knife go, even though she didn't have a strong, capable grip at the moment.

What had hit the side of the camper?

And then she heard a fluttering sound.

Sammy held her breath again and then began to pant. Her breaths were coming fast now, and if she didn't settle down, she'd wind up having a full-blown panic attack.

The woodpecker or whatever had made that noise must be inside the barn too and must've misjudged the distance, hitting the side of the camper. What else could it have been? She stood nervously with the knife in her bundled hands, waiting to pounce, and she noticed again how hard her hands were shaking.

She stilled her breath by counting. *One . . . two . . . three, out. One . . . two . . . three, in.* She didn't move a muscle until she was sure it was all quiet. When she felt confident Marty wasn't near or on the other side of the flimsy door, she hopped back into her original seat in the kitchenette. She scanned to her left and right to see where she could hide the knife if need be, and decided she'd tuck it between the side of the seat and the wall and hide it with her leg. She just hoped she wouldn't injure herself or be forced to use it on Marty. Truth be known, she wasn't sure she could go through with it, even if she felt forced. She decided instead that she'd hit him on the head with a frozen water bottle and knock him out. That she could live with. She figured he had just stepped out momentarily to retrieve something from the car, so she didn't think she'd have time to free herself, but the waiting seemed endless.

The minutes ticked by, and Sammy's eyes watched the door eagerly. Waiting. Eyes wide.

Waiting.

Waiting.

Still waiting.

Sammy had no idea what was taking Marty so long to return. It seemed like at least fifteen minutes had passed, although she had no concept of how to gauge the time, except from the rapid beats of her heart, which seemed to easily outpace the second hand on her imaginary clock. She decided at last that she'd try to release her hands and feet. She attempted to pick the knife up off the seat beside her three times before she was successful. She jammed the wooden handle of the knife between her knees, pressing them together hard in an attempt to keep the sharp blade upright. She began to saw away at the zip ties that had bound her fingers and hands together. Slowly and methodically, she moved her hands back and forth.

Back and forth.

Back and forth.

The job was tedious, and if she wasn't careful, she would deeply wound herself. She gripped her knees tighter to the knife handle to keep it from slipping. She kept sawing at the plastic strings on her fingers, simultaneously eyeing the door, looking for Marty to reappear and catch her in the act.

Sammy's adrenaline pumped as she moved her hands back and forth on the blade until she accomplished her goal. The sight of her unbound hands caused her to squeal out in relief. She clenched and relaxed her fingers to get the blood flowing in them again and then rubbed them together until they felt workable.

If Marty reappeared, he'd notice her unbound hands. She'd have to be prepared. She eyed the door again before leaning over and setting to work on the zip ties binding her feet.

As soon as she released her feet, she sighed audibly. It felt like the first real breath she'd taken through the whole ordeal.

The only noise Sammy could hear was the thumping of her heart beating wildly, throbbing inside her ears. She jumped from the seat, sending a jolt of agony through her ankle. The pain didn't stop her from rifling through cabinets for a pot, pan, or alternate hard object with which she could disarm her opponent upon his return. She moved quickly from cabinet to cabinet, looking for the perfect object. She decided she would knock Marty out, steal his keys, and make an escape in Wanda's car. The potential of escape made her heart soar, as she felt this might be a doable task. It was her only hope.

When she finally found a cast-iron skillet and held it in her hands expectantly, Sammy heard the muffled sound of a car engine starting in the distance. Either someone else had arrived or Marty was leaving. She quickly realized he must've been digging the car out of the snow instead of preparing to brandish a weapon. A nervous giggle seeped from her lips. She waited a few minutes, her hand held to her thumping heart, as if she could manually stop its rapid beats. She flung the door open wide, banging it hard against the side of the motor home.

Sammy needed a few moments to adjust her eyes in the unlit barn. She blinked them a few times before rushing toward the barn door, causing a new thrashing pain in her ankle. When she slid it open, all she saw were the recent tracks in the snow, where Wanda's old Volkswagen had been parked, and the sun sinking into the western sky, creating a beautiful magenta-and-purple backdrop.

A different type of panic began to rise in her throat. Where was she, and how was she going to get out of there?

Chapter Twenty-Three

Sammy stepped out of the barn, and the bitter cold immediately needled her cheeks and caused her nose to drip. She had stood at the threshold of the barn door for a long time, numb with shock, contemplating her latest predicament. She wiped her nose as best she could with the back of her hand, but it continued to stream. The snow wasn't yet falling as the radio broadcaster had earlier predicted, and the sky was turning inky and cloudless. She wondered if she was that far past the broadcast's limits. The lack of sun would cause the temperatures to plummet even deeper. She realized walking any distance in the bitter cold, with a throbbing ankle, wasn't even remotely an option. Especially with the farm isolated from any neighbors—at least from what her own eyes could see.

Hot steam escaped her mouth, sending her breath out like that of a heavy smoker. She'd have no choice other than to camp out where she had heat and wait until daybreak to figure out a safer plan of escape.

She covered her bare ears with her chapped hands to prevent the cold wind from causing them to internally ache. She should be elated. Marty hadn't ended her life. *Why?* Maybe he hadn't murdered his wife after all? Or maybe he was planning to return. She wasn't sure, but her gut told her he was gone. Long gone—never to return.

Sammy's eyes glanced toward the yellow farmhouse in the distance, which seemed to be vacant. Very little light emanated from the home. The farmer must be either on vacation or snow-birding down south in Florida or somewhere warm. Marty had been smart enough to take her somewhere no one was expected to return for a long time, of that she was sure. Not to mention, there were zero tracks in the snow around the house. Nearby were the tracks left behind from Wanda's Volkswagen and Marty's boots. The only other evidence of life Sammy could make out, in the light of the rising moon, was the trail of a deer or rabbit that had crossed the yard after the storm passed and left a winding track.

The cold wouldn't allow Sammy to remain outdoors another minute, as mere breathing sent an instant throbbing to the lungs. She quickly made her way back inside the barn and closed the door behind her to keep the heat inside for the long night ahead. Her teeth chattered as she made her way through the unlit barn, a hand outstretched in front of her to help her find her way as her eyes adjusted to the dark. She followed the dim light emanating from the camper and was thankful that at least she wouldn't be left alone in the dark or cold all night long. She wondered how much propane was left in the tank and if it was even safe to run it while inside the barn, but she had no choice but to reenter the mobile home. It would be her only refuge for the night.

Sammy looked at her surroundings, now seeing them through a different lens. She was no longer afraid for her life, and the adrenaline that had pumped through her veins the entire afternoon had left her depleted and a little hungry. The temperature had dropped within the confines of the motor home, and she wondered if her fears were already becoming a reality. The camper might be running low on propane. She shivered and ran her hands up and down the side of her coat in a pathetic attempt to warm up.

Sammy didn't know the first thing about running a recreational vehicle. What she did know was that, if the propane ran out, she'd be up a creek, looking at a long, cold night ahead. The barn would offer some protection from the cold and biting wind; however, as cold as it was, it wouldn't take long to dip below freezing inside too. She'd always dreamed of going on a camping trip in an RV. This wasn't exactly the way she'd planned it. *After this experience, I might just take that idea off my bucket list*, she thought with a roll of her eyes. The muted gray walls seemed to close in on her, and she knew the feeling of claustrophobia could easily take over if she allowed it.

Sammy resigned herself to the fact that she wasn't going anywhere and decided the best thing she could do was try to settle down for the night. The idea of sleeping in a strange bed inside a strange camper didn't sit well with her, but she tried to push away the negative thoughts clouding her mind and instead began to search for items to make her stay as comfortable as possible. She took a few steps deeper into the space and began to rifle through drawers and cabinets. With unbound hands, the task was much easier. There was nothing worth eating besides the can of peanuts Marty had found earlier. She surmised that he'd at least done a good job of removing food to keep rodents at bay.

Sammy stepped into the bedroom area, and when she sat on the edge of the bed, she knew she couldn't do it. She'd have to sleep by the door in case Marty returned. She had to remain vigilant and ready for anything, like a soldier prepared for battle. She rolled the army-green sleeping bag off the bed, bundled it into her arms, and stuffed it onto the gray pleather kitchen seat. After reclosing all the cabinet doors and drawers that she had randomly left ajar, she sank into the seat and wrapped up in the sleeping bag. Her nose curled along with her stomach when she noted that the sleeping bag was in desperate need of a wash. After trying without success to get a little water from the frozen bottle, she closed her eyes, and before long the weariness took over and she succumbed to it.

* * *

The next morning, Sammy awoke with a stiff neck and a runny nose inside a cold camper. She shivered, even with the sleeping bag tucked tight around her. Her only hope of survival was finding someone with a phone, because there was no way she'd last long under these circumstances. Not helping to alleviate her fears, she realized the camper must've officially run out of propane overnight. She pushed the musty-smelling sleeping bag aside and took a sip of water from the frozen bottle. The ice had melted a bit overnight, giving her at least a quarter of a cup.

When she attempted to stand upright, her ankle buckled, vertigo kicked in, and she thought she might suddenly fall. The stress from the previous day and having little to eat made her feel lousy. The lack of coffee, and no hope for a cup in her near future, made her grunt in frustration. She breathed in deep, centered herself by placing her hand on the nearby table, and then brushed her tangled hair from her eyes.

When the vertigo subsided, she flung open the metal door of the camper and limped into the dim barn. A beam of sunlight peeked through the cracks, giving her the ability to see the interior of the barn better than she had the previous night. The faded gray boards had protected her overnight, and she touched a center beam with reverence as she stepped past. She wouldn't have survived the night outdoors—not a chance. This barn had been her refuge.

The space inside the barn was unnervingly quiet. No trapped flapping birds this morning, and Sammy missed the comfort of her dog. She hoped Bara was tucked in somewhere warm.

She felt as if she were helpless and alone on a desolate glacier, not knowing which way to turn, and she suddenly felt a desperate need to reach out in prayer. As she was pleading with her Maker to help her out of this mess, something reflected a beam of sunshine, catching her attention. A crack in the faded gray wooden walls allowed the light to penetrate. She tented her eyes with her hands to follow the shiny object. Something behind one of the large beams was reflecting the light. Sammy's curiosity won out, and she abandoned her prayer and went to investigate. What she came upon caused her mouth to drop in surprise. A shiny silver key was nailed to the beam, along with a few others. Her heart leapt in excitement, and she looked up to her Maker with a smile of thanksgiving.

Sammy plucked the keys off the wooden beam one by one, tucked them inside her jeans pocket for safekeeping, and turned to exit the barn. One of these keys had to be the key to the farmhouse next door.

It has to be.

The trek through the crusty snow was arduous, as the bitter cold the previous night had caused a sheet of ice to form on top. Sammy pushed her feet hard to penetrate the glaze as she made a path toward the house. Steam rose from her breath, and she tucked her hands into her jacket like a turtle as she trudged across the frozen tundra. When she arrived at the front door, she had to blow on her hands several times to get her frozen fingers to cooperate. She desperately attempted each of the keys in the lock until one finally made the door pop open. Sammy sighed with relief and held a hand to her fluttering heart.

The door opened with a creak, and natural light flooded the interior of the farmhouse. Sammy noted that the furniture was covered in white sheets, as if the owner was keeping the dust at bay while absent. Whoever owned this home wasn't planning on returning anytime soon. The house would probably be cold, but not nearly as cold as it was outdoors. She doubted the heat was turned off completely; otherwise the pipes would've burst long ago.

Sammy tentatively stepped inside the entryway and wondered if the water was turned off, as she desperately wanted a drink. She followed the aged hardwood floor to the back of the house until she found a deep porcelain farm sink in the kitchen. She flicked on the faucet, and after a few sputters, the water shot out full stream. She sighed in relief, cupping her hands beneath it to take a drink. Then, turning her head sideways, Sammy put her mouth directly in the water flow until she was satisfied. After wiping her mouth with the back of her hand, she turned the faucet to hot, and when the water began to steam, she plunged her cold, aching hands into the stream to relieve the pain. She held them there until she could move her fingers with ease. But it wasn't just the cold that had caused her hands to ache. As she studied her fingers, she remembered how tightly her hands had been woven together the previous day. By day's end, a few fingers were sure to show a bruise.

Sammy looked over her shoulder for a towel or even a sheet of paper towel but found none. Instead she wiped her wet hands on her jeans and then tucked them beneath her armpits to keep them warm.

The search for a landline began. She moved out of the kitchen and stepped into a formal room, where she located a telephone beneath a dust sheet covering a long mahogany desk. Unfortunately, when she picked up the receiver, the lack of a dial tone confirmed that there was no service.

Defeat settled in as she pondered her next move.

Sammy didn't ponder long. As she was placing the bedsheet back atop the long desk and adjusting it neatly back into place, her eyes caught sight of a trash can beneath the desk. Prickles moved up her spine. On top of the receptacle lay a magazine with letters cut out of it. Letters that had most likely created the note Jackson had received asking for $100,000— Marty's ransom note.

Chapter Twenty-Four

Finding the cut-up magazine with letters removed led Sammy to one conclusion: either Marty had been inside the farmhouse, or the owner of the property somehow had something to do with Wanda's death and her husband's so-called kidnapping. Was it just a ruse? Had he faked his own kidnapping? There was just no other explanation. Was there? Why would Marty bring her to the very place his captors had created that note, though? The mere thought made her shiver as she realized how narrowly she had escaped death.

A roaring noise booming from outside the quiet farmhouse caught Sammy's attention, and it took a few moments for the sound to register. Her eyes widened like silver dollars.

A snowplow!

Despite the pain coursing through her ankle, Sammy turned on her heel and sprinted for the front window, tore open the heavy, dated drapes, and watched as a large county snowplow made its way down the country road. She tried to gauge how far the house was from the road, and it wasn't close, a few hundred yards. But she'd have to at least try. She bolted out the front door and waved her hands frantically over her head just as the plow was passing the front of the house. She cupped her hands to her mouth and screamed for the plow to stop, but the sound only boomeranged off the trees across the street to echo in her own ears. The roaring of the snow's heaving and pushing deafened her cry for help. After taking a few more steps forward, she realized her ankle wouldn't allow her to run and catch it. Her shoulders sank in defeat as she watched the truck grow smaller. Her body began to tremble from the cold. In her effort to rush outside, she'd tripped through a deep snowdrift. The snow had seeped into her winter boots, causing a stinging chill to creep up her legs and feet. She needed to hurry indoors and remove her wet footwear or potentially suffer frostbite.

Sammy was just about to retreat toward the farmhouse when she noticed something out of her peripheral vision. She turned her head and saw Heidi's black Jeep racing behind the plow in her direction like a black stallion. Sammy's eyes widened to register what she was seeing, and fat tears formed, clouding her vision. She wasn't sure if the tears were from the cold or instant relief that she was about to be rescued. Heidi's Jeep pushed through the unplowed driveway, effortlessly kicking up soft powder despite the glaze-topped snow, and came to an abrupt stop. Suddenly, Heidi and Ellie were racing toward her, tripping their way through the snowdrifts with arms open wide.

"How did you find me?" Sammy murmured as the three held each other in a group hug in front of the farmhouse.

"Wanda's quilt! You left it in the front seat of your car, and so we followed the trail map. You mentioned you thought each of her quilt blocks coincided with one of the blocks painted on the sides of these barns, so we got ahold of the trail map and followed it. Each of the quilt-block patterns is printed on the map, with an address written below it. It took us a while, but we finally found you," Ellie said after the three released each other. She searched Sammy's eyes and refused to let go of one of her arms. Then she began to shake it hard, as if to see if she was really standing next to her and not a figment of her imagination. "Don't ever do that again. You had us scared half to death."

Sammy's facade began to crumble, and she started to tear up again. "I can't tell you how happy I am that you guys are here," she said, wiping her eyes. "To be honest, I was really starting to worry that I'd never get out of here."

Heidi's nursing skills kicked in, "Let's get you inside out of the cold before those tears turn to icicles. Whose house is this?" Heidi looked up at the farmhouse and then turned to Sammy searchingly.

"I have no idea," Sammy admitted, which caused Heidi and Ellie to look at each other with mirrored looks of confusion. Then their eyes flew back to Sammy.

Sammy summoned them to follow with a wave of her hand. "Let's just step inside for a few minutes before we get outta here for good. I think I've got some explaining to do."

The three of them turned toward the front door of the farmhouse, and Ellie asked, "How did you get here? We're so confused. You abandoned your car and came all the way out here? For what?"

Sammy turned to them before they crossed the threshold. "Marty brought me here."

Ellie and Heidi audibly gasped.

"What?" Heidi asked, stepping inside the farmhouse after Sammy. "Marty? You found him? Where is he?" Heidi and Ellie each peeked over their shoulders, searching for him.

"Wait a minute . . . I'm so confused." Ellie reached for her sister and took hold of her arm to encourage her to turn and face them.

"He brought me here against my will."

"Noooo." Ellie shook her head and placed a gloved hand over her mouth. Her eyes widened and her jaw dropped.

"Wait, I have to know. Before I explain one more thing, have you guys seen Bara?" A lump threatened to close Sammy's throat.

"Don't worry, Lynn has him." Heidi placed a comforting hand on Sammy's shoulder. "Lynn called Ellie because someone came into Heartsford Credit Union and mentioned that a golden retriever was wandering around outside the bank with a blue tartan scarf around his neck. Lynn instantly knew it was Bara and brought him inside the bank. She knew something was off since you weren't with him in this bone-chilling cold."

Ellie interrupted. "Then Lynn called me, wondering where you were, and that's how our search for you began. We wouldn't even be here if Lynn hadn't called."

Sammy held her hand to her heart, and a fat tear fell from her cheek. "So Bara's fine?"

Ellie wiped Sammy's tear with her glove. "He's more than fine. Lynn took him home after work last night, and she's keeping him safe until your return. Lynn's obviously worried about you, though, as no one could find you, and Community Craft was locked up tight."

"And you didn't involve the police?" Sammy asked in complete surprise.

"Not yet. Of course, we did a drive by Wanda's house. We found your car. I took the quilt, hoping it would give us a clue as to where you went. Thankfully it did," Heidi said. "To be clear, it was our last-ditch effort before calling the authorities for help."

"Yeah, when Bara was missing, and then we found your abandoned car . . . the whole scene made us really scared." Ellie threw up her hands.

"And then we stopped by your house, and you weren't there . . ." Heidi added. "And you weren't answering your phone. That's when we really started to get nervous. We thought if we involved the police, it'd only get the three of us into more trouble. Especially with Tim and I on a break. The last thing we wanted to do was involve the police and have them arrest us without an opportunity to find you ourselves. We had *no idea* Marty brought you here! We figured you were out somewhere digging for intel, though." Heidi smirked and placed her hands on slender hips.

"My phone is in my car," Sammy said. "I left it in the glove compartment. Stupid move on my part." She rolled her eyes.

"We didn't even think to search your glove compartment," Heidi admitted, lifting her hands in defeat.

"Wait a minute, you slept here? Whose house is this anyway?" Ellie asked, finally taking in her surroundings as the three stood in the foyer of the farmhouse.

"No, I slept in the barn." Sammy jutted a thumb toward the front door.

"The barn?" Ellie's voice elevated a few octaves. "You slept in a *barn*? In the frigid cold?"

"To be clear, in Marty's old motor home inside the barn. And by the way, I think my romanticized idea of a camping trip is officially over. But here's the thing, you guys, Initially I thought Marty was bringing me out here to do me in. But then he sort of convinced me that he really did escape his captors. I mean, if he killed his wife, what would stop him from killing me? Right?" Sammy paused, and Heidi and Ellie looked at her expectantly.

"But then I found something." Sammy pointed in the direction of the trash can. "I mean, I found it long *after* Marty abandoned me here. Just now, while I was searching for a phone to call for help."

Heidi's eyes narrowed, and she leaned in closer. "What'd you find?"

Sammy beckoned her sister and cousin to follow and led them to the dust sheet covering the desk. She lifted it up just enough to point at the trash can. "Look there."

Ellie gasped and placed her hand to her heart. "Oh dear. Is that what I think it is? Oh no . . ."

"What?" Heidi asked, and then it suddenly dawned on her too. "I must admit, it's a bit unusual, and it looks like only the letters are cut out. Either it's one weird coincidence or . . ."

Sammy stopped her with a lift of her hand. "You know what Nash would say? He doesn't believe in coincidences. Nor do I, honestly. That's the magazine that was used to create the ransom note. It must be. So, here's the problem. Who put it there? Marty? Is he that stupid to bring me out here and hope I wouldn't discover this? Plus, he said someone held a gun to his head. Unless he made the whole thing up and was lying to me. What do you guys think?"

Heidi's eyes moved away from the trash can to take in more of her surroundings, and she knit her brows. "Who owns this place? We need to figure that out right now. None of this is making sense."

"That's the thing. I don't know." Sammy tugged at her winter coat as if suddenly feeling suffocated. "I literally just came inside here a few minutes ago looking for a phone to call for help, and I haven't found anything with a name on it yet."

"Well, what are we waiting for?" Heidi said, displaying jazz hands. "Let's find out and then get the heck out of here. You must be starving. Have you eaten anything since yesterday? Besides, Ellie and I've been up most of the night again. We could both use a nap." Heidi yawned and stretched her arms high above her head.

Ellie nodded in agreement, but Sammy was surprised that, despite her pregnancy, her sister looked more alert and awake than she had the other night. Maybe it was due to the adrenaline of finding her. Maybe Ellie was about to crash.

"No, I haven't had anything to eat since yesterday, and I'm dying for a cup of coffee. I can't remember the last time I woke up without one to start my day," Sammy admitted. "If I don't get one soon, I may end up with a headache." She pressed her fingers to her forehead.

"Let's hurry up then, collect our intel, and get out of here," Heidi said. "Where should we start?"

"Did you see any paperwork with a name on it in the desk?" Ellie asked.

"I didn't get that far." Sammy opened a drawer.

"Wait a minute!" Ellie slapped a hand to her forehead. "We're idiots! The exact address of where we are right now is written on the trail map. All we need to do is Google the address, and it should show a homeowner's name. No?"

"Nah, Google won't share a name, I don't think," Sammy said, shaking her head.

"No, Google won't—but county tax records will. I bet Randy has access to that." Heidi flung a finger in Ellie's direction. "Let's get outta here before we get in trouble for breaking and entering yet *again*." Heidi and Ellie turned in the direction of the front door.

"Don't you think the police would believe me about Marty kidnapping me and leaving me here to die out in the cold?" Sammy said as she watched her sister and cousin move away from her. "Don't you think they'd understand why I entered this house in the first place?"

"No," Heidi and Ellie said simultaneously, then looked at each other and laughed.

"With the three of us here inside this house, that is highly unlikely," Heidi added over her shoulder as she looped her arm through Ellie's to guide her forward. "We seem to be on the not-so-hot list with the Heartsford Police Department at the moment."

Sammy couldn't argue with that one. "Yeah, I suppose. I'll have to call Nash on the way home and fill him in. I have to be honest, I'm not looking forward to that conversation."

Especially since she was hungry, tired, cold, and desperately in need of a cup of coffee and a hot shower. She didn't think Detective Nash would let this latest fiasco go easily. She'd much rather curl up under the warm covers of her bed.

Sammy was closing the drawer and looking up at a collage of photographs covering the ghastly old-fashioned wallpaper when a snapshot tucked in the corner of the frame caught her eye. The photo depicted a young man standing by a large pig holding a 4-H ribbon, a buddy's arm wrapped around his shoulder. The two were grinning from ear to ear. The young man was tall, but his features looked oddly familiar. Where had she seen this kid before?

Recognition hit like a bolt of lightning.

Jackson?

Heidi and Ellie were already walking toward the front of the house and were just about to reach the door when Sammy stopped them with a squeal. "You guys! You'd better come back here!"

"What is it?" Heidi unlooped her arm from Ellie, turned, and slowly retreated into the room.

Sammy shook a finger in the direction of the collage. "The photo. On the wall. I think that's Jackson," she uttered in almost a whisper, covering her mouth as if trying to contain the shock. "The other kid looks familiar too."

"Jackson? Why would there be a photo of Jackson on the wall in this house?" Ellie scrunched her nose and scratched the side of her head as she followed Heidi back into the room.

Sammy's eyes darted around the open space as she tried to put the pieces together in her mind. She pointed an index finger toward the dark wooden frame. "Jackson and a buddy from 4-H. Heidi, do you recognize them? This must be his friend's house or a relative or something. You guys, something weird is going on here." Sammy chewed the inside of her cheek nervously.

Heidi looked at the photo and then made eye contact with Sammy. "Yeah, it's Jackson. And swine boy." She returned her gaze to the collage and squinted her eyes to confirm. "That's definitely Adam." She cleared her throat. "It is an odd coincidence to find a photo of them on the wall, but Jackson did mention Adam is one of Marty's card buddies, did he not?" Heidi placed her hands on her slender hips and sighed heavily. "This isn't looking good, is it?"

"Uh-uh." Sammy said.

"Actually, I'm not really surprised. Jackson said Marty and Adam were card buddies, and Jackson is Marty's brother-in-law. These guys are all intertwined somehow."

"Well then, why is one of them inside this house cutting up magazines and crafting weird cryptic ransom notes?" Sammy's lip curled in confusion. "And I just thought of something else. How could I be so stupid? When Adam came into my shop, he said pharmacy drugs are like lethal poison! Don't you find it weird he was talking about poison, even if it was only in jest? Why would he say something like that?"

"We'd better get out of here." Ellie caught on to her sister's apprehension and encouraged her with a tug of her coat sleeve. "Come on, you guys, we need to leave this intel to the police."

"Ellie's right." In spite of herself, Sammy found herself acquiescing, because something weird was going on. But one thing was for sure: either Marty, Adam, or Jackson had had something to do with Wanda's death. There was just no other explanation. The question was: which one of the three? And why?

Chapter Twenty-Five

The return journey to Heartsford was quiet. Both Sammy and Ellie dozed in and out of consciousness, despite the bumpy ride in Heidi's Jeep. The cat nap was just what Sammy needed, as she knew Detective Nash would be meeting with her at home in less than an hour and she needed to prepare herself both physically and mentally. As soon as they'd locked up the farmhouse and the barn, she'd borrowed Ellie's phone to call him and received an expected earful from the officer.

Due to the winter parking restrictions during severe weather, her car had been towed away from the front of the Wadsworths' Queen Anne Victorian. The plows hadn't been able to get a proper sweep through the narrow road, apparently. Nash patiently informed her that she'd broken the law yet again and would have to pay a fine to retrieve her car. He also mentioned he'd been trying to get ahold of her via cell phone and he'd done his best to warn her ahead of said fine. And his biggest question: why was her car located there in the first place?

Now they needed to meet to discuss things. Especially with the latest development, she had decided not to share everything over the phone. If she did, he might go totally ballistic and put a warrant out for her arrest. Even though in her eyes her kidnapping wasn't the least bit her fault, she doubted the detective would see things from her point of view. She thought seeing him in person might be a way to diffuse the situation.

When the Jeep arrived in front of Sammy's house, Heidi looked through the rearview mirror and said, "I'll run over to Lynn's and pick up Bara for you and drop him off here, since you don't have a car. Then when I bring him home, I can take you to the tow lot to pick up your car. I might take a nap first, though." She chuckled. "Hopefully by then, your meeting with Nash will be over. Sound good?"

"Sounds terrific." Sammy clasped her hand to her heart. "Thanks, Heidi. I miss my pup so much!"

"Oh, and you'll be happy to know there's a surprise waiting for you inside the refrigerator," Ellie said, shifting in her seat to regard her. After interrupting herself with a muffled yawn, she added, "Meatball soup that was en route to church for our potluck event, but when Heidi and I began looking for you and came over here, I quickly abandoned that idea and stuffed it inside your refrigerator. I called the church office and told them I couldn't drop off a meal, as I had a family emergency. You're welcome." She smirked and then shifted back to gaze out the windshield.

Sammy jutted a thumb in the direction of her rented Cape Cod. "Are you sure you don't want it back? I can go get the soup for you." Although she secretly hoped her sister wouldn't want it back. Warm soup in front of the fireplace sounded very appealing.

"Nah." Ellie swatted away Sammy's offer with a hand. "You know I always make a double batch of everything and freeze whatever's left over. I would've brought the other half to the church, but it was already frozen. No worries. Enjoy it. Hopefully it'll warm you up after this crazy excursion." She leaned her head back on the headrest and closed her eyes again.

"Okay then, I won't argue about it. I don't think I have much in the way of groceries in the fridge anyway." Sammy unclicked her seat belt and opened the back door.

"Trust me. You don't." Ellie laughed, but her eyes remained closed.

"Thanks, Ellie. I think soup is just what the doctor ordered. Now that I'm home, my appetite is definitely returning too." Sammy stepped from the Jeep. "Thanks for the rescue, girls. You both get some rest, okay? I'll see you later." She shut the back door, smiled, and waved as the Jeep retreated from her driveway. Her sister and cousin returned the wave.

Since Sammy's keys were lost in a snowbank in front of the Wadsworths' Victorian, she was thankful she'd left a spare house key beneath the fake rock on the porch. She didn't even have to kick the snow off to reveal it, as Ellie and Heidi had evidently used the spare key recently to enter her house. Somewhere in the house she'd stashed a spare for her car too; hopefully she'd be able to locate it before Heidi returned.

Sammy opened the front door and felt the comfort of home surround her like a warm hug. She removed her coat and hung it on a nearby hook, then switched on the gas fireplace. A whoosh of warm air filled the living room with instant coziness. The events of the last few days had left her weary, and suddenly her muscles seemed to ache, as if she were suffering from the flu. She abandoned the licking flames of the fireplace, hauled herself up the oak staircase that led to the bathroom at the top of the stairs, and stripped off her disheveled clothing. As soon as she turned on the shower, the steam from the faucet filled the small bathroom, and she took it in reverently.

Sammy stood under the hot water with a whole new appreciation. If she'd had the time, she would've stayed in there all day, trying to rid herself of the feeling of the germy camper. She shuddered at the disgusting thought as she lathered up her favorite handmade citrus soap from Community Craft. After her body was finally thawed and refreshed, she stepped from the shower and wrapped up in an oversized towel. She combed her long auburn hair with a pick, removed the wetness with a few swipes of the blow-dryer, and looked at her reflection in the mirror. The shower had eased her aches and pains, which revived her at least enough to function under the impending firestorm of Liam Nash. However, she certainly didn't look rested, as heavy dark-gray shadows had appeared beneath her eyes. Would he blame her for being kidnapped, or would he have compassion on her? She wasn't sure but suspected it wouldn't be the latter.

Her body began to shiver again as the steam quickly evaporated and morphed to cold air, so she removed the wet towel, reached for her bathrobe on the hook behind the door, and wrapped herself in luxury. The soft fleece seemed to hug her, and if the detective hadn't been on his way over, she would've stayed wrapped in the robe for the remainder of the day. Unfortunately, that wasn't an option and she'd have to change clothes. She rubbed a little blush on her cheeks to brighten her slightly pallid complexion after her ordeal. Her eyes were tired and gritty, so she decided she didn't need to impress the detective with liner or mascara. She did, however, dab the gray circles with cover-up as best she could, though it scarcely hid the shadow. She smirked at her reflection and gave up.

Oh, why was she worried about it? Detective Nash had seen her look far worse. Besides, she had made peace with trying to impress Liam with her looks—that was coming to an end, and soon. It wasn't her style to be some made-up beauty queen anyway, so what was she trying to prove? He could take her as she was—or not at all. Not that it mattered. She didn't see any chance for their relationship to progress, especially when he had seemed so disappointed in her the other day.

She almost didn't want to spend any additional time with him for fear of seeing that reaction again. That wasn't an option either. If she didn't explain herself fully and tell him why her car had needed to be towed away from the Wadsworths' estate, she'd never earn the respect of the detective again. Plus, she had pertinent information related to his case, and she wouldn't hold back this time. She just wasn't sure how she'd explain it all without him losing his cool.

After brushing her teeth, Sammy looked at her image one last time before abandoning the bathroom and stepping into her nearby bedroom to get dressed. She chose her most comfortable pair of jeans, the ones with the hole in the knee, and long-sleeved white Cuddl Duds beneath a pale-pink zip-up. She hoped the pink would help lift the color to her tired, washed-out face.

Before she even had a chance to slip on her socks, the doorbell chimed, alerting her that her guest of honor had arrived. She breathed deep and stepped into her fuzzy slippers as she ran her hands nervously though her damp hair and brushed her long bangs away from her eyes. She took another deep breath before making her way down the oak stairs.

When she opened the door, the detective was playing around with the buttons on his cell phone and seemed distracted. She gestured him inside and then closed the door, hoping to keep the cold air out and the cozy fireplace heat in. “I was just about to reheat some homemade soup. Do you have time? Would you like some?” she offered.

Nash rubbed his hands together as if to warm them. “You know what, I think I’ll take the time and take you up on that offer.”

He smiled, but it seemed strained. Was that because he was still frustrated with her or because he was frustrated with the job? This was concerning, because she didn’t want to get off on the wrong foot yet *again*.

“Why don’t you warm up by the fire and I’ll bring you a cup?” Sammy gestured a hand toward the fireplace, and he followed her direction and stepped farther into the room.

“Where’s the pup?” His eyes darted around his feet and then back at her.

“Well, as I mentioned over the phone, I have some things I need to share with you. I thought it best to share them in person.”

Confusion swept across the detective’s face. “What does that have to do with Bara? Is he at the groomer? The vet? I hope he’s not sick.”

“No, I’ll explain everything. Just give me a moment, okay?” Sammy moved quickly into the kitchen and opened the refrigerator door. She retrieved the Tupperware container of soup, dumped it into a saucepan, and flicked it to simmer. While the soup slowly warmed, she returned to the living room and sat down on the love seat. The detective was seated comfortably on the recliner, scrolling through his phone.

"Any word on Marty?" Sammy asked tentatively.

"No. As you know, the FBI is involved and has been searching for him, and we have a BOLO out on his wife's car. A BOLO is . . ."

Sammy put up a hand to interrupt. "I know, 'be on the lookout.'"

"Yes," he interjected. "We've been keeping our eye on the Wadsworth home, and his wife's car seems to be missing suddenly. You didn't happen to steal it, did you? Although I didn't see it in your driveway, I suspect you're smarter than that." He held his arms tight to his body and then smirked, seeing the shock on her face. "Hey, I have to ask. After all, it was *your* car abandoned out in front of *their* house, and I'd really like to hear why. This better be good." His eyes grew intense, and he shifted forward on the seat and leaned on his arms with his hands folded, waiting with bated breath.

"What? Me?" Sammy held a hand to her heart. "Heavens, no!"

The mere suggestion almost knocked her from her seat. She wondered if his friend Ginger from the FBI had insinuated that Sammy was the reason Wanda's car was missing from the Wadsworth household. She decided to check on the soup. Maybe giving him something to eat would soften his reaction when she fessed up to what had really happened. She had a feeling this wasn't going to go well.

Sammy rose from the love seat. She was overtired and unprepared for an argument. If only she could retreat to her bedroom, lie down, pull her comforting quilt around her, and rest.

"Where are you going?"

"To the kitchen. I need to check the stove."

Sammy limped out of the room and tried to catch her breath before reacting poorly, as she felt her temper beginning to flare. How could he accuse her of such a thing? *Is this really what he thinks of me? Capable of grand theft auto? For heaven's sake, really?*

Instead of giving her a moment alone to calm herself, though, he followed her into the kitchen.

"What's going on with you?"

Sammy stood at the stove, reached into a nearby drawer for a large spoon, and began to stir the soup bubbling in the saucepan, her back turned away from him. "What do you mean?" she asked lightly, trying hard to calm her tone.

"I mean you're acting strange."

Liam moved closer, so close she could feel his warm breath on the back of her neck. Her body reacted to the closeness, and she wanted to turn from the stove and fall into his protective arms. She desperately wanted to feel what it would be like to be held by him for more than just a second, especially now, after all that had happened had left her raw.

But she wouldn't allow herself. Instead she continued to stir and said, "What do you expect? You basically insinuated I was capable of stealing a car, like I'm some sort of criminal!" She moved the spoon more rapidly and harder in the saucepan, and the soup spattered, causing it to splash and scald her arm.

"Ow!"

The detective reached over her shoulder, removed the spoon from her hand, and turned her away from the stove as she licked the warm soup from her arm.

"Talk to me."

"I'm going to talk to you, but to be perfectly honest, I'm a little afraid." Sammy paused. "Because, truth be known, I don't want to disappoint you again."

There, she'd said it.

"Disappoint me?"

"Yeah, that's right. I *care* what you think. Despite what you believe . . . I really do care." She bit her lower lip nervously. "That really hurt, what you said in there." She flung her hand in the direction of the living room. "Maybe I'm just overtired," she added under her breath.

After a pause, she continued, "I'm not a criminal, Liam. I'm only trying to help find justice for Wanda. I've only ever tried to help. That's who I am to the core." Her lip trembled slightly, and she thought if she didn't get it together, she could actually start to cry. "And you insinuating that I could be capable of a crime . . . What? *Really*? You don't know me at all." She turned her back on him, her shoulders drooping, and plunged the spoon back into the saucepan.

The detective turned her to face him again by placing a hand on her shoulder and encouraging her to turn around. "Please just tell me what's going on, will you?" His eyes softened. "This isn't helping. You need to talk to me."

Sammy didn't answer but reached for a nearby cabinet, fished out two large glass-handled mugs, and proceeded to fill them with a ladle that she removed from a hook hanging on the side of the cupboard.

"It smells delicious."

The detective stood over the stove, waved his hand in front of the saucepan, and breathed in the wafting steam. Sammy thought this was his way of deflection to get her to open up and talk again. He was darn good at his job.

"It sure does. I wish I could take the credit, but my sister actually made it. Meatball soup is one of her specialties. She cooks it every winter, and it's one of the few things that makes me look forward to January. It's like a hug in a mug. Here you go." Sammy handed the detective his oversized glass mug along with a spoon and then took hold of her own. "Let's go and eat our soup in front of the fireplace, okay? I've got a chill in my bones I can't seem to shake." When they arrived back into the living room, she signaled for him to take the leather recliner. "There's a table beside the chair if you need it." She indicated the wooden TV tray with a nod of her head as she sank into the nearby love seat, balancing her soup.

Before saying another word, she simply held the mug in her hands and felt the warmth of the heat emanating from within. It felt so good to be home. She hoped whatever she was about to share with Liam wouldn't take her away from the comfort of home and land her in a cold jail cell.

The detective was taking his first spoonful of soup when she said, "I saw Marty."

He nearly spit the soup from his mouth. "Excuse me?"

Sammy proceeded to tell him all that had happened, from the moment she parked her car in front of the Wadsworths' Queen Anne Victorian to her horrific ordeal during her kidnapping, and she didn't stop until she had unloaded the entire day's events leading up to that point. After she had finally relayed all that had occurred, she noted he hadn't gotten angry with her. Instead, he had only encouraged her to keep talking and seemed to grow more compassionate. She felt lighter, as if a weight had been lifted and the opportunity to talk openly with him was now back on the table. Maybe he wouldn't throw her in jail after all.

"And Marty let you go?" The surprise on the detective's face was priceless when he finally spoke. His reaction made her feel as if he'd thought Marty might somehow be involved in Wanda's death. He dug his spoon deep into the mug, came up with chunks of potato and meat, and dove into it heartily, which made her smile. Evidently she wasn't the only one who loved her sister's soup recipe.

"Yeah, he did. Which leads me to believe he's telling the truth. I don't think he poisoned his wife. Wouldn't he have made sure I didn't get out of the camper alive if that were the case? Besides, he told me someone held a gun to his head. Of course, he could have just been lying to me to create an alibi. Anyhow, I think something else is going on here. I found a picture of a guy named Adam with Wanda's brother, Jackson, at the farm where Marty brought me. Has Adam Boyd hit your radar yet? Allegedly, he's a friend of Marty's, and from what I understand, Adam was involved in the card games Marty was into. Apparently, large amounts of money have been changing hands at those gatherings. There's a chance this could be about money. Maybe a few of the guys he's been playing cards with wanted their money back? Although I'm not exactly sure what this would have to do with Wanda—unless they felt she was getting in the way."

Sammy's demeanor turned pensive. "What I can tell you is that Adam is somehow connected to the farm where Marty took me. Otherwise, why would there be a photo on the wall of him and Jackson? And I recently met the guy at Community Craft. He came into the shop and compared medicine to lethal poison. Interesting timing, in my opinion. Like maybe he knew something about Wanda being poisoned. How would he know?

The detective set his empty mug on the tray table beside the recliner. "The department has been following up on a few leads, but to be honest, the name Adam Boyd hasn't crossed my path yet. I did, however, find an interesting link between a few farmers that seems very disturbing and might possibly be a motive. But again, I'm not sure why Wanda would've been targeted and not Marty." The detective steeped his fingers and held them to his lips.

"How so? I mean, what's the link? Because I also heard Craig had some work issues going on with Marty too, and some important papers were tossed in the fire. Maybe Craig's involved somehow? There was a pretty big argument at my shop between Cheryl and Craig the night of Fire and Ice," Sammy said thoughtfully. She set her spoon aside and drank the tomatoey liquid until it was gone. She'd have to call Ellie and thank her again for leaving the food behind, as it hit the spot perfectly.

"Well, from some of the people I've interviewed, it seems there are a few farmers who are pretty ticked off about the seed Marty's been selling to their neighbors." The detective adjusted in the leather recliner, causing it to groan.

"Just to clarify—not seed Marty's been selling to them, but seed he's selling to their neighbors?"

"Exactly. Several of the farms adjacent to the ones that purchased seed from Marty seem to have a connection. They all lost more than half their crop this year. When the farmers began to exchange stories, they realized what they have in common, Marty's name keeps popping up. On all the neighboring farms, all but one, has lost acres of crop this past fall."

Sammy set down her empty mug and then snapped a finger. It was as if a lightbulb had gone on in her mind. "I think I know why."

The detective waited expectantly.

"Dicamba. I think Marty was selling dicamba-ready seed instead of Roundup-ready. When seed grows and it's been doused with dicamba, the pollen or parts of the plant grown from that specific seed have the potential to blow onto neighboring fields. The chemical is so strong, it can wipe out an adjacent crop. I don't think it's even been legally tested, or at least the testing hasn't been finished yet through the FDA. I think he's been selling test seed without the neighboring farms knowing it, and they have no way to protect their fields."

"How do you know all this?" Shock riddled the detective's face. "Since when did you become an expert on farm seed?"

"My aunt and uncle had a farm growing up—Heidi's parents were farmers. She knows a lot about seed, and I happened to find research on the Wadsworths' computer when I was . . ." She cleared her throat, realizing she'd taken the conversation a bit too far, and closed her lips and held them tight.

"When you broke into their house. Yeah, I heard about that." He eyed her. "Tim told me. Which, by the way, I have every authority to throw you in jail and toss away the key." He raked his hand through his thick hair.

Sammy grimaced. "I'm sorry. Are you going to arrest me?"

The detective didn't answer. Instead he lifted the empty mug off the tray table and peered into it with longing for more. "That was amazing, by the way." He set the mug back down and wiped his mouth with his hand. Sammy handed him a Kleenex, which was the closest thing she had to a napkin, since she'd forgotten to grab any when she was in the kitchen. "Can I get you a refill?"

"Nah, I'd better not. I don't have a lot of time. But thanks."

Nash didn't say any more on the subject of arresting her, so Sammy pushed forward. "Did you happen to get the toxicology report back yet? Do you know what poisoned Wanda?"

The detective paused and breathed deep, as if considering whether he should share. "It looks like a honey made with mountain laurel is the culprit."

Sammy stood from the love seat and began to pace the room. "*Mountain laurel*? Where does mountain laurel come from? Is it an herb supplement or something?"

"No, it's a wildflower grown in the Smoky Mountains, and—"

Sammy stopped midstride. Her heart began to pound, and she put up a hand to stop him midsentence. "Wait. Wanda and Marty took a trip to the Smoky Mountains this last summer with her extended family. Oh, it couldn't be, could it? That someone on that trip could've used something they picked up on their vacation? How horrible! Wait a minute! Adam had a Smoky Mountain key chain when he stopped in Community Craft!" Sammy whispered under her breath, more to herself than to Liam.

The detective stood from the recliner and moved close to her. "Sammy, listen to me. You've gotten in way over your head on this. I'm going to need you to stand down and trust me to do my job." His voice softened. "I'm worried about you. I think you've been through enough already." Their eyes locked, and for a moment, their self-protective walls came tumbling down.

Liam intimately brushed the hair away from her eyes. He looked at her with growing intensity and leaned toward her, and their lips were just about to touch when his cell phone rang, instantly jolting him back to the present moment. He reached for his phone and answered the call.

"Nash," he said curtly as he placed the cell phone to his ear. "I'm on my way."

Sammy searched him looking for answers.

"It's Marty. The FBI picked him up, and they're bringing him back to the police station. I've gotta go." He swiveled on his heel toward the door.

The close call of their kiss was over. Sammy felt the air seep out of her like a deflated balloon. She followed him to the front door and held it open for him. The detective turned to face her.

"I have to ask—do you want to come in and file a kidnapping charge, or can you hold off?" He reached to touch her gently on her cheek and rubbed it with his thumb, sending a new tickle down her spine. "I would never put you in danger, Samantha, but I think keeping Marty in custody is going to hamper my case. I need to be able to follow him after my interrogation to see what's really going on here."

"No, I can wait. Do what you have to do to get to the bottom of this. I understand," Sammy said with deep resolve. She reached for his hand beside her cheek and gave it a tight squeeze before he let go.

Sammy's eyes dropped to the floor, and a pause came between them. Then the detective reached for her chin so their eyes would meet and gave her a penetrating stare. "Trust me when I say, there will be a tail on Marty the minute he leaves the station. Not to worry. Keep your doors locked, though, and call me anytime, night or day, if you feel your safety is in jeopardy. Do you hear?" He waited for her nod before stepping out the door.

After he left, she realized there was one important thing she'd forgotten to mention before his abrupt absence—the cut-up magazine she'd found at the farmhouse.

Chapter Twenty-Six

Sammy paced in front of the storefront window at Community Craft, trying desperately to settle down and focus on her work. Her mind was otherwise occupied. Looking at the display window was a constant reminder that she hadn't yet put the final pieces together to determine who had caused Wanda to perish within the confines of her shop. Had Marty confessed? Did Nash think the man had faked his own kidnapping as a ruse? And what had happened between them during his interrogation? The detective had almost kissed her. She held a hand to her cheek as she felt a sudden rush of crimson rise to her face.

"What's with you today?" Deborah stepped in front of Sammy midstride to block her incessant pacing, grabbed hold of both her arms, and gave her a teasing shake to gain her attention. "You okay?"

"What do you mean? I'm trying to fix the display. Something's wrong with it; I just can't put my finger on what." Sammy frowned and lifted a finger to rest on her lower lip.

"Nothing's wrong with it." Deborah waved a hand of dismissal. "It looks great, and as a matter of fact, we've sold a lot of quilts because of it. Or maybe it's just because of the sudden rush of cold weather that we're selling so many quilts now. It's been freezing, which is quite good for blanket business! In any event, you look like a caged animal at the zoo longing to escape." She chuckled. "I'm wondering if people walking by on Main Street see the same thing." Deborah pointed out the window at a passerby, who lifted a hand in greeting at the sight of them.

Sammy laughed. "I won't argue that this weather has me feeling a little cagey. How many more days do we have until spring?" she sang out, stepping away from Deborah to adjust the soy candles on a nearby rack to ensure that all the labels were facing front and center.

"We've got quite a while before tulips will be popping around here," Deborah remarked with a laugh. She then returned to the cash register, where a customer stood patting Bara on the head and waiting patiently.

Sammy always smiled when she noticed her dog bringing a customer joy. She was so relieved and happy to have Bara back with her and in good health. Lynn had taken such good care of him that she'd have to take her to lunch, or at the very least coffee, as a token of gratitude.

She returned her attention to the display window and noticed Tim heading in the direction of Liquid Joy. She rushed out the door, lifted her hand to the side of her mouth, and yelled the officer's name until he turned in her direction and crossed the street to join her.

Sammy rubbed her hands up and down her sweater sleeves, shivering as she waited outside for the officer so she could have a private moment with him.

"What are you doing out here? Get back inside where it's warm, Sammy." Tim opened the door to Community Craft and stepped in behind her. "Look, if you're looking for intel by calling me over here, you're barking up the wrong tree."

Sammy looked over her shoulder to see if they were alone and could talk without anyone overhearing before she placed her hand gently on Tim's arm to diffuse his thought. He looked down at her hand on his arm and shook it loose, shrugging her off.

"I'm done sharing anything that goes on within my department with *all* you S.H.E.s." He gave her a dirty look. "Don't ask me another thing. I'm tired of getting in trouble over you three." He lifted three fingers and held them close to her nose.

"I know." Sammy brushed his hand away from her face. "I called you over here to sincerely apologize. For all three of us S.H.E.s. It's my fault. H and E would never have gotten so far involved in this if it weren't for me. I'm completely and totally one hundred percent responsible." She held a hand to her heart. "And it's crushing me to know the damage I've caused," she added sincerely.

The officer's thick blond brows narrowed, creating one continuous line across his face. He looked at her with growing suspicion, shaking his head. "I don't believe you. You're all consenting adults; how could this be solely your fault?" He flicked a finger in her direction. "Although you three do seem to revert back to your youth when you're in each other's company, I highly doubt you can control Heidi like a puppet."

"Tim, please," Sammy pleaded as she took his arm again. "I think you're making a big mistake blaming Heidi for this. She loves you, and I know for a fact she feels horrible for causing you any trouble with your job. She wouldn't have done any of it if she wasn't so loyal to me, though, which is why I think you should cut her some slack. You know, I'm convincing when I want to be with both my sister and cousin." She gave him a sly smile. "I've gotten both of them into a lot of trouble in the past, and I think I've finally learned my lesson."

The officer regarded her warily. "I highly doubt that. That you've learned your lesson, I mean. Even though your latest excursion led to your being kidnapped and might have gotten you killed, I don't see you stopping your sleuthing anytime soon." He tucked his hands inside his thick police belt and held them there firmly.

Sammy wasn't surprised he'd heard about Marty taking her against her will. "Please just think about what I've said and take it into consideration?" Sammy nudged him playfully with her elbow. "Promise me at the very least you'll marinate on it?"

"Okay, okay, I heard you. I appreciate what you're trying to do, Sammy, really I do." Tim's eyes left her as his attention was diverted by something on the other side of the glass front door. He opened it and yelled across the street. "Nash! Hey, Nash, over here." He signaled Liam with a whistle, caught his attention, and beckoned the detective to join them with his hand.

Sammy hadn't seen or heard from Liam since their near kiss. Her heart fluttered at the thought of it. She also wondered about the latest intel on Marty, but true to her word, with Officer Tim Maxwell present, she'd have to keep a tight lip. She watched the detective navigate the traffic to cross the street and join them. It wouldn't be easy . . .

"Greetings. What no-good thing are you two discussing?" Nash said in a teasing tone, giving a nod of his head. When Tim looked out the window for a moment at a passerby on Main Street, Liam winked at her, causing heat to rise in her cheeks. She hoped it wasn't noticeable.

"To be honest, I was just sincerely apologizing, and I'm hoping Officer Maxwell will reconsider things with my cousin," Sammy blurted. Why did she always say exactly what she was thinking the second she thought it? She wondered a little too late if this was something Tim had wanted to keep private, if he indeed kept his personal life separate from his work.

"Ah." Nash raised a brow and placed his hands on his hips.

"And you, Detective?" Sammy asked. "Jonesing for some afternoon pick-me-up over there?" She gestured a hand toward Liquid Joy.

He agreed with a smile.

"I forgot to tell you something very important. A significant detail that shouldn't be overlooked. The farmhouse where Marty took me had a magazine with cut-out letters in a wastepaper basket, like the ones used to create the ransom note. You may want to get a warrant and check it out," Sammy said, rubbing her hands up and down her arms in an attempt to warm up. She couldn't seem to get the chill out of her bones.

Nash took in the information and then studied her carefully. "Would you care to join me for a cup of Liquid Joy? Now that you've called me over here, I think I just figured out a way that you can help me." The detective looked pensively at her as he pondered and raked his hand through his curls.

"Pardon?" Sammy raised a hand to her ear to be sure she was hearing correctly.

I'm heading to Liquid Joy to grab a cup of coffee before my stakeout. Would you like to join me?" He crossed his arms across his chest and waited expectantly.

"Huh?" Sammy's heart beat with eagerness. "Do you want me to go with you? On a stakeout? Or just join you for coffee?" *Oh, please let it be the stakeout he's asking me to join.*

Tim took all this in with pure amusement, and Sammy swatted him with the back of her hand.

"Get your coat," Liam urged.

Sammy turned quickly on her heel, before the detective had the chance to change his mind, and rushed toward her office. "Deborah," she called out over her shoulder. "Can you cover for me this afternoon and close up on your own? I've been summoned on official police business." Sammy grinned as she rounded the corner to step inside her office and reached for her coat.

"Sure, no problem." Deborah shadowed, poking her head just inside the office door as Sammy was placing her knit hat on her head. "Does this have anything to do with the investigation into Wanda's death?"

"Yeah, and it sounds like the police are onto something pretty big and they need my help," she said as she buttoned up her winter coat and then slipped on her gloves.

"Get going then, Sammy. Please be careful though, okay? We kinda need you around here. Make sure and listen to that detective and don't put yourself in any more compromising positions," Deborah added warily.

"Thanks. I'll be back before close to pick up Bara. If something comes up and I can't make it back, I'll send Ellie over to get him."

She patted her dog on the head before meeting Liam by the front door. Tim was already across the street, stepping into Liquid Joy ahead of them.

"What's the plan?" Sammy's eyes searched the detective's penetratingly.

"I can't believe I'm saying this out loud." He chuckled. "I think I could use your help to set a trap. Are you up for that?"

"Absolutely!" Sammy beamed. "What do you want me to do?"

"Walk with me," he said, opening the front door of Community Craft. Sammy clutched the top of her winter coat and kept stride with him willingly. Together they crossed the street to Liquid Joy, where Tim was soon exiting with three covered cups in a coffee carrier.

"Looks like you finally got your wish." Tim eyed Sammy as the three walked along the sidewalk toward the alley leading to the police department. Sammy assumed they were heading to the back lot where the detective's car was parked.

"How do you mean?"

"I mean, your assistance is required in an ongoing investigation by our lead detective here." Tim jerked his elbow toward Liam, careful not to spill the coffee he was carrying.

"Yes, I guess I did get my wish. I must have worn him down," Sammy teased back. "Officer Maxwell, does this mean you won't be so hard on my cousin then?" she hinted.

"Let's keep Heidi out of this," Tim said with a warning smile as he removed his coffee cup and handed the other two that remained in the carrier to Sammy. The officer moved toward a patrol car and opened the door. "I'll meet you over there." He regarded the detective with a quick nod of his head and slipped into the SUV.

Sammy hurried to catch up with Liam, as she'd fallen a few steps behind due to the recurring pain in her ankle. "So, is it true? Have I really worn you down?" she asked.

"Something like that," he answered with a lopsided grin.

Sammy followed the detective to where his silver Honda Civic was parked. He opened the passenger door and held it for her.

"Sorry for the mess," he said as he quickly sidestepped in front of her. He brushed off the seat with the sleeve of his jacket and removed a potato chip bag, all before Sammy climbed inside, and then shut the door.

Liam slid into the driver's seat and settled in next to her. "Click it or ticket," he said. As soon as Sammy set the coffee in the cup holders between them, she followed his lead and clicked on her belt.

"Do you have your phone with you?" he asked as he started the engine.

Sammy removed her cell phone from her pocket and waved it in front of her. "I almost thought I'd have to get a new one, with this little puppy having been left inside my glove compartment in the cold overnight. Thank goodness it thawed. These things cost an arm and a leg." She grimaced.

The detective drove the Honda Civic to the very edge of the parking lot of the police department, put the car in park, and turned his head to face her squarely. "Before we start this, I need to be perfectly clear. Under no circumstances do you leave the safety of this car unless I allow it. Understood?" He held eye contact with her until he felt he had been clearly heard.

"Yes, you have my word." Sammy crossed her heart with her finger. "Where are we going? I feel like I'm being kidnapped again, minus my hands being tied." She lifted her hands to illustrate her freedom. "Do you want to let me in on what's going on?" She giggled nervously, though her nervousness came from excitement that he'd *finally* asked her for help in an ongoing investigation. This was epic. Not knowing what was coming next, however, left her breathless.

"As I mentioned, I didn't want to hold Marty last night. I had to let him go." Liam let out a whistle. "Keeping him in custody isn't going to lead me to the perp. So, I think I have an idea that might work."

"Okay?"

"Following him is my best bet."

"Do you think it's possible Marty faked his own kidnapping as a ruse? You think he was the one who poisoned his wife all along, don't you?" She turned to face him and watch his demeanor for confirmation.

"I'm not entirely sure," he admitted. "Marty was vague when I questioned him last night, and I just want to rule him out as a suspect so I can move on to others to interrogate if it isn't him," he said, tapping his fingers along the steering wheel. "Either way, elimination will help, I think."

"Okay, do you plan on letting me in on your plan of attack on how you want to do this?" she teased as she watched the familiar landmarks pass through the car window, trying to gauge exactly where they were going.

"Last night, before I left your house, do you remember what you said to me?" He turned his attention from the windshield to look at her, and suddenly she felt cornered. The only thing she remembered is that they had come dangerously close to kissing. As a matter of fact, she had dreamed about it all night. Her heart leapt at the thought. She didn't think that's what he was referring to, though, so she remained quiet in hopes that he would clarify. She could feel her face getting hot.

His eyes left hers and returned to the windshield to focus on driving. "You mentioned that Marty went to the Smoky Mountains with his extended family. That's where we believe he would have come up with the mountain laurel and turned it into a toxic honey, with which he potentially poisoned his wife." The detective paused.

"Yeah, so . . ." Sammy turned to him and watched the corner of his temple pulsate as if he was in deep thought.

"After hours of interrogation, he didn't give up anything regarding Wanda's poisoning. I began to think, I need to go at this from a different angle if I want a confession, or at the very least, I need substantial evidence. And since I don't want him on merely kidnapping charges, our best bet is to set a trap and hope he'll walk right into it."

"Sounds like a smart plan. I see where you're going with this, I think."

"To be clear, I want him on murder charges, not just kidnapping, if he did indeed poison his wife. There's no way I'm letting him get away with just a slap on the wrist. But then last night during my interrogation, every which way I tried, I couldn't get him to spill or slip up. So, if it really was Marty behind all of this, the only way to get the evidence I need to make it stick is to trap him. Either way, by process of elimination, I'll know whether or not he was indeed involved."

"Okay?" Sammy tried to piece together all that he was saying in her mind, but she wasn't sure she was totally following. "What do you want me to do? Where do I come in?"

"Here's my idea. I need you to make a phone call."

Chapter Twenty-Seven

"Who am I calling exactly?"

"Give Marty a call and tell him what you found inside the farmhouse. Tell him about the cut-up magazine and tell him you left the evidence exactly where you found it. Ask him if he thinks you should tell the police." The detective said this as if he was considering his plan and executing it in his own mind, yet he was letting her be privy to it all unfolding.

"I'm still a little confused. I think you're going to have to spell it out for me as clearly as possible so that I don't make a mistake." She looked down and unbuttoned a few buttons on her coat, as the adrenaline was causing her to sweat nervously.

"I want you to call Marty and tell him you found the magazine with the missing letters while you were looking for a phone to call for help. Tell him you know that whoever was in that house must be involved. You can even accuse him if you'd like. Which, to be honest, is one of the others reasons I wanted to bring you with me. If I know exactly where you are, I can protect you if he is indeed the killer and might try to retaliate during this ruse." He leaned over and tapped lightly on her hand.

Sammy flipped her hand in his and took hold of his hand, giving it a light squeeze before letting go. She loved that he was protecting her and considering her safety above all else.

"Here's the thing. When Marty shows up to remove the evidence, we'll know for a fact he's trying to conceal it and we'll know he's our killer. We'll have him cornered. Otherwise, why would he try to remove it? If he wasn't guilty and he didn't create his own ransom note, then his immediate instinct would be to call the police, right? We'll just have to sit and wait. I have dispatch ready to deploy additional backup if need be."

"Oh wow." Sammy fidgeted with her phone nervously. "Okay, I can do this." She evened her breathing. "Should I call him now?"

"Yeah, I have his number right here." The detective scrolled for Marty's phone number and then handed over his iPhone. "Here. If you call him now and it is indeed him behind all this, he'll rush over there to remove the evidence, but we'll have a few minutes' head start, so go for it. Use your phone, though, so he doesn't trace the call back to me."

Sammy's hands were trembling as she dialed the number. Marty answered on the second ring.

"Hello, Marty? It's Sammy Kane." She swiped the phone to speaker, filling the car with the sound of his voice. Maybe the detective could use Marty's words as evidence as well, if need be.

"I see you found your way home," Marty said sarcastically.

Sammy's phone almost slipped from her clammy hand as she chuckled and tried desperately to lighten the conversation. "Yeah, especially after all you put me though. You're lucky I didn't freeze to death out there. Did you know I ran out of propane in the middle of the night? Despite what you put me through, I've decided not to press charges." She eyed the detective, whose eyes left the windshield momentarily and looked at her intently before returning his eyes to the road ahead.

"Yeah, well, I'm not going to feel indebted to you for that. You seem to think it's okay to be in everybody's business, so you kind of brought it upon yourself. Look, I'm packing to get out of here. I'm not sure why you called me, but I have to go."

"Wait!"

"What is it? Why are you pestering me? You really are a tenacious one, aren't you?"

Sammy tapped the detective on the thigh while saying, "I called to help you. I think whoever owns that farmhouse might be responsible for everything that's happened. Maybe even your wife's death."

"What did you say?"

"I found a cut-up magazine with letters missing. Just like the letters in the ransom note your brother-in-law Jackson was sent."

"Did you tell the police?"

Sammy's eyes darted to the detective, and he shook his head no.

"No. No, I wanted to call you first. Should I go ahead and notify the police?"

The detective nodded and patted her arm encouragingly.

"Where did you find it?"

"Inside the farmhouse. I found a key in the barn and went in to use the phone."

"Thanks. I'll pass on the information to the police—not your concern. Goodbye, Sammy."

"'Bye." Sammy clicked the phone off and then took a deep breath. She hadn't realized she'd been holding her breath through the entire conversation.

"You okay?" The detective held the steering wheel with both hands but turned toward her briefly to check on her.

"Yeah, I'm fine. Now what? We wait, right?" Sammy unbuttoned the remaining buttons on her coat and opened it beneath the seat belt.

"Right. Something you're not very good at," he teased with a lopsided smile.

Sammy responded with a toss of her hand. "Did you catch that Marty said he was packing?"

"Yeah, and that's interesting news, since I told him not to go too far. I'm not worried about it; the FBI is hanging close to him to see if these mysterious kidnappers show themselves anyway. I doubt he could use the bathroom without them knowing it. He's just not aware that their presence is all around him."

The remainder of the ride was eerily silent between them as Sammy wrestled with one last thing she hadn't yet shared.

"Liam?"

"Yeah?"

"There is one more thing that may or may not be relevant to this case."

"What's that?" His eyes remained on the road rolling endlessly before them. They must be getting close, as the houses were becoming fewer and farther between. Sammy instantly flashed back to the desolation and fear she'd felt when Marty had taken her against her will. Goose bumps rose on her flesh—and not from the cold.

"You okay? I lost you for a second." The detective reached out and nudged her lightly.

Sammy smiled, returning to the present and the man sitting next to her, who would surely protect her this time from any impending danger.

She deflected her fears by returning to the subject at hand. "Yeah, I'm fine. Sorry, I was just thinking about whether I should share something that was hidden and private to Wanda. I found a cryptic rhyme inside her quilt. The quilt Wanda draped across her lap the night she died. I'm not exactly sure what she was trying to say with that message, but the quilt was also part of a trail map that someday I think she hoped someone would figure out. Or maybe it was just some weird way of keeping herself sane."

"Rhyme? How odd. What'd it say?"

"*The blocks pieced on this quilt release me of guilt,* or something along those lines. You haven't uncovered an affair or anything during your investigation, have you?"

"No. Everyone I interviewed confirmed the opposite, that Wanda was very loyal in her marriage. Apparently, her husband was the jealous type and constantly accused her of infidelity. Maybe because she was fit and attractive, he felt insecure, but everything I've heard thus far is that she was loyal and trustworthy."

"So, what else do you think Wanda felt guilty about? And why piece together a quilt of a trail map if it meant nothing? It had to mean something for her to stick that rhyme in there. Don't you think?"

"What I think is, I like the way your mind works." He turned and winked at her before easing the car to a stop alongside the road in front of a familiar landmark. Tim pulled up alongside and rolled down his window as the detective did the same, sending a rush of cold air into the car.

"I'll take the back of the farmhouse on foot," Tim said as he rolled ahead to conceal the SUV patrol car far in the distance.

Sammy shuddered from the cold and from dread. She didn't know how she was going to feel returning to the farmhouse, and she was surprised at her amount of unease. Her eye caught the painted quilt block that hung on the barn, and she tried to focus on the intricacy of the log-cabin pattern instead of her growing anxiety. *The painted quilt blocks have to mean something . . . what do they mean? What else do all these farms have in common?*

"All right, we need to find a clear stake out position where we can still see the front of the house, since Officer Maxwell will take the back. Where do you think we should hide, partner?"

"Partner?" Sammy's eyebrows wiggled in amusement. "I like the sound of that."

"I thought you would." He smiled wide, sending a pleasant ripple down her spine. She wondered if they'd ever get the opportunity or the right moment to attempt that kiss again.

Sammy pointed to a group of trees on the opposite side of the road. "You think you can sneak your little Honda in there?"

"I can try."

The detective swung the steering wheel hard and turned the car in the direction of the trees. Luckily, because of the great low canopy of pine branches, there was just enough room to tuck the car beneath them without shoveling. Anyone who was paying attention would see the tire tracks and find them. Hopefully, whoever was about to show up would be much too preoccupied with removing evidence than to notice someone watching them.

When parked, the detective stretched across her lap to reach the glove compartment. "Excuse me," he said, and Sammy caught a slight whiff of aftershave as his arm passed in front of her. He reached inside, pulled out two miniature sets of field glasses, and handed her one. "It's official. Go ahead and spy. Since you're so into this, wake me when you see something," he added, before he set his head back on the headrest and closed his eyes.

Sammy nudged him playfully. "Seriously? You're going to let me do all the dirty work here?"

She placed the binoculars up to her eyes and peered out of them. She turned to view the side of the farmhouse to see if she could catch where Tim would be hiding, but she couldn't locate him. Apparently, he was doing a very good job of it. She dropped the binoculars to her lap momentarily and gazed over at the detective, who looked relaxed in the seat next to her. It felt as if eons of nothing but quiet ensued before they spoke again.

"Are you awake?" she whispered.

"Uh-huh. Why, you got something?" he said, keeping his eyes shut.

"Yeah."

He scrambled to attention, wiped his eyes with the back of his hands, and fumbled for his binoculars.

"I'm only kidding," she said sheepishly, feeling bad that she'd jolted him from his comfortable state. "Go back to resting. Can I ask you something, though?"

"What's that?" Instead of heeding her advice, he reached for his coffee in the cup holder and took a sip, then balanced the cup on his lap.

"What evidence do you have against Randy? I'm just curious."

"Oh, you haven't heard yet? I thought for sure you'd be the first one called after we spoke with him."

"So you did bring him in?"

"Yes, just before meeting you this morning. And don't worry, we cleared him."

"So, what'd you have on him, then? You know I'll find out eventually!"

The detective chuckled. "His fingerprints were on a metal fireplace box we found located inside the Wadsworths' closet. Apparently for good reason. Randy hid it in the closet for a showing appointment. He assumed there were valuables inside, and he thought it wasn't wise to leave it out in the open. But when we found it, it was empty."

"Ah. So, I'm guessing you wanted to make sure Randy hadn't been the one to empty it?"

The detective nodded.

"I'm glad he's cleared, then." Sammy was sure Ellie would be thrilled too.

The detective let out a yawn and then sighed. "I'm beat." He rubbed at his tired eyes with his fingers. "I didn't exactly sleep well last night knowing I had potentially let a murderer walk right out of my department after his interrogation."

"A lot of pressure, huh?"

The detective smiled and wiped his face with his hand as if to will himself awake. "Let's just say, some nights are better than others."

"I'm just curious, why didn't you invite your friend Ginger from the FBI on this little excursion?" Sammy hinted with a smile.

Nash chuckled. "The FBI was only involved because Marty was a missing person and his wife's death had been ruled a homicide. Once Marty was brought in, our need for their assistance was pretty much over. The only thing they're now paying attention to is Marty to see if these so-called mystery kidnappers show. Personally, I get the feeling Ginger's thought pattern is that the guy was never kidnapped in the first place. He's a liar, and hopefully we can prove that today. Besides, you don't bring a whole cavalry when you're trying to be discreet. I would've thought you of all people would understand that," he said teasingly, and lifted the coffee to his lips again.

"Look, here comes a truck." He pointed a finger out the windshield and set his coffee back into the cup holder.

Sammy peeked through the binoculars, and just as the detective had said, a blue truck was pulling into the driveway and parking next to the farmhouse. Whoever it was, the person wasn't concerned about being discreet. Although she could understand why, as it wasn't exactly Grand Central Station around here. No one was within sight for miles.

"Who is it?" Nash nudged her with his elbow, causing the binoculars to shift and skew her view.

"I don't know. I can't tell. I can only tell you it looks like a man based on his height and the way he's dressed. He's opening the front door of the farmhouse now."

The detective confirmed that his weapon was sitting correctly in the holster that crossed his chest before he opened the car door.

"Please let me go with you. Whoever it is isn't expecting anyone. It's highly unlikely this could get dangerous. Please?" Sammy hoped her begging didn't sound like a whine. "Besides, it's getting cold inside the car without it running, and I'd be safer with you than without you. Don't you think?" She wondered if her puppy-dog eyes would have any effect on his answer.

"No, Samantha," he said firmly.

The detective closed the car door carefully so as not to make a noise and put his fingers to his lips to signal for her to remain quiet. She followed his lead and sank down in her seat but proceeded to peak over the dashboard. Nash moved quickly across the street, and even in the snow, he seemed spry. He removed his weapon from his holster and held it at his side while he signaled her to stay inside the car. The detective waited a few minutes to ensure the person was deep inside the house. After a few moments, he entered the front door of the farmhouse, his weapon drawn.

Sammy sat in the car, looking through the binoculars, and grew frustrated at not seeing a thing. She dropped them to the seat and wrestled a moment with her decision but then quietly opened the car door. Before thinking it completely through, she found herself racing across the street to follow Nash and stepping through the front door.

At the sound of Sammy closing the screen door, the man turned, and Liam said, “Don’t move.”

Jackson stood holding the magazine in one hand. When he looked in her direction, confusion contorted his face, as if he couldn’t place her.

Detective Nash gave Sammy a frustrated glare warning her to stay put. He then turned to face Jackson. “Is this your place?”

Nash knew it wasn’t, but Sammy figured he was trying to get the suspect to relax and open up. He put his weapon back in his holster to befriend his opponent instead of coming off as threatening, now that he knew Jackson was most likely unarmed.

“No, no, it’s not,” Jackson answered, and then regarded Sammy. “Wait. You’re related to Heidi. You brought food over for my family the other day. You’re the owner of the craft shop. Community Craft, right? What are you doing here?”

Jackson scratched his head as he tried to figure out why she was standing in the middle of the living room of a farmhouse that didn’t belong to either of them, accompanied by a detective asking pointed questions.

“No, Jackson, what are you doing here? Are you still friends with Adam after all these years? I saw the 4-H photo from your youth on the wall. This must be his family’s farm.”

"Yes, Adam's father is down south for the winter. Marty suggested I help them out to earn a little extra winter money. They needed someone to check in from time to time, and that's why I'm here. What are you both doing here, and who are you, anyway?" Jackson's eyes left Sammy and traveled to the detective. "Quite an entrance you made there with guns blazing!" He chuckled nervously.

Sammy gestured a hand toward the officer, and he introduced himself. "Detective Liam Nash, Heartsford Police Department." Nash thrust out a hand for Jackson to shake, and Jackson took it willingly. "We were wondering why someone was entering this home that is obviously vacant. We thought it might be a break-in."

The detective stopped short and eyed Sammy as if he had a plan. She had no idea where he was going with this. She wondered if Marty had confided to Jackson that he'd brought her here. That would blow everything. Sammy remained quiet and let him take the lead.

"So, that's why you're here?" Nash asked. "To check in from time to time on your friend's family's farm?"

"Yep," Jackson said innocently. "Just making sure the pipes don't freeze in this bitter cold."

"And the ransom note that you just 'happened to drop' while we were at your house?" Sammy threw up her fingers in air quotes. "That was written with the magazine in your hand," Sammy blurted. "This is where *you* wrote it, didn't you? The question is, why? Why kidnap Marty? Did you want the large amount of money you mentioned he had hidden in his gun safe from all his card winnings? You didn't care who you showed the fake ransom note! Just as long as it gave you a solid alibi. Is that it?"

Jackson's eyes flew to the detective to gauge his demeanor. "I don't know what you're talking about," he said, holding up the cut-up magazine in a defensive stance.

"What've you got there?" The detective nodded in the direction of Jackson's hand, and he looked down at what he was holding as if he knew he was busted. His face turned instantly ashen.

Jackson fumbled for the right words. "Hey, Marty knew what he was doing was wrong . . . and he wouldn't stop. Craig showed him the test results, proving in black and white that he was destroying people's lives with what he was selling. And what does Marty go and do? He tosses the results in the bonfire. He *knew* the seed he was selling was doused in poison. Poison! He knew it, and he refused to fess up to what he'd done. Marty's a fraud and a thief! No one could stop him, including my sister, so I did what I had to do."

"Oh nooo." Sammy's hands rose to her cheeks. "I just figured it out. Wanda wasn't your intended target, was she? Marty was. Marty sold seed to the farm adjacent to yours, didn't he? And that resulted in you losing more than half your crop, leading to a huge loss in profit. I remember you telling us you didn't know why you lost half your crop this year. Actually, you had a pretty good idea, didn't you? Because Wanda told you—didn't she? She knew what was going on, she knew her husband was selling experimental seed, and so she created a map of all the farms affected. She was waiting for the perfect time to expose her husband, but you couldn't wait, could you?

You meant for Marty to be poisoned, but your own sister used the honey. You didn't want Marty to do any more business in the farming industry, and you hated the way he treated your sister, but you poisoned the wrong person. You accidently poisoned your sister."

Jackson looked like a deer in the headlights. He dropped the magazine to the floor and bolted for the back door.

"Not so fast." Officer Maxwell popped out from behind a nearby wall, drew his weapon, and blocked Jackson. He kept the gun steady, pointing directly at the man's heart. "Put your hands above your head where I can see them. Do it now," Tim added firmly.

While Tim clicked on the handcuffs, Sammy asked, "So why kidnap Marty? Was it all about the money in the gun cabinet? Were you really going to kill him too?"

Jackson lifted his eyes to meet her gaze, looking defeated. "I had no choice. If I didn't stop Marty, he would've continued destroying farms across the state of Wisconsin. I planned to kill him after his capture, but I choked. I couldn't take another life. And then the jerk escaped anyhow."

"Where's the money?" Nash pushed.

"Hidden. My plan B was to try and make it look like Marty was using the money to flee after killing Wanda."

Sammy interjected, "After Marty escaped, you stole the money from his gun cabinet, knowing full well the police would find it empty, and then you lied to me, Heidi, and Ellie. Correct?"

Jackson didn't answer. His eyes dropped to the floor.

"What about the magazine?" Nash asked.

"I came here thinking Marty must have been hiding out in his camper, but I couldn't find him. I looked everywhere, including inside this house, which is when I got the idea for the ransom note. And if I had been smart enough to burn this magazine, we wouldn't be having this discussion, would we? No one would ever think in a million years it was me. I'd hoped the kidnapping at least would bide me some time. Guess that really worked out as an epic fail." Jackson hung his head.

Sammy watched in numb shock as Tim dragged Wanda's brother out the door and across the snow-covered lot into a recently arrived squad car. She wished she felt better, but watching this unfold had left her cold and traumatized.

"You know the sad part?" Sammy asked as she moved to stand next to Liam.

"What's that?"

"Jackson's inherently a good guy. He let bitterness toward his brother-in-law get the best of him, leading him to spin an alibi completely out of control. If his guilt hadn't led him to this twisted cover-up, you probably never would have caught him, would you?"

"You'd be surprised how many convictions I get due to a guilty conscience and the incessant need to try and cover things up."

"Does it ever go away?"

He turned to face her. "Does *what* ever go away?"

"The underlying sadness that finding the truth uncovers. Does it ever help to know the truth? If only people could reach out and talk to one another . . . and really listen to what the other had to say . . . wouldn't a lot of this be avoided, then?"

"I'm afraid it's not that simple."

"If only people could communicate." Sammy pushed her hands deep into her coat pockets.

"Yeah." He turned to her. "If only people could listen and follow directions." He bopped her on the nose with his finger.

"Touché." She smiled sheepishly.

Chapter Twenty-Eight

The resolution behind the mystery into Wanda's tragic death set the town of Heartsford back on its axis. Folks passed in and out of Community Craft with less chatter on their lips regarding her untimely passing and began focusing on the life she'd led, thus beginning the healing process. Everyone recalled the kindness and warmth Wanda had added to their sweet little town. Her lap quilt hung in a prominent place above the back door as a reminder of the life she'd shared willingly and the quilts she'd made and selflessly given away within their community. Since her husband was now serving time on kidnapping charges and Jackson was headed for life in prison, Sammy felt it fitting to keep the quilt where Wanda's "chosen family"—the quilters and seamstresses of Community Craft—spent the most time.

Heidi stepped through the back door and eyed Sammy looking at the quilt. "Wanda's work of art looks perfect up there. I like that you can see it immediately if you walk in off Main Street." She pointed toward the front entrance of the building.

"Yeah, me too. It's a pretty amazing quilt too. The fact that Wanda quilted those blocks together to atone for her husband's wrongdoings. She wanted the farmers affected to at least be part of the trail map. She felt they all deserved something to make up for her husband's bad judgment. She convinced the committee to paint barn blocks for each and every one of them."

"She was pretty amazing that way."

"Yep, she sure was," Sammy said with a lump forming in her throat. "The quilting group decided that instead of quilting something in her honor, we'd each sew a block and patch it together to donate to someone special. That's what Wanda would've wanted."

Heidi wrapped her arm around Sammy's shoulder and gave it an encouraging squeeze, then looped her by the arm. The two stepped deeper into the shop and met Ellie by the cash register.

"I just locked the front door. Another day in the books," Ellie said, rubbing her abdomen. "Time to get home and make supper."

"How are things with you and Randy? Getting back to normal, I hope?" Sammy asked cautiously.

"Yeah, we're getting there." Ellie smiled. "You think you know everything about a partner, and then you learn you don't." She sighed. "Life is full of surprises, isn't it?" She looked down at her belly. "Randy's been sweet lately, though. He's even agreed to paint the nursery. Gender-neutral of course," she added with a gleam in her eye.

"Any word on Wanda's house?"

"Randy thinks he might have a potential buyer. We'll see. Looks like the money from the sale will go to pay Marty's lawyer. As well as the money Jackson stole from Marty's gun safe. How's that for irony? I still can't believe Jackson deliberately dropped that envelope with the ransom to solidify his alibi in front of witnesses. Apparently, he was waiting for just the right group of mourners to cement his case, and there we came. Seriously, if Marty hadn't had the smarts to escape and hop in the back of that freight train to Heartsford and go into hiding, he might not have survived either. Jackson had already taken one life; his conscious wouldn't allow him to take two, but if he'd had more time, he might've got the courage. He thought for sure the police were on to him, and the truth is, he probably would've gotten away with it!"

"Crazy. Jackson went back to Adam's family farm looking for Marty, and he must've literally just missed him! Do you know how close to death I was?" Sammy shuddered and shook her head in disbelief. "I can only think of poor Wanda and what her own family did to her. First her husband, then her brother. What a shame."

Heidi piped up, "Can you imagine that one bad move led Wanda to drink that poison? Apparently, she never added honey to her morning tea. That was Marty's routine. For some strange reason she decided to sweeten her tea that one day—huge mistake. That's where Jackson really messed up, making that mountain laurel honey concoction. Can you imagine hurting your own sister like that by accident? He'll have to live with that for the rest of his life behind bars. Hopefully Teyla and the kids will be okay."

"That's what makes me really sad. Jackson's kids losing their aunt, and now their father is headed for life in prison. Their uncle will do some time also. So sad." Sammy hung her head.

"And what about you, Miss Heidi?" Ellie rose a brow and nudged her cousin playfully with an elbow.

"What do you mean?" Heidi asked.

"You're all dressed up in those knee-high boots." Ellie took her cousin by the hand and spun her in front of them. "Perfect makeup . . . and your hair looks beautiful tied back with that bejeweled butterfly pin. What gives?"

"I'm on my way to meet Tim at the Corner Grill for a pizza," Heidi said, fluttering her eyelashes as a cautious smile rose to her lips.

This news grabbed Sammy and Ellie's attention.

"Just talking . . . we'll see." Heidi chuckled. "Thank you, Sammy. I heard you talked to Tim on my behalf, and I do appreciate it," she added seriously. "I stopped by here before dinner because I'm actually curious about this one." She nodded her head in Sammy's direction. "Rumor has it you have plans for this evening?"

"I'm on my way to meet Nash. I've been summoned." Sammy shrugged.

Heidi and Ellie exchanged an amused look.

"What?" Sammy asked innocently.

* * *

For the life of her, Sammy couldn't understand why Nash had asked her to meet him at the south end of the Ice Age Trail. The trail had been named after the landform dated some ten thousand years ago during the Ice Age when a series of ridges had formed from glaciers in southeastern Wisconsin. These mile-long ridges spanning over a hundred miles featured craterlike depressions created from melting ice, and the trail connected across the entire midwestern state. Hikers had the opportunity to enjoy the vastness of nature, from tall pines and prairie grasses to rivers, lakes, and wildflowers. But during the winter, it was a frozen sea of white where hikers kept on with their fitness plans despite the bone-chilling weather.

Dress warm, he'd told her. *I have a mystery I need help solving.* His cryptic message had left her guessing. Had he found a body out on the trail? A clue to an unsolved mystery from a cold case? An abandoned wallet or key left behind, for which he couldn't determine the owner? What case was he working on that he needed her help with? The fact that he had asked for her assistance was mind-blowing. She was surprised he was willing to give her that kind of opportunity again. Maybe she'd impressed him and he appreciated her help in solving Wanda's murder after all.

Sammy noted the familiar brown sign at the edge of the road with the golden words painted deep within their lettered crevices: *Ice Age Recreational Scenic Trail.* She turned her car in the direction of the plowed lot and parked next to Detective Nash's familiar silver Honda Civic. She looked to her left through the driver's side window to greet him and found his car was empty. Sammy frowned and then looked around in confusion. She'd assumed he'd be waiting for her in a warm car. She was wrong. Sammy adjusted her hand-knit hat tighter to her head and tucked her scarf around her neck before giving her coat a final button to the top and exiting her vehicle.

She closed the car door, and the silence was deafening. Only two cars, hers and Nash's, were parked in the lot; the remainder was empty. Tall pines towered above her head, framing a magenta sunset painted across the western sky. The temperatures had warmed to a balmy twenty-five degrees, but she still couldn't fathom why the detective would ask to meet her here, especially when it'd soon be dark. Could it not wait until morning? She looked over both shoulders to locate him and turned around on her heel. Nothing.

Where was he?

She was just about to return to her car and retrieve her cell phone out of the glove compartment to text him when she looked down and saw something red standing out from the white of the snow at her feet. Her eyes sought to identify the foreign object, and as she leaned closer to retrieve it, she realized it was a rose petal. *That's odd. How did a rose petal survive out here in the cold? And how did it get here among this sea of white?* She tucked the petal into her coat pocket and moved toward the foot of the trail, where the trees opened to a wide clearing.

That's when she saw it.

The pines were lined with luminaries on each side, lighting the trail as if she were in a glowing dream. She blinked her eyes to confirm what she was seeing. Scattered along the center of the trail, rose petals were dropped like bread crumbs leading directly through the center, where Liam Nash stood with a lopsided smile.

"You found me."

Sammy smiled wide. "What's this, Detective? I thought you said you needed help with a mystery." Sammy looked beyond him and noted the luminaries far surpassed where he was standing. It seemed as if the entire trail was lit, all the way to the bend in the path.

"Yes, I do." He nodded slowly and didn't move. Instead he waited for her to come closer to where he stood among a scattering of rose petals grouped around his feet.

"What's the mystery, then?" she asked when she was nearly a foot away from where he stood. She tucked her glove-covered hands into her coat pockets and smiled.

"For someone who's so astute, I'm surprised you haven't figured it out," Liam teased.

"Well, I guess you have me stumped!" Sammy admitted with a laugh.

"The mystery is why you and I can't seem to communicate, even though we both know we feel something for each other. Someone had to take the first step, and I thought this might help." He gestured to the lighted path. "I think it's time we blaze a new trail, Samantha. Leave our past behind and find the light in our world as it is—here and now." His tone grew serious, but his eyes were wells of liquid chocolate. "I want us to be able to share who we really are, and this is me." He held his arms out wide before dropping them to rest at his sides. "I've shown more of myself to you than anyone. This is me." His voice grew hoarse.

Sammy smiled. "You've witnessed my true self and didn't seem to appreciate my finer qualities," she teased, her smile widening. "You know, my tenacity seems to get on your nerves a little."

"Well, when it comes to my work, some of your *finer qualities*, as you call them, could use a little fine-tuning." He smiled, showing the tooth that jutted out just a little on his lower jaw.

"I suppose . . ." she agreed. "I tend to get in the way of your job sometimes, and I do apologize for that. I'll work on it."

He held up a gloved hand to stop her. "But when it comes to my personal life, you're exactly what I need." He spoke with a shyness Sammy had not yet experienced from him.

"Okay then, since we're being completely transparent and honest with each other, I have something that's been bothering me. Just a tad." Sammy pinched her fingers together to show him how little as her eyes crinkled into half-moons.

"What's that? I can take it. Bring it on. Tell me." He stood proudly with his hands on his hips, smiling expectantly down at her.

Sammy chewed her lip. She wanted the words to come out honestly and vulnerably, not accusingly, but this was who she was, someone who didn't hold back. This would be a true test. Would he appreciate her honesty? She decided to go for it.

"The other day, when you introduced me to Ginger from the FBI, it sort of hurt my feelings to know you had been speaking ill of me behind my back. If I'm being honest, as we are right now . . ." She paused. "I don't like it when people talk about me behind my back. I'd rather you just say it to me. Right to my face." Sammy waved a hand between them and then waited. "Be who you are . . . with me and without me. Be the *same*, all the time," she reiterated. "That's really important to me in relationship."

The detective cocked his head in surprise. "I'm not sure I understand what you mean. Talking badly about you? I'd never utter an unkind word about you."

Sammy cleared her throat. "When Ginger said, 'You're the one . . .'" Sammy closed her eyes and breathed in to center herself, but when she opened her eyes to continue, she noted a wide smile across the detective's face. "What's so funny? I'm being serious right now!"

"Sammy, Sammy," he said, shaking his head.

"What?" She threw her hands up innocently, and he grabbed them and pulled her in close, so close that his warm breath was on her. He leaned over, cupped her face in his gloved hands, and kissed her.

When their eyes finally met, he whispered, "Don't you know yet, Samantha? You *are* the one."

Patched Flight

Original Quilt Block Pattern by Carol Jensen
For questions on this pattern, email:
CaradoraDesign@yahoo.com
Or visit her on Facebook: Caradora Design

Lap quilt is twelve blocks with a finished top size of 42 inches wide × 57 inches long

Materials

2¼ yards light-colored fabric
2¼ yards dark-colored fabric
¾ yard medium-colored fabric for sashing

Block assembly

Each block will need four light and four dark 3½-inch squares and eight pieced triangle squares. Finished block size is 12 inches.

First Row

1. Cut light and dark fabric into 3½-inch strips and 4-inch strips.
2. Cut each strip into 3½-inch squares and 4-inch squares.
3. Take the 4-inch squares and cut on the diagonal to make two equal triangles.

4. Sew together one light triangle to one dark triangle on long diagonal edge.
5. Sew a light square to the pieced square along the leg of the dark triangle, with the dark triangle on the top.
6. Piece together another square from one light and one dark triangle. Sew the pieced square along the leg of its light triangle to a dark square, with the light triangle on the bottom.
7. Sew together the two sets with the solid squares on the outside, creating one strip of four squares.

Second Row

1. Sew a pieced square along the leg of the light triangle to a dark square, with the light triangle on the bottom.
2. The second set will be a light square sewn to the leg of a pieced square, with the dark triangle on the bottom.
3. Sew together the two sets with solid squares in the middle. Now you will have the second strip in the block.

Third and Fourth Rows

1. To form the third row, repeat the second strip, but turn so that solid squares are alternated in the middle.
2. The last strip requires the same assembly as the first strip, but turn so that the dark square is on the bottom left.

Now sew together the four strips to create your block.

Sashing

Cut three 3½-inch strips of medium-colored fabric. Cut the strips into eight 12-inch pieces that will be sewn between each block in each row. Now cut three more 3½-inch strips of medium sashing fabric and sew a strip between each row. This should complete your quilt top.

Recipes

Sammy's Crustless Spinach Quiche (for a cold, snowy morning)

Ingredients

1 tablespoon olive oil or butter

½ sweet Vidalia onion, finely chopped

½ small package fresh cremini mushrooms, sliced

1 clove fresh garlic, minced

Few handfuls fresh spinach, washed and dried with a paper towel

5 organic eggs from a local farmer

Salt and pepper

3 cups Wisconsin cheese: 1 cup shredded cheddar and 2 cups pepper jack (if this is too spicy, adjust cheeses to taste; for example, flip amounts to 2 cups cheddar and 1 cup pepper jack, or use all cheddar)

4 to 6 slices crisp cooked bacon, crumbled

Assembly

1. Preheat oven to 350 degrees.
2. Lightly grease a 9-inch pie pan.
3. Heat oil or butter in a skillet.

4. Sauté onion and mushrooms in the skillet. Add garlic and wilt spinach.
5. In a large bowl, scramble the eggs with a fork and then add salt and pepper.
6. Fold the cheese into the eggs.
7. Add the spinach mixture and crumbled bacon into the bowl of eggs.
8. Pour into the greased pie pan.
9. Bake 30 minutes or until set (check every 15 minutes). When there is no liquid in the middle, the quiche is ready!

Ellie's Meatball Soup (best for days when temps dip below zero)

Ingredients for meatballs (purchase frozen meatballs to skip this step)

1 pound ground chuck
1 pound tube Jimmy Dean sage sausage
1 egg
½ Vidalia onion, finely chopped
¼ cup premade apple sauce
¼ cup bread crumbs
½ tsp basil
½ tsp oregano
Lawry seasoned salt to taste

Assembly

1. Preheat oven to 350 degrees.
2. Mix ingredients in a small bowl. Form into walnut-size meatballs.
3. Bake until no longer pink. Freeze meatballs in freezer bags until ready to prepare soup.

Ingredients for soup

1 46-ounce bottle V-8 juice (or 1 quart Ellie's Aunt B's gardened canned tomato juice)
32-ounce container beef broth

1 sweet onion, finely chopped
2 cloves garlic minced
1 or 2 stalks celery, chopped
1 or 2 carrots, chopped
2 or 3 golden-yellow potatoes, peeled and chopped
15-ounce can petite diced or diced chopped tomatoes
⅓ green pepper, finely diced
bay leaf
½ teaspoon oregano
½ teaspoon basil

Assembly

1. Place all ingredients except potatoes on high in slow cooker until it comes to a simmer.
2. Add potatoes after the mixture is bubbly so they don't become too mushy. Cook until potatoes are fork tender.

Note: Can replace potatoes with white minute rice if desired. And if Aunt B's canned green beans are still available, add a mason jar's worth to taste. Cook on low until veggies are tender. Enjoy!

Acknowledgments

I always thank you first, my dear readers, specifically those who've started with book one of this Handcrafted Mystery series and followed this story from day one. *Thanks so much.* Thank you for following my journey through Heartsford and falling in love with these three quirky S.H.E.s along with me. I hope they always keep you guessing and laughing too.

As always, thanks to Sandy Harding; your support is priceless. I appreciate your guidance more than you know, and thank you for keeping my love of the written word alive and in print! Thanks to Faith Black Ross, my amazing and talented editor extraordinaire, who elevates my writing to a whole other level (any mistakes are entirely my own). Thanks to all those who work tirelessly on my behalf at Crooked Lane Books: Jenny, Sarah, Ashley, and those unnamed behind the scenes. And thanks to the cover artist, Ben Perini; I'm so lucky to have been paired with you.

Thanks to Jamie Conway for his guidance and information on farming and farm seed (any misrepresentation is my own). Thanks to Patti, who was also a great resource on farming questions. Speaking of which, I can't forget my fellow book clubbers from JRML, who've come along on this crazy journey with me.

And of course, the lead at JRML, Jennifer, who I adore and who makes herself readily available with a hug and a smile when I need a break from my writing cave. Thanks Ty Morgan, I'm so glad our paths crossed! I appreciate your eagle eye.

Thanks to Carol Jensen, who created a unique and special quilt block in honor of this book. Please send us pictures of your finished project; we'd love to see them!

To all my followers on my author Facebook page, bloggers, reviewers (yes, you . . . even the harsh ones), and friends from "Save our Cozies," thanks for keeping this writer sane after hours of being left alone. I enjoy your friendship and online conversations. Lisa Kelley, Dru Ann Love, Lori Caswell, thank you for working tirelessly in support of me and other cozy authors.

To my peeps, who not only inspired this series but inspire me daily, just by who they are and the way they choose to live their lives in community: Wendy, Jason, Zoey, Patti, Jennifer and my porch visit pal Debbie K.

To Jared, Sara, Jesse, Aubrey, Heather, and Karl, extended family, and last but certainly not least—not ever! Mark, you really are my number-one fan. Thank you for your ongoing respect, tireless support of this craft, and LOVE. I love you.